A Murder Among Friends

RAMONA RICHARDS

Steeple
Hill®

Published by Steeple Hill Books™

STEEPLE HILL BOOKS

Steeple
Hill®

ISBN-13: 978-0-373-44232-4
ISBN-10:   0-373-44232-7

A MURDER AMONG FRIENDS

Copyright © 2007 by Ramona Richards

www.SteepleHill.com

Printed in U.S.A.

"Please," Maggie whispered. "I didn't kill him."

Reaching up, Fletcher let one finger stroke gently under the two stitches near her left eye. "The M.E. has released the body. There's this memorial service planned. Do you want to go?"

Maggie pressed his hand against her cheek. Fletcher's gut tightened as she held it there briefly, then let go. "No. Not yet. I need to stay here."

They looked at each other for a moment, and Fletcher wanted to say something, anything to explain how he felt. And what he couldn't let himself feel. Not until he cleared Maggie as a suspect.

* * *

RAMONA RICHARDS

A writer and editor since 1975, Ramona Richards has worked on staff with a number of publishers. Ramona has also freelanced with more than twenty magazine and book publishers and has won awards for both her fiction and nonfiction. She's written everything from sales training video scripts to book reviews, and her latest articles have appeared in *Today's Christian Woman, College Bound,* and *Special Ed Today.* She sold a story about her daughter to *Chicken Soup for the Caregiver's Soul,* and *Secrets of Confidence,* a book of devotionals, is available from Barbour Publishing.

In 2004 the God Allows U-Turns Foundation, in conjunction with the Advanced Writers and Speakers Association (AWSA), chose Ramona for their Strength of Choice award, and in 2003 AWSA nominated Ramona for Best Fiction Editor of the Year. The Evangelical Press Association presented her with an award for reporting in 2003, and in 1989 she won the Bronze Award for Best Original Dramatic Screenplay at the Houston International Film Festival. A member of the American Christian Fiction Writers and the Romance Writers of America, she has five other novels complete or in development.

Ramona and her daughter live in a suburb of Nashville, Tennessee. She can be reached through her Web site at www.ramonarichards.com.

I've told you these things for a purpose: that my joy might be your joy, and your joy wholly mature. This is my command: Love one another the way I loved you. This is the very best way to love. Put your life on the line for your friends.

—*John* 15: 11–14

Special thanks:

To Nancy Zottos,
who opened up New Hampshire to me.

To all my friends who made it possible for me to
go out on my own, especially Sunny, Phyllis, Jeff,
Marcheta, Jamie, Teri, Marilee—and Pat, who
introduced me to the real Ciotka Cookie.

To Carol Lynn Stewart, Corbette Doyle and
Terra Manasco, my fellow struggling writers and
critique partners. Thanks for pushing me ever harder.

To K, the one who—from the first "A"
to the latest "Z"—has offered me the most
hope-filled inspiration and encouragement.

Finally, to my mom, Jimmie Lou Pope, who has read
every word, amazed, thrilled and sometimes puzzled
that her daughter could write like that.

Special praise:

To God and His astonishingly glorious Son.
I took it to heart when someone once told me,
"Your talent is your gift from God. What you do
with it is your gift to Him."

I couldn't do it without You.

ONE

Autumn looks like death, sometimes, with the bloodred leaves fading to burgundy and finally to rust and brown. Maggie Weston thought about such death as she stared steadfastly out the window at the swirl of leaves, despite the rumble of a male voice that sounded behind her.

"Maggie."

Go away. Maggie crossed her arms tightly as she continued to focus on the bright colors of the New Hampshire fall landscape. The back wall of the A-frame lodge house was almost entirely glass, spreading the scene before her in a cheery panorama. The trees were brilliantly dappled in the rich sunlight, but all Maggie could see was death. Death in the trees. In her heart. On her back steps. *Help us, Lord,* she prayed silently. *Help* me.

"Maggie." The voice tugged at her.

It's over and done with, she thought, anger and grief curling into a tight knot in her stomach. *Just go away and leave us alone.*

The staccato clicks of feminine heels tapped into the room. "I'm very grateful you've decided to stay, Fletcher," said a quivering voice. Without turning, Maggie knew that newly widowed Korie Taylor Jackson would be touching the tall man's arm, stroking it and preening in a slight flirt, as if she couldn't stop herself.

Yeah, right. Maggie's thoughts were cold. *Just wait until he starts asking* you *questions.*

"Thank you, Korie." The man's voice was deep and as mellow as the darkest mahogany, and Maggie's throat tightened as he spoke. "But I really don't think I should be doing this—"

"Nonsense!" Korie interrupted him. "You were Aaron's friend. What better way to start your new business than with solving Aaron Jackson's—" She stopped and cleared her throat. Maggie heard the tears being forced back into Korie's voice as it dropped to a whisper. "Solving your best friend's murder. Everyone in the world knows what a good detective you are."

Maggie couldn't quite believe Korie saw her husband's death as a marketing opportunity. An involuntary growl escaped her throat.

Korie snapped. "Maggie! If you have something to add, just say it!"

Maggie turned and looked slowly over the couple before her. Even in her widowhood of one day, Korie couldn't resist the affectations of her flowing, oversize skirts and bohemian blouses, which swooped as her slender arms darted through a conversation, making her look like a colorful, earth-bound parrot. Korie had probably been *born* an incorrigible coquette. At twenty-four, Korie had had two successful shows of her art in New York City and had snagged Aaron Jackson, reveling in his popularity as a bestselling novelist.

Part of the reason for Aaron's success stood next to Korie. Fletcher MacAllister, who until two months ago had been a detective with New York's finest, was the model for Aaron's series hero, Judson MacLean. The charming and meticulous Judson, who had carried his author to the top of the *New York Times* fiction list on a regular basis, had paid for most of Aaron's worst habits, including his booze, his cigars and his wife of three years. Of course, the books had also paid for all of them to be here, in this writers' colony that Aaron had so modestly called Jackson's Retreat. His dream. His life.

His death.

Maggie took a deep breath to steady her voice. Aaron's character, Judson, with his Nordic looks and his tastes for lovely women, fine cooking and expensive suits, looked nothing like the man in front of her. Fletcher's features and dark hair reflected more of his Thai mother than his Scottish father, and he had obviously slept in his suit, probably more than once. His eyes, a rich brown instead of Judson's piercing blue, were almond shaped and questioning, waiting for her to respond. She took a deep breath and ran her hands through her tangled curls, all too aware that her fingers were trembling.

"He's right, Korie. Don't you think New Hampshire is more than a bit out of his territory, even if he has started his own business? He doesn't know this place, doesn't know us, and the fact that he was staying with you and Aaron doesn't make him any more capable than Tyler and his folks. They may be a small-town department, but they're not idiots."

Trying to appear calm, Maggie walked to the counter separating the main room from the kitchen and reached for one of the cups she had stacked next to the coffeemaker. "And I don't think you'll win any points with Mr. MacAllister by lying. Aaron's books aren't yet translated into—" Maggie paused, waving her hand as she searched for the most obscure language she could think of "—Burmese. I'm sure there are some people in the world who would not feel the need to swoon in the presence of the 'real life' Judson MacLean."

"I'm not Judson." Simple, straightforward and delivered with finality before Korie could fly into a protest. Just as Maggie remembered from her first meeting with Fletcher five years ago. That one hadn't gone very well, either.

Maggie slapped the cup down. "And I'm not going to stand around while Korie tries to convince you that Aaron's death was anything more than an accident. It can't be—" Maggie's voice cracked. Blinking hard, she turned and strode out, leaving the community room of the large lodge behind her and stepping out onto the back deck. She paused, shivering slightly in the cool fall air. She rubbed her arms, feeling the chill through her light sweater. She should have stopped for a jacket, but right now she didn't care if she froze half to death. She brushed away a single tear, then took another deep breath. *God, please help me,* she prayed again, this time fighting back the wave of grief that threatened to swamp her the way it had last night. *Help me handle this.* Maggie started down the steps, then hesitated. The deep color on the bottom step reminded her of what she had found just after midnight. Her own insistent words echoed in her mind, almost as if she were trying to convince herself of something she didn't quite believe. *It had to be an accident!* She bit her lip and stepped over the stain.

The mat of leaves crunched and mushed under her feet as she walked out through the woods. The newly fallen leaves on top were dry, while the layers underneath were damp from the frosts they had already seen. The ground beneath all the layers was uneven and a challenge for walking. Maggie loved the effort it took to hike the land, and she almost always wore a stylish but practical pair of boots in case she got the urge to get out of the house. This was her refuge, ever since she'd arrived here at Jackson's Retreat. Her eyes stung as she remembered her first day here, but she kept walking as briars and low plants tugged at her long woolen skirt.

Jackson's Retreat. It had been Aaron's dream to build this colony of cabins scattered across ten acres of his New Hampshire home. The A-frame lodge, with its high glass wall at the back, basement game room and large living area, formed the center of the small community. Aaron had set up an escrow account substantial enough that the interest funded the usual operating expenses, so that the writers who were accepted here could live rent-free in small one-room cabins. Where they lived, that is, as long as they met Aaron's stringent requirements of production. Their only out-of-pocket expenses were for personal items and food.

When Aaron had called Maggie four years ago and asked her to run the retreat, she had been doubtful at first. Although she and Aaron had been friends for years, since Maggie was in college, she had not seen him in almost a year. They had met at the bookstore where she worked as an assistant manager, and their friendship had later deepened into a turbulent—and brief—romance. After their relationship fell apart, they promised to remain friends, but Maggie had intentionally stayed away from him, unable to forget the intense feelings he had stirred in her heart. These emotions were still raw when he asked her to run the retreat, even though she knew he was dating Korie at the time. After much prayer, Maggie had accepted the job, and Aaron married Korie shortly thereafter.

Aaron. Maggie tripped over a root and stopped, realizing that her vision was beginning to blur with tears. She wiped them away, then pressed her lips to stop their quivering. Thoughts of Aaron flooded her mind. His unbridled laughter, the bigger-than-life way he'd enter a room and take over the conversation. The tenderness with which he had once held her.

The insistence with which he refused to take no for an answer. Maggie had turned down the job at first. Firmly. Surely, he should get someone else to run the retreat. Maggie suggested several other people to him, but he persisted. It was Maggie, with her finely honed management skills and understanding of the writer's soul, that he wanted in charge of his dream. Finally, she had relented.

Maggie walked on, relishing the feel of the spongy ground under her boots. How she adored this land! Leaving her job in New York, she'd moved here and fallen in love with the land and the dream. Now she lived full-time in the lodge house, overseeing the care of the cabins and their temperamental inhabitants.

Maggie looked up through the dancing leaves as the sun played in patterns on the ground and her face. She sighed, feeling some of the tension ease away. It had been this way almost from the beginning. The comfort she had felt when praying about the job had opened the door; the peacefulness of the location and the constant demands of her job were a great combination. She felt at home and content, and the proximity to Aaron had allowed her finally to put her feelings for him in perspective.

Aaron, who lived with Korie in an old Victorian down the road from the lodge house, stopped in twice a day to check on things. He liked being involved with his dream and his writers. *His* writers.

She frowned as she pushed aside an overgrown bush next to her favorite trail through the woods, a few of the dried branches breaking as the bush snapped back into place. Aaron's arrogance hadn't always sat well with "his" writers, but they couldn't argue with the success that came from being here. All of the residents—past and present—had achieved far more success financially and artistically than they had before their time at the retreat. They may have battled Aaron, but his edge became their driving force. *So why would anyone want to kill him? Why did she*— Maggie shook her head, unwilling to acknowledge the thought that hung at the back of her mind. Instead, she went over the events of last night's dinner, trying to pull *anything* forward that might answer her questions.

Was he leaving—or coming back—when he died? It had not been a pleasant night. Aaron had been angry. In fact, he had been angry a lot lately—at her, at his wife, at—

No, she told herself again. Maggie knew what she had done was wrong, but it was for the right reasons. *I know what they would think. Besides, what's done is done.* Still, her conscience nagged at her. *Tell him.* Maggie took a ragged breath. Her mother used to say that your conscience was God's finger on your back, poking you in the right direction. And God never gets tired.

Her mother. Aaron. Lil— Tears clouded her eyes again, the grief unstoppable this time.

Maggie had found Aaron when she had taken out the trash for the night. *Why didn't I hear anything? I must have been in the kitchen cleaning up.* Maggie stopped, unable to see for the tears, unable to walk from the weakness in her legs. *All that blood!* She sank down next to a tree and drew her knees tight against her chest, then leaned her head on them and sobbed. The grief she had been trying to restrain for the past twenty-four hours poured out of her in lung-wrenching gulps that seemed endless. *Oh, dear God, help me!* The sobs ceased only when her nose became so clogged that she started to choke and cough. She grabbed the bottom of her skirt and started to wipe her face with it.

"Here, use this."

Maggie gasped and snapped backward, hitting her head against the tree. Her screech echoed through the woods as she jerked and stared up through tears at Fletcher, who was calmly holding out a handkerchief to her. He tipped his head sideways in apology. "I didn't mean to scare you."

Maggie stared at him, still shaky, and rubbed the back of her head. "How did you find me?" she asked, her voice hoarse.

He waved absently behind him. "I've known moose who left less evidence of their passage." He shook the handkerchief at her again. "Go ahead. It's old, but it's clean," he said.

She hesitated a moment, then snagged the soft worn cloth, wiped her face and eyes and blew her nose. She peered briefly at the smears of makeup on it. "Great. Now I looked like a sleep-deprived raccoon." She crushed it into a ball, then peered back up at the man she'd only known as a New York City cop. "What do you know about moose? You're a city boy," she said.

He nodded. "For fifteen years. But I grew up in Verm—" He stopped and cleared his throat. "I need to ask you some questions."

"Read the police report. I told them all I know."

He sat down in the leaves next to her and she frowned, scooting away. "I did," he replied.

Maggie twisted the handkerchief viciously. "I *really* don't want to go over this again, okay?" Her voice was harsher than she intended, but she didn't apologize.

Fletcher was silent. His eyes seemed focused on something in the distance. After a few moments, he said softly, "He was my friend, too."

Over her head, Maggie could hear a squirrel chewing on a nut. A breeze brushed the branches around them lightly, and the remaining leaves whispered to her. Maggie turned her head slightly to look at Fletcher. He seemed totally comfortable sitting here next to a tree, even in his business suit. He sat with his long legs crossed, guaranteeing the most stains per square inch on his pants, but he didn't seem to care. Maggie suddenly remembered a description that Aaron had written about Judson MacLean.

> Judson was a man who always surprised people. He caught them off guard. With his size, with his intelligence, with his wit. And with his ability to ferret out information from the least likely of suspects.

Aaron had been right about that part. Fletcher was a large man, tall with a lean figure that belied a personal strength. Sitting here, even without speaking, Fletcher had taken charge of the scene. And what surprised Maggie was both the ease

with which he did that as he sat with a woman who was virtu-
ally a stranger—and the odd twinge that ran deep in her gut.
Don't start liking him, girlfriend, she cautioned herself. *He's
not here because he wants your company.*

"Is that why you're doing this?" she asked. "Because he was
your friend?"

Fletcher looked directly at her, locking her in his gaze. "Par-
tially. Are you grieving *only* because he was your friend?"

Maggie's eyes widened, and she felt her anger building
again. "Am I a suspect?"

"So you don't really think it was an accident."

Anger flashed through her, a raw combination of grief and
the denial she so desperately wanted to hang on to. She stood
up, tossing the handkerchief into the woods. "Aaron fell! And
you will *not* try and convict me in my own home!" Turning on
her heels, she started back toward the lodge.

He called lightly after her. "Yes, Maggie, I will." She
stopped but did not turn. "If you're guilty."

Fletcher watched her stomp away, unaffected by her anger.
She was fighting against the truth too hard, as if she knew
someone had killed Aaron, yet she didn't want to believe it. He
released a deep breath. It wasn't an uncommon reaction to the
murder of someone you love, but there were more facts that
bothered him than just her behavior. According to the police
report, she'd found Aaron, but she had *not* called the police.
The groundskeeper, Tim, had called them after he'd found
Maggie next to the body. Fletcher wanted to know why Tyler
Madison, the local police chief, had blithely overlooked that.
The amount of blood indicated Aaron had died on the steps,
but the body had been moved, rearranged to make it look like
a fall. Taking a deep breath, he stood up and pulled a small
brown paper bag from his coat pocket. He stepped over a few

broken branches and lifted his handkerchief by one corner, bagging it carefully. *DNA,* he thought casually, *can be handy to have around.*

As he turned to go back to the lodge, he could still hear Maggie crashing in the leaves. "Maggie Weston, you are most definitely a suspect," he muttered, as he followed her wide swath through the trees. "Right now, everyone who was here last night is."

Maggie slammed into her office at the south end of the lodge. She paced, her anger seething but with no outlet. *How* dare *he! How dare he accuse me of killing Aaron? He has* no *right here! None! Tyler has ruled it an accident, and Aaron is gone. Why couldn't Korie just have accepted that? She didn't love him—* Maggie stopped abruptly, her mind caught on a thought.

Love.

When she'd first met Fletcher five years ago, she and Aaron had been in the blush of love. They hadn't seen each other since. *Does Fletcher think I killed Aaron because he didn't love me anymore?* Maggie sank down in her office chair, her manager's brain kicking into gear. It was a motive. And not a bad one. And it might keep Fletcher off guard long enough—

That's illegal, girlfriend. It's called obstruction of justice. And immoral. And against your beliefs. Maggie sighed at the nagging inner voice. God's finger. *But it's not evidence,* she insisted to herself. *Not really.* "And aren't some risks worth it?" she asked aloud.

A knock on her door brought her attention back around, and she called out for her visitor to enter. Fletcher opened the door and was followed into the office by Korie. They sat in the chairs on the front side of the desk.

"I want Fletcher to stay here, in one of the cabins," Korie announced, expertly swinging her blond hair back over her shoulder. "Surely you have one that's empty. It doesn't look right for him to keep staying with me, and I want him to get to the bottom of this. And I want you to call Chief Madison and tell him you're behind it as well. He cooperated with Fletcher about the reports, but he's acting like you're queen of the estate and he's deferring to you."

Silence.

Maggie looked from one to the other, and she knew they were waiting for her to protest. After a moment, she opened her center desk drawer and pulled out a key with a numbered key chain on it. She tossed it lightly at Fletcher, who caught it with no effort. "Number four," she said, handing him a map and a brochure. "You might have to clean it. The previous occupant left this weekend after a fight with Aaron, and I haven't had a chance to get the cleaning service down there yet. The map will help you get around the estate, and the brochure will familiarize you with our routine."

She paused and looked at Korie. "I'll call Tyler as soon as you two are out of the office. I'm sure he'll be more deferential to you, Korie, when he realizes how much you'll inherit."

Korie froze and Fletcher's eyebrows arched. Maggie started her mental list. *A mad writer who left in a huff and a wife who will inherit. No lies, but a bit of mud on the picture.* Maggie felt a tightening in her gut, and she glanced briefly at the Bible on the corner of her desk. *It's worth it,* she thought insistently, her faith at war with her loyalty.

Korie stood, muttering under her breath, and turned to leave. "Come on, Fletcher, I'll help you get settled."

Fletcher got to his feet, watching Maggie. He said quietly, "You go ahead, Korie. I'll be there in a minute."

Korie slammed the door behind her, but neither of them jumped. Fletcher turned and went to the window near her desk, staring out. Maggie turned in her chair to watch him. There was mud on his pants that he had not bothered to brush off and a leaf stuck to the back of his coat. But there was nothing sloppy about his movements or his intentions.

Maggie blinked first. "What do you want?"

"What risk is worth it?"

Maggie stood and went to his side. "Is eavesdropping part of your job?"

He was still looking out the window. "When necessary."

"So do you just expect me to blithely confess that I know something about Aaron's *accident* that I'm not telling you?"

Fletcher turned to face her, and Maggie was surprised by the intensity in his eyes. He stepped closer, and Maggie wanted to look away but didn't dare. He loomed over her, his height and closeness overwhelming her. She took a deep breath in an effort to remain calm and only succeeded in inhaling a scent that was purely masculine, acrid and intense, like freshly tanned leather. She trembled as he leaned forward and whispered at the side of her face.

"Don't do this, Maggie. We both know he was killed. We both know that someone moved his body so it would look like an accident. And I promise you I will find out who and why. Whatever—or *whoever*—you're hiding is not worth it. Understand?"

Maggie let out her breath, her voice shaking. "Perfectly," she whispered back.

He stepped back and smiled. "Fine," he said, his voice light. "Then we'll get along famously." He turned and went to the door.

"Dinner's at six," Maggie said firmly. He stopped and looked at her, puzzled. She tilted her head back, regaining as much pride as she could. "Since you've been staying with Korie, I thought you might not know. Everyone at the retreat eats dinner in the lodge. Every night. It's required. One of

Aaron's little dictates. Everyone who's on the property, no matter who, eats at the lodge at six. He thought it reflected small-town life. You can meet everyone then. But I hope you'll be gracious enough to talk to them about Aaron in private."

He looked her over, nodding in agreement. "I will," he said, and he shut the door behind him.

Maggie let all the air out of her lungs and sat back down in her chair, her legs unable to hold her any longer. She reached out and stroked the edge of her Bible. *Is deception always wrong? Isn't it allowed,* she thought, *to protect your own family?* She wanted to believe she was right, but every fiber of her body seemed to twitch. Leaning her head on her desk, she let the tears flow one more time.

Fletcher ignored Korie's protests and went out the back door to stand on the deck. He needed to be alone and he needed fresh air. He inhaled deeply, relishing the late-afternoon chill that stung his nostrils.

She had smelled like sandalwood, all spicy and sweet. He closed his eyes, but all he could see was the way her auburn hair had clung in small curls to her shoulders and the gentle curve of her neck. He was also struck by her almost unnoticeable glances at the Bible on her desk. Clearly, her morals, her faith, were playing hard on her heart, which tugged at something deep in the back of Fletcher's mind, a sensation he had ignored for a very long time.

Fletcher opened his eyes and leaned heavily against the deck rail, gazing out over the November landscape, wondering if he should bow out now. His gut still ached from knowing his best friend lay on a morgue slab, and he had never expected the impact Maggie's emotion would have on him. Her strength, her grief, drew his attention right away, and now he fought the idea that she was involved in Aaron's murder. But her anger hid something that ran deep, and all of his experience, all of his instincts, told him that she knew who the murderer was. Or she thought she did. Fletcher knew he had to get his own grief back under control if he was going to find any answers at all.

Because Maggie Weston was grieving not just for Aaron but for the person who had killed him. Fletcher just hoped that it wasn't her.

TWO

Judson was meticulous, insisting especially on a spotless kitchen in which to cook the gourmet meals he cherished. Three maids in the last year had quit, unable to live up to his requirements.

Fletcher dumped the clothes out of his hastily packed bag onto the rumpled bed and sorted them into piles of clean, dirty and suits. He hung the suits in the tiny cabin closet, then dumped the clean pile into one drawer of the dresser, the dirty into another. He sat on the squeaky bed, trying to ignore the smell of sour food and stale sweat in the cabin, and pulled a small notebook and a pen out of his jacket to look over the notes he'd taken so far. As he went through the list, his left heel bounced nervously against the floor, and the pen clicked as his thumb snapped up and down on its release.

Aaron Jackson's body showed that he had apparently died from a severe blow to the right side of his head, crushing his temple. He had been discovered by the estate manager, Maggie Weston, around midnight Monday, lying facedown on the back steps of the lodge house deck. His head was on the last step, his feet near the top. She was found about half an hour later by the groundskeeper, Tim Miller, sitting on the steps beside the body in total shock. He and another resident, Scott Jonas, had to carry her inside.

The pen clicks picked up speed as he went down the list, and he paused, taking a deep breath, looking at his left hand. *This is harder than I thought it would be.* Even the pen brought back sharp memories that threatened to break through Fletcher's tightly restrained emotions. Aaron had hated the clicking pen, recognizing it as one of Fletcher's control mechanisms. The older man's voice echoed in his head.

"Why don't you go ahead and just lose that Scottish temper, me boyo? Emotions are good! They make life more intriguing."

"I'm a cop. I can't get emotionally involved with my cases."

Aaron clucked his tongue. *"So you're made of steel, are you?"*

Hardly, Fletcher thought, forcing his heel to stay flat on the floor and his feelings for Aaron to the far reaches of his mind. He took a deep breath. "Focus," he murmured, looking down at the notebook again.

Fletcher's brief examination of the body at the coroner's showed that the wound to Aaron's head was rounded—not flat or sharp—which was the impression a step, or the edge of a step, would have left. His body position was also odd and not that of a man who had fallen down steps. Bits of blood had been found approximately six feet out from the deck, with a few smears between that had been hastily covered. The wound was dotted with tiny bits of some material the ME couldn't identify and contained almost no sign of wooden slivers. The coroner's preliminary findings had confirmed this. They were still waiting on a final report.

Fletcher underlined his next note. *So he was murdered and the body moved. No accident. Now, why would anyone want him dead?* Fletcher took a deep breath and stood up, stretching, an odd weariness in his bones. He hadn't slept well while he was at Korie and Aaron's. Aaron was a midnight prowler, and Korie never seemed to shut up. No wonder Aaron spent dinnertime at the retreat with his writers and Maggie.

He frowned. Korie and Maggie. Both had been involved with Aaron, and the contrast between the two women was so stark that it was ludicrous. Korie, the flamboyant flirt, was the wild party child in New York and a restless, wandering artist here in New Hampshire. Maggie was stronger, more reserved. He remembered meeting her five years ago, when she and Aaron had been lovers….

Fletcher stood very still, a memory reaching through. An argument. Maggie and Aaron. About their relationship. *Well, what else do couples fight about?* But this had been different. *How? Had Maggie still loved him? Was she jealous of Korie?* Maybe. But Fletcher couldn't remember anything else, and he shook his head to clear it.

He sat back down, turned the page in his notebook, clicked the pen twice and started another list. "Who would hate him enough to kill him?" he asked aloud.

"The list is endless," Maggie said from the doorway.

Fletcher stood, his eyebrows raised. "Is eavesdropping part of *your* job?" he asked.

She smiled wryly. "When necessary." She carried a large paper sack. "I brought you some things I thought you might need, since you aren't one of our regular guests. They usually come prepared." She set the bag on the desk and looked around at the small room, which had a tiny kitchenette in one end. The furnishings were simple: a desk with phone and computer ports, two comfy, overstuffed chairs, a bed, a dresser, a small eating table with two chairs. Maggie frowned at the bed.

"I brought clean sheets, for starters." She began emptying the bag. "Jamie left in something of a hurry, and he was notorious for being a slob. I found an extra phone in one of our guest rooms, so you won't always have to use your cell. Some of them won't pick up a signal here, anyway. And I've got towels and soap."

Fletcher stood back as she started stripping the sheets, wrinkling her nose. "Jamie was also notorious with the local girls. I just hope I don't find one tied up in the bathroom."

"No, it's clean," Fletcher replied. She paused and looked up at him, doubtful. He shrugged. "Well, not *clean* exactly."

She laughed and tossed the dirty sheets into a pile. "I called the cleaning service and they should be here this afternoon. I'm sure Korie made promises to help, but she wouldn't know which end of a broom to hold." She grabbed the clean sheets and shook them out. Fletcher tucked his notebook back in his coat and reached to help her. "Thanks," she said. "There's a washer and dryer at the lodge if you need it. Have you looked over the brochure?"

Fletcher shook his head, watching Maggie peripherally as he shoved the corners of the sheets under the mattress. Pleasant, but too efficient. Too cooperative. *What are you up to, Maggie?*

"There aren't a lot of rules around here," she said, her voice taking on a routine note. He could tell she'd given this speech before. "But the ones we do have are enforced without fail." She tucked a pillow under her chin and slid on a case. "One, everyone eats dinner in the lodge. Nights out have to be pre-arranged. You are on your own for breakfast and lunch. There are several restaurants in town, or you can keep groceries here, as long as you keep the place clean. No personal visitors except at the lodge, and no overnight guests who are not spouses. Aaron's library, as well as the local public library, is available for research, and we ask that you make any long-distance calls from the lodge. There's also an Internet connection, if your service doesn't have a local number. There's no long-distance service available in the cabins. We also keep up with the ones that are business and the ones that are personal. You won't be charged for business calls. Cell phones, of course, are permitted, but they are not allowed at the dinner table." The pillow landed on the bed with a fluff of scented air, and she went to the closet for blankets, her voice maintaining its monotone. "Please keep the thermostat at seventy-two degrees. You can come and go as you please, as long as you maintain the required production quota for the week. Aaron reviews everything on Saturday, so make sure you—"

Maggie froze and her eyelids fluttered. "You're not a writer. Sorry." Fletcher watched as she blinked away the glassiness from her eyes and took a deep breath. She crossed her arms over her stomach and bit her lower lip. Fletcher thought again about the two women who had loved Aaron Jackson so passionately. Korie, told of Aaron's death, had wailed and flailed for an hour or so, with nothing but polite tears since. Maggie's grief ran deeper, more consuming, and it looked as if it was going to last for a long time.

He gave her a moment, then spoke softly. "Tell me about the production requirements. Were they harsh?"

Maggie took a deep breath and seemed grateful. She nodded, sniffed and spoke evenly. "Yes. The application to get in here discourages most writers from even trying. They must have at least one mainstream novel published, with more than five thousand copies sold, with good reviews. They have to produce at least two short stories or a hundred pages of a novel a week, with a rough draft of a book, play or script per quarter. Flighty temperaments—and that covers a *lot* of writers—aren't allowed. Aaron's philosophy was that you were here to work, not be trendy. He also encouraged them to form critique groups, which meet in the lodge. He didn't expect everything produced to be perfect—or even *good*—but you had to show you were serious about the work."

"How long did most people stay?"

Maggie laughed. "Most leave within a couple of weeks. Aaron could be nasty about it. Aaron the Arrogant. That's what a lot of them call him. And worse."

"And the ones who stay?"

Maggie sat down on the bed. "They do some amazing work in the long run," she said quietly. "It may look casual around here, but this isn't a weekend conference of workshops. The cabins are only allotted out in three-month increments. They remain empty if someone leaves early. I've helped a lot of these folks write grants so they can stay here and still pay their mortgages, feed the kids. It's hard work, very solitary and driving, and one reason Aaron requires everyone eat together is to force some type of community on them, so they won't hole up in their cabins. It pays off. We've already produced two Pulitzer nominees, three Edgar winners, and two National Book Awards nominations. Aaron really is tough on them, but the ones who stay respond to his…" Her voice trailed off again, and she cleared her throat. "I guess I'm not used to the past tense yet."

"Why did Jamie leave?"

Maggie sat up straighter. "Aaron. Jamie kept going out at night, bringing home the girls. Not allowed." She smiled. "James Henry. Young and talented, but too immature. As arrogant as Aaron. Thought he was Henry James and that it would be easy. He chafed under Aaron's rules. Told him to stay out of his personal life. They had a fight over the weekend, and Aaron tossed him out on his gifted behind."

"This is not in the police report. Did you see the fight?"

Maggie shook her head. "All I told them was what I knew about Monday night. It was an accident, remember? As to the fight, I was at church with a couple of the others." Fletcher raised an eyebrow, and Maggie scowled at him. "Don't look so surprised, Fletcher. Not everyone who comes out of New York is decadent."

Fletcher wiped his mouth, her words triggering a memory of a morose Aaron after his breakup with Maggie.

"She even got me going to church again."

"What? And the roof stayed up? No lightning strikes?"

"Humph." Aaron shook a smoldering cigar at Fletcher, scattering a few ashes. *"You're not the decadent you'd like people to think. It wouldn't hurt you to darken the door of a church again."*

Fletcher brushed the ashes off the table to the floor. "What makes you think I don't go?"

Aaron smirked. "'Cause I know you, and I know why you don't go. And that hasn't changed."

Fletcher looked away. He didn't want to talk about it.

Or think about it now. He cleared his throat. "Did anyone see the fight?"

"I doubt it, unless Tim overheard something. You could ask him. There are times I think he overhears everything. The fight did happen up at the lodge. Jamie, as you can see, left in a bit of a hurry. You'll probably find leftover pizza in the fridge."

Fletcher frowned. This was too easy; she was leading him somewhere, and it wasn't where he wanted to go. "Who's been here the longest?"

Maggie got up and peered into the bathroom, then winced. "I'll see if the cleaning folks can't get here sooner. And the microwave will probably be safer than the stove. We didn't expect to move anyone in here for a week or two."

"Maggie..." Fletcher nudged.

"Scott and Lily," she said.

"A couple?"

Maggie nodded. "Scott Jonas is the writer. He's been here several years now, almost from the beginning. Lily came and went for a while, then started staying here steadily about six months ago. Scott and Aaron fought a lot, but they seemed to understand each other."

Fletcher stood a bit straighter. "Lily Dunne?"

Maggie stared at him. "Please don't tell me you're a fan."

He shook his head. "No. I know Scott's novels. Aaron had me read them. His bio said he was married to Lily Dunne. I know who she is, of course."

Maggie nodded, chewing a bit on her lower lip. "Lily stays here, too. It's a bit unusual, but Scott's almost a permanent resident. They have the largest cabin, which is closest to the lodge."

"Must be quiet here for her, after the lights of Broadway and L.A."

Maggie responded by gathering up the dirty sheets and dumping them into a bag. "You'll get to meet them tonight. Don't forget—dinner's at six."

"Anyone else here who isn't a writer?"

Maggie paused. "Me. And Tim, of course."

Fletcher paused. Tim Miller was the retreat's groundskeeper and the one who had found Maggie on the steps. Tyler had mentioned to him that Aaron had confidence in Tim, even though a background check had turned up a misdemeanor trespassing charge in Tennessee. Tim had said it was a political protest, something about taxes. The charge had been dismissed, and Aaron had never reported any problems. "He must help you a lot."

Maggie's eyes glistened with tears. "Yes."

"Who else would hate Aaron?"

Maggie looked at him. "He's alienated dozens of writers who thought this was paradise on earth. Aaron has—*had*—a temper that could shatter steel, but you know that, Fletcher. You knew him. You were one of his best friends. Who do *you* think would kill him?"

Fletcher looked her up and down, taking in every inch of her anger. His voice was quiet. "Anyone who despised or feared him."

Maggie looked disgusted. "You have a gift for the obvious." She stuffed the bag under her arm and started out the door.

"Or loved him," Fletcher finished.

Maggie paused, then looked over her shoulder. "Do you always have to have the last word?" She repositioned the bag and tramped out, letting the door slam behind her.

Fletcher grinned. "Always." He walked to the screen door of the cabin and watched her slender figure disappearing through the trees, wondering how much of her grief was real and how much was a calculated act. He knew she had intentionally handed him three major suspects on a silver platter, all without lying or stretching the truth, and he was aware that whomever she was protecting had probably been carefully excluded from the conversation. He sat down on his now-clean bed and took the notebook out, adding a few sharp scribbles to it, pausing only to click the pen twice. *You're playing a dangerous game, Maggie,* he thought. *And you're not as good at it as you think you are.*

Aaron flopped down on Fletcher's ancient sofa, the bottle of Green Label Jack Daniel's held loosely in his hand. "Men should stick together, me boyo," he said, exaggerating the fake Irish brogue he always adopted when intoxicated, or when he wanted to appear intoxicated.

Fletcher noticed that the bottle was open but still full, and he wondered if it was the first bottle...or the second. He went to the kitchen to make a pot of coffee anyway, hoping to distract his friend from the whiskey. "You aren't going to try to convince me you have women problems, are you?"

Aaron wagged his finger in the air, at no one in particular.

*"I am not as much the ladies' man as my publicist would have
the world believe, dear Fletcher. It is far more hype than
history."*

*Fletcher returned to the dimly lit living room and sat op-
posite Aaron in the sagging leather recliner he refused to get
rid of. "So those thousands of women you've dated…"*

Aaron shook his head. "Less than a hundred, I promise."

*Fletcher laughed. "More than most men can claim. Or
would want to."*

*Aaron sat up and peered at the bottle, clearly wanting to take
a swig. "Well, most men could claim a bit of love along the way."*

*Fletcher leaned back in his recliner. "If you're expecting
sympathy from me, you're going about it in the wrong way."*

*Aaron shook his head. "Nope. No sympathy. Just want to
crash on your couch tonight. Don't feel like driving back up
to the retreat."*

Fletcher frowned. "What about the apartment? Korie—"

*Aaron laughed abruptly. "Korie?" He paused and finally
drank from the bottle, but the swallowing seemed painful and
he grimaced. "Korie is… Korie is 'en salon' tonight. She
couldn't care less."*

"'En salon'?"

*Aaron put the bottle on the floor, lay down on the couch and
propped his feet up on one arm. "Holding court with all her
'artistes.' She has illusions she's the reincarnation of Mabel
Dodge. Has dreams of re-creating a salon society and influ-
encing the art world the way Dodge did a hundred years ago.
They are all over the apartment. She won't miss me until it's
time to order something, pay for something or tip someone for
carrying something she's bought."*

*Fletcher was silent. After a moment, Aaron sat up. "I'm
going to be sick now. Can I still stay?"*

"As long as you want."

Aaron laughed again as he headed for the bathroom. "Judson, my dear fellow, you may regret that offer."

Fletcher grimaced as the door shut. Judson, the one name he hated hearing, the one name Aaron teased him with the most. It was going to be a long night.

The night turned into a week, and Korie had never once called or checked up on Aaron once during those seven days. Aaron's anger and disgust at his wife dulled to a quiet cynicism, and at the end of the week, they had returned in separate cars to New Hampshire. Now she stood to inherit everything. If—and it was a big *if*—Maggie was right.

Fletcher threw his notebook on the bed and opened the door. Gazing up toward the lodge, he could see Maggie on the deck, looking in his direction. After a moment, she walked down the steps and disappeared along one of the trails. *But if Korie were the killer, why would Maggie protect her? They hate each other.* Fletcher smiled wryly. *Perhaps, Maggie, me dear, you've muddied the water more than you realize.*

Her feet cold and her mind numb, Maggie tramped through the woods behind the lodge again. She'd tried to do her job, had called the restaurant about tonight's dinner and the cleaning service for Fletcher's cabin, but nothing else. Her anger and grief of the morning seemed to have faded away, but it left nothing behind except a nagging twinge of guilt. Work should be her therapy, but she felt frozen, and everything in her office reminded her of Aaron. Thinking some cool air might help, she had gone out on the deck, then realized she just wanted to walk. She'd started down one of the trails, then left it, wandering aimlessly at first over the soft ground, relishing the last of the tiny white and purple wildflowers that dotted the ground in between spots of bright orange fungus on the tree roots. This land had been farm country until about seventy-five years ago, so the trees were relatively young and sparse, allowing for a lot of undergrowth. Maggie liked spotting new plants and trying to identify them, making almost every trip a bit of an adventure. She stopped, pulling a slice of bark off a birch tree. Breaking it into tiny bits as she looked around to get her bearings, she realized she was gradually heading west toward the edge of the property and an old logging road that only had one destination: Cookie's.

Cordelia Holokaj, but all her nieces and nephews called her Ciotka Cookie. Maggie had found the Hansel-and-Gretel cottage on one of her first escapes into the woods to get away from the flaring temperaments of the retreat's writers. Cookie had taken her in, served her hot chocolate and fresh gingersnaps, and told her stories from the world wars that made the retreat's resident writers sound like poor amateurs. Cookie's had been *her* retreat ever since.

The cottage always smelled like wood smoke, ginger, fresh bread and cabbage, and today was no different. Maggie stepped across the threshold and inhaled, much of her tension flooding away. "It's so good to be here," she murmured as Cookie gave her a hug. She bent down and scratched Cookie's ancient mutt, Pepper, behind the ears. The overweight dachshund/sheltie mix grunted her contentment with the gesture.

"I was wondering when I'd see you," Cookie said, her voice like gravel in a blender from her almost eighty years of cigarettes and New England winters. She motioned for Maggie to sit in one of the doily-covered horsehair chairs that crowded a tiny living room clustered with pictures, icons and books. A rickety upright piano sat against one wall, its stool covered with a well-worn blanket and its ivory keys yellow from years of enthusiastic fingers.

Maggie sat, curling her long legs beneath her, in one of the chairs next to the fireplace. Pepper waddled over to a spot between the chair and the fire, turned around once, then sank to the floor with a satisfied sigh. Pepper's low, broad body was a perfect match to Cookie's comfortable and huggable size.

Maggie took the offered cup of chamomile tea and found herself staring blankly into the gentle blazes of Cookie's low fire. Cookie waited, stirring her tea and munching on a gingersnap.

"I didn't realize how much it would hurt now that he's gone," Maggie said, finally. Cookie merely nodded and handed the younger woman a cookie. Maggie held it, then laid it on the arm of the chair. "I mean, I hadn't loved him—I mean, been *in* love with him—for a long time. But, I mean, to have Korie acting like…and Fletcher MacAllister running around as if…" Maggie's voice trailed off. Her numbness was giving way to confusion. What had happened to the resolve she'd felt earlier, to keep Fletcher at bay?

"What are you afraid of?"

Maggie was silent, uncertain if she should even tell Cookie.

The old woman cleared her throat. "This is a small town, Maggie. Never forget that. Never. Jackson's Retreat does not exist in a vacuum. Word gets around. We mostly know who's sleeping with whom, married or not. Or married to someone else. We also tend to know who's trying to make a move, and whether the proposition's been accepted."

Maggie stared at her. "What are you saying?"

Cookie's gaze was steady. "I'm saying most everyone around knows who Korie was sleeping with, and I don't mean Aaron. How long are you going to keep quiet about it?"

"As long as I have to. Enough people have already been hurt."

Cookie nodded. "One of them even killed."

The tears slid from Maggie's eyes and she set her cup aside. She got up, then knelt in front of Cookie, burying her face against the old woman's knees. "Cookie, I was so angry! But now it just hurts. And I'm so scared."

Cordelia Holokaj's Polish parents had been killed in the concentration camps of World War II, and her only son had disappeared into the jungles of Laos, never to return. She knew grief, and fear, like few other people. She stroked Maggie Weston's auburn curls. "You've gotta keep your head clear, baby. Don't let what you felt for Aaron get in the way here. Don't be lying to Fletcher MacAllister. Not only is it wrong, but it'll come back to haunt you quicker than anything else you can do."

Maggie raised her head, her eyes pleading. "But he could destroy everything I love."

Cookie shook her head. "Not him. What's done is done. He's gonna shine some light on it, but his being around doesn't make it more or less true." She wiped Maggie's face with her apron, and pushed her shoulders back. "You're stronger than this. Be who you are. And stop lying to the man."

Maggie got up and sat back in her chair. "I haven't lied to him."

Cookie raised both eyebrows. "Why didn't you call the police?"

Maggie chewed her lower lip.

Cookie nodded. "Small town. *Very* small town."

Maggie picked up her cup and stared into the tea.

Cookie watched her for a few moments. "What else, baby? This isn't just about Aaron."

Maggie sat up a bit straighter. "Not sure. Maybe Fletcher. I tried to lie to him, but I couldn't—"

"Good thing. You're a lousy liar. God's too close to your heart."

"Mama said it was 'God's finger' poking at you."

"Good mama. She knew you. When you believe as strongly as you do, it's hard to turn your back on what you know is right, what you know God wants you to do."

Maggie's mouth twisted. "Yet I can't let him know about—" She stopped and sipped her tea, her eyes starting to water. "He confuses me. He's different than I remembered."

"What's different?"

Maggie shrugged. "I'm not sure. I saw him in his cabin this morning, and he was so calm, almost as if he were determined to make me talk." She smiled. "And talk I did."

Cookie snorted. "And you didn't lie to him."

Maggie shook her head.

"Just threw a little dirt around?"

Maggie stared at Cookie, a bit of her humor finally breaking through. "Now why in the world would I want to do that?

The old woman wagged her finger. "Now don't think you can start trying to fool me either, baby. I know you too well." She then stood up, motioning for Maggie to follow. "Come on. I have some dough rising on the stove. Let's go whack some bread around."

Maggie smiled finally and followed the old woman into the kitchen.

A local restaurant catered the retreat's evening meals. Every day Maggie would help them set the trays of food on the counter separating the kitchen from the open and airy main room of the lodge, and the writers would go down the buffet line. Today was no different. As the restaurant workers left, Maggie started the coffeemaker, set out plates, napkins and glasses, then pulled assorted soft drinks, carafes of tea and Scott's requested spring water out of the refrigerator.

She looked over the spread once more, then frowned. Three of the coffee cups were missing. She found one in the dishwasher, and she washed it and put it on the counter. She crossed the lodge to Tim's room, knocking softly. He occasionally took coffee to his room after breakfast.

There was no answer, and she pushed the door open slowly. She hated invading his privacy; this was his home, too. Tim had only been here a few months, but he was as much a part of

Aaron's "extended family" as she was. She, for one, was grateful for Tim's patience. They'd lost two groundskeepers before due to Aaron's temper.

Tim's room smelled faintly of machine oil and freshly mowed grass, but it was relatively neat. A computer that she had given him took up most of his desk, surrounded by printouts from landscaping sites and veterans groups. *I didn't know he was a veteran,* Maggie thought. She tried not to look at the other papers, already feeling like a spy.

The two missing cups were on the nightstand, and Maggie grabbed them quickly and hurried back to the main room. She washed them, put them on the counter then checked over the table one more time. Sighing, she poured herself a cup of coffee and plopped down on an overstuffed couch in front of the fire, grateful for a few minutes of peace.

She looked around the room, feeling a melancholy sense of pride in what she saw. The A-frame lodge had been Aaron's idea, as had many of the rules for the retreat. But the rest had been hers. She'd moved into the house when it was newly finished, still smelling of fresh wood and paint. She'd decorated it, shipping in some items from New York. Others were from local artisans. In addition to the main room, there were five bedrooms and a game room with a big-screen television in the basement. An extensive library and computer had been set up in the main room's loft. A laundry and kitchen, which were open for anyone's use, were at the beginning of the north wing, with her office on the other side of the main room from the kitchen at the end of the south hallway. One of the bedrooms was for visitors, with one each reserved for her, Tim and Aaron. The fifth one was reserved for one of the writers, and was a perk that was assigned on a first-come, first-deserved (in Aaron's opinion, of course) basis. Currently, Tonya Marino, who had been at the retreat for almost two years, lived there, but she was so quiet and reserved, Maggie often forgot the young writer was even in the house.

Maggie had done it all, but the main room was her true source of pride. The room was perfectly square, with floor-to-ceiling panes of glass on the front and back walls and heavy oak paneling on the others. A fireplace interrupted the glass on the back wall, as did a door that led out onto the wooden deck. The sitting area Maggie had arranged in front of the fireplace was cozy and filled with fat pillows and thick throws to hold off the chill of the New Hampshire winters. The dining table, which could seat fifteen, was near the front, where the sloping front lawn could be seen during meals. That wall also let in the best sun of the day and gave the residents a view of gorgeous sunsets in good weather.

The colors throughout the house were rich and dark, more masculine than feminine, and the art of both sculptors and painters from the nearby town of Mercer dotted the walls, adding a dramatic brightness to the atmosphere. This was Maggie's home as well as her workplace, and she cherished each piece. And she was terrified she was about to lose it all.

When Korie inherits... The thought was a weight in her head that both hurt and angered her as well as adding to her confusion. *What would I do?* New York was no longer home. She loved this place more than she'd believed she could. She loved Mercer, with its conservative yet artsy ways. The reserved but loving people there. And Cookie. She'd made a lot of friends here, far more than Aaron, who had stayed to himself, and Korie, who was seldom around except on the occasional weekends. Maggie swirled the coffee around in her cup, watching the brown liquid lap up the sides. A few drops spilled over. She watched them hit the hardwood floor, but she didn't care. *Why should I care about anything?*

"Should I get you a mop?"

Maggie leaped to her feet, sloshing the coffee down the front of her skirt. "Fletcher MacAllister! Don't you *ever* knock?"

His left eyebrow cocked. "I didn't realize we had to."

Maggie's fist clutched the soaked fabric. "No, no. You don't have to. But could you at least have the courtesy to make a little noise so you don't scare a person half to death?"

He scuffed his feet.

Maggie glared at him, fighting a smile. He stared back, amusement lighting in his eyes.

"I'm starved! Let's get this show on the road!" Scott Jonas's voice rang out from the back door, and Maggie blinked first, turning to look at him. Lily, his wife, followed, tripping a bit as she stepped through the door. She grabbed the door frame with her right hand, since her right tightly gripped an open bottle of Dom Perignon champagne. Maggie winced, and glanced at Fletcher, whose eyes narrowed as he looked over Scott and Lily, head to toe. His focus lingered on the bottle, and Maggie felt a chill move through her. She started forward, forgetting about the wet spot on her skirt.

"Here, Scott, help me take the foil off the trays. Everything just got here, so it's still hot." Maggie opened up one tray after another, putting tongs or large spoons into each of the dishes.

"I'm not really all that hungry," Lily announced. "I just came because we have to." She plucked a glass off the bar and poured the last drops of champagne into it, frowning. Then she smiled sweetly at Maggie. "Sorry, hon, looks like I'll have to go get another one."

Maggie's stomach cramped. She went to Lily and took the shorter, darker woman by the arm, speaking softly. "Don't you think you should wait?"

Lily flipped her long hair over her shoulder. "No," she said, in a loud stage whisper. "Why should I?"

Maggie closed her eyes. "Out of respect. And we have company," she said, nodding at Fletcher.

Lily glared at her. "Respect? Give me one good—"

Maggie grabbed Lily's wrists suddenly, locking eyes with her and startling the young actress. "Just because," Maggie said firmly.

Lily froze, then slowly relaxed under Maggie's gaze. Her eyes softened. "I'm sorry, Mitten. I know he was special to you."

Maggie let go of her and pulled the empty bottle away. "Thank you. Please promise me that you'll eat." Lily nodded, looking suddenly very small and young as she sank down into a chair at the table.

Maggie went into the kitchen and paused, staring at the bottle in her hand. Most people would look at the expensive drink with affection. It was a symbol of so many celebrations. But Maggie despised it, despised what it had done to one of the most talented actresses she'd ever seen perform. And when Maggie refused to stock it for her, Lily had it shipped in, two cases a month, storing it in the cabin. It was an image that everyone at the retreat knew well: Lily and her bottle, wandering through the morning mist, like Catherine searching for Heathcliff on the moor.

Lily had promised she would try to cut down, but Maggie knew, all too well, that Lily used it to cope with her marriage recently—as well as other things. Maggie also knew that Lily sometimes appeared drunk when she wasn't, just to keep Scott at bay. He hated it when she drank, and these days, Lily preferred him to be angry instead of affectionate.

Scowling, Maggie flung the bottle into the trash, where it landed with a leaden thud. She grimaced at the sound, and she felt flushed, as if her blood were racing. *Please let her be acting. She promised to lay off it tonight.*

Maggie returned to the great room, then realized that the room was much noisier. The rest of the residents had arrived and were gossiping and filling their plates. Maggie stopped, looking around.

They sat and started eating, talking about the day's work. No one seemed to notice Aaron's absence. Only a day had passed, and it was as if nothing had changed, and that any minute, the tall blond man who had so captivated her a few years ago would open the door and stroll into the room with that casual lanky way he had about him.

Maggie felt like screaming. *How can you all be so callous?* She stared out over the room, feeling numb again. Lily came to her, distracting her. The younger woman leaned close, whispering, "You didn't tell me he was a cop."

"He's not anymore."

Lily's lips pursed. "Very funny, Mitten. Why is he here?"

"Korie wants him to be."

"Korie!" Lily's suddenly loud voice echoed, and several people stopped talking. Over her shoulder, Maggie could see Fletcher watching them.

Maggie nodded. "Yes—Korie," she said, in her normal voice. Stepping away, she announced generally, "Korie won't be here tonight. She called this afternoon, and she's going to a show opening in Boston. She'll be back tomorrow night, and will stay until—"

"Yeah, right." Scott's cynicism was undisguised. "I doubt we'll see much of her ever again. She's finally free."

Fletcher had finished filling his plate and sat down on the opposite side of the table from Scott. "Why do you say that?"

"Who are you?" Scott asked, as he broke open the cap on a bottle of spring water.

"Fletcher MacAllister. I'm—"

"Judson MacLean," Scott finished.

Fletcher reached for the salt. "Not exactly."

"Fletcher is going to be our guest for a while," Maggie said, setting a plate of food on the table and slipping into her chair. She glanced around, wondering who looked the most guilty. "Fletcher, meet our current retreat residents. To my left are Lily Dunne and Scott Jonas. Next is Patrick Stanfield, cabin three. Dan Jameson, cabin—" She stopped and smiled weakly. "I'll give you those later. Carter Everson, Tonya Marino, Frank Petersen, Laura Baker and Mick Lovett. And down at the end there is Tim Miller." Maggie went through the names of the nine residents and the groundskeeper slowly, noticing that Fletcher made distinct eye contact with each of them. "Fletcher is here, at the request of Korie, to look into Aaron's death." The table fell silent as they all stared at Fletcher.

"I thought it was an accident," said Patrick, a writer who'd been at the retreat almost as long as Scott and Lily.

Fletcher opened his mouth to speak, but Maggie beat him to it. "It was, Patrick. But you know Korie and her drama-queen ways. We just want to make sure there are no loose ends. Don't be surprised if Fletcher asks you about Monday night, just to see what you remember."

"But I don't remember anything," Lily said.

"You never do," responded Scott.

Dual pink flushes colored Lily's cheeks, and there was a brightness to her eyes that everyone tried to ignore. She picked up her fork in her left hand and tried to eat, but mostly moved food from one side of the plate to the other. Maggie knew from long experience that she would probably be silent the rest of the night.

At the far end of the table, Tim Miller stood up suddenly, taking his plate back to the bar. Second helpings hit his plate with mushy slaps, as Fletcher said evenly, "I won't bother anyone unnecessarily. Tyler has completed his report. This is just for Korie's peace of mind."

"In other words," Scott said hoarsely, "she thinks one of us killed him."

Maggie bristled. "Scott, I don't think—"

"Oh, Maggie, just shut up," Scott said. "Stop protecting her. You know what she's like. She wants us out of here. What better way than to stir up the idea that we're all killers?"

Maggie flared. "No, Scott, I will *not* shut up. You're being obnoxious. *Again*. No one knows what's going to happen to the retreat, but Korie has said nothing at all about closing it."

"What about that offer?" Scott demanded.

"What offer?" asked Dan.

"Yeah, Maggie," Scott continued. "Why don't you tell us all about the offer? Especially Korie's point man here."

Maggie took a deep, calming breath. She looked at Fletcher, but he showed no emotion in response to Scott's gibe. He merely looked at her, waiting.

"A few weeks ago, Aaron and Korie received an offer from a developer who wants this property. It was a fairly good one, but Aaron turned it down flat. He doesn't—didn't—need the money, and he wanted to keep the retreat up and going."

"But Korie didn't agree."

Maggie looked at Scott patiently. "Korie knows what this place means—meant—to him, Scott. Even more, Korie is all about image, and the awards associated with this place mean image to her. She may change it, but I can't see her closing it."

"She's also about money," Scott answered.

"She will have plenty of money," Maggie answered. "Aaron was heavily insured."

"Enough to run this place?" asked Dan.

"Probably not," Scott snapped, "but enough for Korie to want him dead."

Maggie took a deep breath but ignored Scott. *This is getting out of hand.* "The retreat is self-supporting. Aaron set up an escrow account large enough that the operating expenses are covered by the interest earned every year. He once told me that he was having that handled separately in his will, but I don't know for sure what that meant."

"Maybe he meant he'd leave it to you. He does seem to take care of all his toys."

Maggie slammed her hand down on the table. "Scott!"

"So who else do you think would profit from his death?" Fletcher asked quietly.

Scott slid down in his chair and took a swig of water. "Certainly none of the ones he's tortured over the years." He paused, then looked at Maggie. "Who'll be the judge of the requirements now?" he asked. "Surely not you or Korie. Neither one of you knows diddly about literature. Or did you plan to claim that part of his fame, too?"

Lily looked up sharply, first at her husband, then at Maggie, who sat without answering. Fletcher cleared his throat and addressed Maggie. "I thought you had worked in the publishing industry."

Scott made a gargling sound. "Yeah, in retail. She managed a bookstore. That's like asking a fast-food manager to judge the food at a gourmet four-star restaurant."

Lily slapped her napkin into her plate, then stood, picked up the plate and her glass, and went to the kitchen. Silence ruled as she left, then Dan chuckled. "Got a couch for tonight, Scott?"

Scott pushed away from the table. "I don't need her. And I don't need this." He stood up and pointed at Fletcher. "Whoever did it should get a reward. Aaron got what he deserved." He strode across the room and left, slamming the door behind him. Tim got up and went to the window, watching Scott disappear through the trees. Then he turned and watched Lily as she started cleaning up in the kitchen.

Dan lifted his glass and toasted Maggie. "Now I see why you spend so much time at Cookie's, Maggie. We are a temperamental lot."

Maggie frowned, then forced herself to smile. She really hadn't wanted Fletcher to know about Cookie. "Dessert, Dan? They sent Boston cream pie and strawberry sorbet."

Dan laughed. "Are you suggesting I eat and not talk?"

Maggie looked innocent. *"Moi?"* she asked, pointing at her chest. "Why, Dan, I *never* get tired of all my lovely writers. They keep things so lively around here."

Fletcher stood up. "I think I'd like some of that sorbet."

Everyone else wandered away from the table. Some to get dessert, some to get coffee and stand by the fire. A few went downstairs to the game room. Frank and Laura left, holding hands, and Tonya returned to her room. As Maggie started to the kitchen, Tim caught her by the arm. "Is she going to be all right?" he asked, nodding toward Lily.

Maggie touched his cheek. "They'll work it through."

"He shouldn't hurt her like that."

Maggie shook her head. "No, but she'll be fine." Maggie glanced at Lily, then back at her groundskeeper. "She always is."

Tim nodded, then retreated to the fire, where he poked at the flames, keeping constant watch on Lily. Maggie paused, then said softly, "I had to get two of the cups out of your room tonight."

He looked surprised, then shrugged and looked back at the fire. "That's okay, Miss Maggie. It's your house."

Maggie shifted her shoulders, feeling weary. Tim sounded unusually Southern tonight. Must be her imagination. "Still, I promised I wouldn't go into your room without telling you."

He shrugged again, poking harder at the logs. Sighing, Maggie went into the kitchen, took a dishrag out of Lily's hands and clutched her fingers in her own, shaking them gently.

Lily's green eyes met her blue, and Maggie wished she could pass some of her own stubbornness and strength through their mere touch. The pain and anger in those green eyes seared her heart.

"Did he hit you today?" she whispered.

Lily shook her head. "Still just that one time…" Her eyes glistened.

Maggie frowned. "No tears, not tonight. Okay?"

Lily bit her lip and nodded.

"Good girl." Maggie took a deep breath and Lily followed her example. An old routine that gave them new resolve. "Go bring some of the dishes off the table. We'll put them in the dishwasher, and I'll run it in the morning. I'm going to see if the guys downstairs need coffee."

Air hockey occupied the two men downstairs, however, and Maggie returned as Lily was loading the last of the dishes. She looked around the room, making one more check. The room was almost clean, and Dan and Patrick were finishing their coffee near the fire. Tim must have gone out for his nightly walk around the grounds. But there was still one other body missing.

Maggie frowned. "Where's Fletcher? Did he go back to his cabin?"

Dan shook his head. "Nope. He helped Lily for a bit, then took out the trash."

Maggie froze, a slice of fear in her stomach. "He did what?"

Dan didn't even look up. "Garbage. He'll be back in a few."

Maggie turned toward the kitchen to find Lily staring at her, puzzled. Maggie just mouthed, *Oh, no,* when the door opened and Fletcher walked in, his face a dark mask and one gloved hand holding an empty Dom Perignon bottle. He stopped, then looked from Maggie to Lily, and back. "Call Tyler, Maggie. Tell him I've found the murder weapon."

From the kitchen came a small gasp as Lily sank to the floor.

THREE

Judson was insistent that the crime scene be secured, since it was far too easy for forensic evidence to be contaminated. He'd seen too many cases lost simply because the investigators had been careless. Catching a criminal was hard enough without sloppy procedure.

"It was in the trash can," Fletcher said.

Maggie sat on the deck steps, huddled in an oversize coat, as Fletcher explained to police chief Tyler Madison how he'd found the bottle. Inside, Lily was stretched out on a couch with an ice pack on her head, but the other residents had returned to their cabins, puzzled and annoyed.

Fletcher frenetically demonstrated his actions as he talked. Tyler's eyes tried to follow him, but Maggie just stared, amazed at the sudden burst of energy in the detective. She now realized his calm demeanor, his control, was a part of his work. Underneath was a strong passion, just waiting to break through. No wonder he and Aaron had been so close, she thought. They'd both shared the same love of life, of their work.

The lights from the house cast long golden pools across the deck and down through the yard, with the rails and slats of the deck creating lines of darkness on the ground. Fletcher walked in and out of the shadows with his pacing, like a large dog behind a fence. "I went to put the bag of garbage in the can," Fletcher said, "and I noticed the neck sticking up. I thought it might poke a hole in the bag, so I went to move it and saw the blood, then the fact that the label was damaged. That's when I realized the flakes found in Aaron's wound might be from the label."

Tyler nodded, his hat a little unstable on his head. "We'll have to send them off for analysis. We're not set up for anything like this here."

"The blood, too."

"Of course." Tyler crossed his arms, and Maggie looked from him to Fletcher, as if they were tennis players. The younger man had gotten his job six months ago when the previous chief had died, since he was the senior member of the five-officer police force. Yet he was still not quite thirty, and his inexperience seemed to shine.

Fletcher paced back and forth a few minutes, then stopped in front of Maggie. "Maggie, *why?*"

Tyler stepped in. "Now, wait a minute, MacAllister—"

Fletcher exploded. "Can't you see? She was alone with him for over half an hour. She threw the bottle away. She moved the body. I want to know why."

Maggie finally exploded in the face of his building temper, his relentless accusations. "I did *not* move his body! He was like that when I found him. He was *dead!* I couldn't even bring myself to touch him. I barely remember what happened! How could I move him?" She stood up. "Don't you *dare* blame me just because you're hurting, too!"

Fletcher stopped, clenching his fists as he stared at her. He took a deep breath and let it out slowly, obviously trying to regain control. "Then why hide the bottle?"

Maggie threw up her hands. "Why do you even ask? You know why!"

Fletcher's words were crisp. "So why are you protecting Lily?"

Maggie froze. "Because she didn't kill him!"

"Didn't she? Don't you think so?" Fletcher bent over her, his questions flying fast, directly at her face.

"No! She couldn't!"

"Why not? Aaron was hit on the right side of the head. That means it was most likely a left-handed assailant. Lily's the only one here who's left-handed."

Maggie shook her head furiously. "No! You don't understand. There's no way!"

"Then why did you toss out the bottle?"

Tears filled Maggie's eyes. "Because I knew how it looked. The blood—but the blood was already on the bottle we'd had earlier. I knew everyone would think like you do—"

"How long has she called you Mitten?"

"Since we were kids—" Maggie stepped back, eyes wide, her hand over her mouth.

Fletcher backed off, staring at her. She watched as he blinked rapidly, studying her, and saw the understanding come over his face. "You're sisters."

"Say what?" Tyler demanded.

"Is that why you're protecting her, Maggie?"

Maggie shook her head, an overwhelming weakness settling over her. She sank down on the steps. "Yes. No. No! You don't understand. It's the other way around. And it's not."

Fletcher sat down next to her. "Explain it to me."

Maggie took a deep breath, resolved for it to come out. "I went to college. Lily went to Broadway. Bit parts, a few films, a show here and there, not a lot of money but enough, for about five years. We didn't see each other much, even though we were in the same city. And there was no press. No one cared. Then she made *Ramsey Place*, then *Blue Ribbon Winner*, then—" Maggie stopped and wiped her face with her hands.

"Her career went up and her personal life went down the drain. She was followed everywhere she went. She was stalked. People broke into her home to steal her clothes!" Maggie sat up straighter and motioned around her. "By the time things really got hot, I was already here. This place has no security, but it's remote and hard to find. She had lied and said she had no family. My dad died before I was born and my mom married Bobby Dunne when I was only one, but they never changed my name—" She stopped, her hand waving away the past. "It's a long story, but it worked. The press left me alone. But we traded off. Sometimes I would hide her here for weeks. That's how she met Scott. She's still being stalked, in fact, which is why she's staying here with him. It's one reason she started drinking. She can't handle the fame, much less the fear."

"What about her career?"

Maggie shrugged. "Right now it's in the drunk tank. Her agent stays in touch, sends her scripts, begs her to go to rehab before it's too late. I hoped being here would help. She's got to stop drinking."

"Who knows you're her sister?"

Maggie buried her face in her hands. "No one. Not even Scott."

Tyler crossed his arms. "But you look so different."

Fletcher waved away the objection. "Just the hair and eyes." He made a circular motion around his face. "Here is the same."

Maggie sighed. "My dad had red hair—I got the auburn from him. Lily has her hair straightened."

Fletcher stared out into the woods. "How long has she been drinking?"

Maggie shrugged. "I'm not sure. Not long, I know. We didn't drink when we were younger. That wasn't how we were raised, and I know she didn't drink until she left the church. Even then it was nothing like this. Sometimes she goes through a bottle a day."

Tyler stared at her. "A bottle a day!"

Maggie looked up at him. "You think we do that much celebrating that we need two cases of champagne a month?"

"How would I know—"

Maggie looked skeptical as she quoted her best friend. "It's a very small town, Tyler. She orders it, it's stored in her cabin, but it's still delivered here. So give me a break, okay?"

Fletcher smiled quickly, but wiped it away with his hand. "But sometimes she doesn't really drink. Like tonight. She wasn't really drunk."

Maggie watched him closely. "How did you know?"

"Because it's my job, Maggie. She has the act down, but not the other signs, the stuff a cop would notice. Why does she pretend?" Shifting uncomfortably on the step, Maggie looked out, her eyes unfocused. When she didn't answer, Fletcher prompted quietly, "Scott?"

Reluctantly, Maggie nodded. "He hates it, so he stays away from her when he thinks she's…which is what she wants…" Her voice trailed off. This wasn't anyone's business.

Fletcher took a deep breath. "Tell me about their fight, Maggie. Tell me about finding Aaron. And this time don't leave anything out."

Maggie hugged her knees to her chest and closed her eyes, remembering and saying a quick prayer for guidance. She really didn't want to relive that moment.

"Lily and I had been cleaning the kitchen. We do that almost every night, just to have some time together. Aaron had been at dinner, his usual arrogant, jerky self. He'd been drinking."

"Green Label Jack Daniel's."

Maggie looked at him then nodded. "It hurt. He told me he'd been trying to stop lately. I thought he was serious about quitting. I hadn't seen him drink for a long time, and he acted…weird, even for Aaron. He'd berated Scott and Patrick for slacking off. I didn't get it. They are two of his favorites. Then he started in on Lily." She shifted, the memory still burning, a vision of a red-faced Aaron shoving Lily backward, snatching the champagne bottle out of her hand.

"This trash will kill you, girl!" Aaron's open hand aimed for the side of her head, but Lily turned into it and his palm landed on her cheek and lips, drawing blood.

Lily fell to her knees with a short screech, but she scrambled up, diving for Aaron. "Like you'd know, old man!" she bit back, grabbing for the bottle with her right hand as her left raked its nails over his neck, drawing blood.

His hand closed on the young actress's blouse, and he pulled her face up close to his, raising her up on her toes, his voice low and hoarse. "You cat! You have no idea. I'm the one person who does know."

"Stop it!" Maggie yelled, shoving her way between them as Aaron pressed his palm to the scratches Lily had left. "Look what this is doing to you! You're acting like children, the both of you. Stop drinking!" She faced her boss, who literally towered over her. "Go home, Aaron. Sleep this one off."

Aaron's glare shook her all the way to her toes, but she tilted her chin up as he raised his hand again, her eyes narrowing to thin slits. "Don't you dare," she whispered sharply. "Don't you even think about it."

Maggie paused and took a deep breath, forcing her eyes to meet Fletcher's. "Anyway, no one stayed around after dinner, not like tonight. At first he acted like he was in pain, but then he just got belligerent. No one wanted to be around him. Then he started in on Lily and me, and I called his bluff and told him to go home and sleep it off. He acted as if he was going to hit me, and I stood him down. He laughed, making a comment that I would never take it from a man like Lily did—"

"Scott hits her?" Tyler demanded.

Fletcher looked up at him. "Pay attention, Tyler. Or does your mother not go to the local beauty shop to keep up with what's happening around town?"

Maggie almost laughed, and she looked at Fletcher, grateful. He smiled briefly and nodded his encouragement. She continued with a sigh. "Scott only hit her one time, but it's left her skittish. It's made things very tough for them, for us. So when Aaron hit her, I can understand why she went after him." She looked up at Fletcher, her eyes pleading. "I thought the blood was from the fight, but I knew how it would look!"

Fletcher was back under control and merely nodded at her. "Keep talking."

She shrugged. "Lily left, and Tim went to bed. I was going to take out the garbage and go to my office to work for a bit. That's when I found him. He was just…there. Lying on the steps with that look. No life in his eyes." Maggie stopped, staring up at the bright stars, which were blurry through her tears. *Are You listening, God? Are You watching? Am I doing the right thing?* The relief she felt from the release of the information was tempered by doubts about Lily, about Fletcher. About herself.

Fletcher took her hand, folding it in the warmth of his. "Go on."

Maggie sniffed back the tears, relishing the comfort of his grasp. "Tim got up to go to the bathroom and realized all the lights were still on. That's when he found me." She paused. "Us."

Fletcher squeezed her hand. "No, Maggie. Before that. What did you do?"

Maggie looked at him, puzzled.

"How did you react?"

She lowered her eyes and tried to call back the memory. "I…I…dropped the trash bag. I remember it spilling all down the steps as I went to him."

"Who cleaned it up?"

Maggie suddenly felt confused. She didn't remember. She looked up at Tyler, who shook his head. "There was no trash when we got here."

"Then Tim must have picked it up before you got here. Or Scott." Maggie racked her brain. "I don't remember anyone else being around." *Why can't I remember?*

Fletcher tugged on her hand. "When did you find the bottle?"

Maggie stared at him. "This morning, just before you and Korie got here. I didn't know how it got there, and I realized how it looked…Lily's bottle close to where he'd died. The blood. Everyone was already saying it wasn't an accident, that the body had been moved."

"So how do you know it had not been in the trash after all?"

"I guess I don't." Maggie studied Fletcher's face. His gaze was distant; she could almost see him processing what he'd been told. *You don't believe me, do you?*

Tyler shook his head. "No. MacAllister, I know we're just a small-town department, but we would have noticed a bloody bottle at the crime scene. There was no trash at all when we got here."

Fletcher nodded. "No doubt. So it had to have been placed afterward. Either to look as if it had been an overlooked piece of your trash…"

"Or to implicate Lily," Tyler finished. "I still don't understand why the bottle didn't break from such a blow."

Fletcher spun on his toe and headed back to the trash can.

"Other brands might have," Maggie said, "but the Dom's bottle is pretty…" Her voice trailed off as Fletcher started digging through the trash, coming up with the bottle she had tossed earlier that evening. "What are you doing?"

Fletcher paused, looked from her to Tyler, then with a sudden jerk, he slammed the end of the bottle down on the ground, the thick glass burying itself several inches into the dirt.

Maggie gasped, then closed her eyes, burning tears leaking through the slits.

"That wasn't necessary," Tyler said softly.

Fletcher crossed to Maggie and leaned over her. "He didn't deserve this," he said, his voice a harsh whisper. "Help me. Don't hinder me."

Maggie opened her eyes. "Please stop. I can't do this."

Fletcher looked into her eyes a moment, then nodded, emotion giving way to business. "We'll finish tomorrow. Nothing is going to get solved tonight. I'll talk to the other residents in the morning. Tyler will get the analysis done. There's a good chance our killer left more than fingerprints on that bottle. We can get elimination prints from everyone here, if they'll cooperate—"

"My fingerprints will be on that bottle."

He nodded. "I know."

"I didn't kill him. Neither did Lily."

Silently, he stood up, pulling her up with him, then he put his hand on her elbow as she climbed the stairs. They were almost at the door when a memory sparked in her brain—just a flash, but it might be important. Maggie turned abruptly at the door, to speak to Tyler.

The pain slapped into her face almost at the same time she recognized the sound of the gunshot in the distance. There was a moment when she wondered where the pain was coming from, almost as if it were not a part of her. Then everything shifted into a slow blur. She felt remote, pulled out of her body, and she heard herself screaming. She was falling, then not, then there was the solid wood of the deck beneath her. At once, the pain hit in full force, a thousand shards of glass against her skin. Then Maggie's vision faded, and with the darkness, relief. She closed her eyes, embracing it.

FOUR

Work was his passion, and Judson pursued it with a relentless sense of perfection. His personal standards were tougher than the department's, and he went through a number of partners before finding one suitable. "My partners," he once told his captain, "keep forgetting that it is the *work* that you are involved with, not the crime victims."

He watched her breathe, his eyes tracing over every contour of muscle and bone, every bit of pale flesh. Every bruise. Every bandaged wound.

It was his mistake, and she had almost paid the price for it. If she had not turned so abruptly—

The bullet had grazed her scalp and blown apart the wooden door frame, embedding a half-dozen shards of wood in the side of her face, near her hairline. Sometimes Fletcher thought he could still hear her screams. Maggie had fallen against him, then to the deck, as Tyler had bounded into the woods after the shooter. The screams had brought out Lily, who surprised Fletcher by taking charge of her sister and yelling at him to go, *go!*

But he and Tyler had not found so much as a shell casing in the dark, and Fletcher had returned to the lodge, his anger barely under control, to find that Lily had called 911, pulled the first-aid kit out of the kitchen and removed most of the wooden slivers. She had stopped the bleeding with pressure bandages, directed the arriving officers into the woods and helped the ambulance attendants load Maggie. Maggie had only remained unconscious a few moments, and it had been Lily who had calmed her, trying to ease the panic with a soothing voice. As they had watched the ambulance leave, Lily had spoken evenly. "Who's going to take me to the hospital?"

Fletcher never took his eyes off the flashing lights. "You're not drunk at all, are you?"

"I *am*..." Lily had said, with an exaggerated pause for effect "an actress."

Fletcher had nodded. "One of the officers will take you. I have to stay here."

"She'll be disappointed."

Fletcher had looked down at her, frowning. "What?"

She had smiled. "Never mind. I'll snag an officer. You'd better stick to Tyler. He looks a little out of his element."

Fletcher had watched as Lily sauntered off. A smile, a flirt and a coy squeeze on the arm later, and she and an officer were headed for the hospital in Portsmouth. Maggie had been treated and kept overnight for observation. She was released this morning, sent home doped up on the appropriate painkillers.

Now, he watched her breathe.

"Not my usual type, is she?" Aaron asked him, as Maggie had headed for the ladies' room.

Fletcher had noticed. He was so used to seeing far too many perfect, rich, trophy-wife candidates on Aaron's arm that Maggie's difference shone—her soft but out-of-control curls, her light use of make-up. He tilted his head as he

*watched her walk away. There was a slight awkwardness to her
gait, a faint limp that Aaron had explained was left over from
a childhood accident, but the sway of her hips still made men
turn and look. Nice legs.*

*He looked back at Aaron. "She's not your typical airheaded
beauty queen, no."*

*"But she's smart. And sasses me back like no one ever has.
She's got spunk."*

Fletcher took a sip of his coffee. "Yeah, I noticed."

*Aaron laughed, his voice muffled by his raised glass. "I like
it when you two fight. I like the way she tries to defend me."*

"You would. Don't you ever fight with her?"

*"Only about one thing, my dear Fletcher, and eventually, I
promise you, I will win."*

*Fletcher looked at Maggie, who had taken a quick sidestep
to avoid a waiter loaded down with dishes. She had to be the
most determined women he'd ever met. "You may have met
your match this time."*

"Never, me boyo. No woman bests Aaron Jackson."

*"You know, Aaron, your humility is one of the things I like
best about you."*

*Aaron had scowled. "Humility is a much overrated virtue,
usually touted by those who have nothing to be humble about."*

*Fletcher studied his friend's face. "Why are you so intent
on this?"*

*Aaron was quiet for a few moments, then said evenly,
"Because if I lose this one, I lose the girl."*

And he had. Aaron and Maggie had called it quits a few
months later, and Aaron had gone on to a series of lovelies, all
of whom bored him within a few weeks. Korie had latched on,
and Aaron had married her quickly, as he had told Fletcher
shortly after the wedding, "out of attrition." *Were you still in
love with him, Maggie?*

Fletcher sighed. This was a mess. He still didn't quite believe everything she had told him, and it was beginning to look as if anyone who knew Aaron had some motive to kill him. Every single resident had opportunity, including Maggie and Tim. He was also bothered by the fact that he didn't *want* to consider Maggie a suspect, even though he had to. He had to eliminate her, if only to shut up the voice in his head that wanted to hold her out separate, treat her special.

He liked her too much.

He sat up straighter, forcing himself to focus on the investigation. He wanted to look at Aaron's finances, talk to the other residents. And why kill Maggie? He squirmed in his chair. If, in fact, the shot was meant for her. He needed more evidence, especially from the woman in front of him, the woman whose blood was still on his coat.

"So what *did* you fight about, Maggie?" he asked aloud, not expecting an answer.

"Most likely love, religion or money," Lily said from the doorway. Fletcher stood as she entered, carrying a small tray that held a steaming bowl of soup, crackers, a bottle of soda and a glass of ice. She pushed the door shut with her foot.

"That smells good."

"Ciotka Cookie made it and sent it over."

"Who's Cookie? That name keeps coming up. And what's a chalka?"

Lily grinned, then set the tray on the table near the bed. "It's pronounced 'Chot-ka.' It's Polish, or something, for 'aunt'...Aunt Cookie."

Going to the window, Lily opened the blinds a bit, and slats of dusty light sliced through the room. Fletcher looked around the room in the slightly brighter light, taking in the practical but feminine decor. Maggie's bed was an antique, with a tall, ornately carved headboard and a mattress that was higher than usual. The matching dresser was narrow, but had a mirror that could be tilted down to check a lady's dress hem. On the opposite wall was a low jelly cabinet, with a top that was lined with books and small photos.

The figure on the bed stirred, and Lily looked down at her, then sat on the edge of the bed, pushing Maggie's tangled hair away from her face. "Cordelia Holokaj. She's a trip. She has this delicious little Hansel and Gretel cottage on the other side of the woods, down a deserted logging road. She's Maggie's best friend, mentor, confidante, you name it."

"Sounds like someone I want to talk to."

"Don't you have someone like that? I think we all should."

Fletcher nodded. "An uncle. He got me on the force. Lives in Brooklyn now. Where would I find this cottage?"

"I'll ask Tim to show you where it is. You'll love it. Just don't assume you'll be in charge of the interview." Lily sat on the bed, lightly stroking a strand of her sister's hair. "Why were you asking about her fights with Aaron?"

"Why do you pretend to be drunk all the time?"

Lily grinned. "My question first."

Fletcher sat down. "Aaron once told me they fought a lot when they were dating."

The dark hair flowed like a silk shawl around her shoulders as Lily nodded, and Fletcher finally saw the elegance and glamour that Hollywood and much of the country had once, briefly, doted on. "That would be the love fight. She drove him crazy with her faith, but that wasn't an all-the-time kind of fight. And she never asked him for money while they were dating. In fact, the only money he ever gave her was to run this place, and then just her salary and expenses. He tried to give her more, but she'd always refuse. She can be very stubborn."

Fletcher snorted, almost involuntarily, and Lily laughed. "And you haven't even run into the really bad moods yet."

Fletcher winced but didn't respond. "Why did they fight about their relationship? Aaron always acted like—" He hesitated, and Lily finished for him.

"Like he was a gift to the fairer sex. Aaron really did think he knew how to please a woman. For the most part, he did." She ignored Fletcher's arched eyebrow and continued. "And he had a hard time with women who knew how to say no."

Fletcher absorbed this for a moment, then his eyes narrowed. "Maggie turned him down?"

"Repeatedly. She never gave in. That's why they fought all the time."

"I can't believe I'm lying here with a face full of wood, and you two are discussing my love life."

Lily and Fletcher stared at each other a moment, then at Maggie. Lily burst out laughing, a gorgeous, crystalline sound that made the room brighter. "Actually, dear sister, we're discussing the total absence of it."

Maggie scowled, briefly, then took her sister's hand. And Fletcher was struck again by how different these two sisters were—and why Aaron had adored them both. Lily was always onstage—every moment was schooled and preened, as if she knew someone, somewhere, was watching her. Her voice had a coached lilt to it, and her makeup was always carefully done. Fletcher recognized now that even the slurred words of her "drunkenness" were cautiously and carefully manufactured. She was worldly and a bit jaded, yet there was a fragility and openness to her that made men desire her and women unafraid of her.

Maggie, on the other hand, with her auburn curls that were almost never completely under control, wore very little makeup and seemed defiant, secure and a bit intimidating. Yet she wasn't as cynical as her sister, and Fletcher saw in her an innocence that was oddly endearing, as if she really believed she could take on the whole world—and win. She used her intelligence as a shield, and she was very protective of her sister and all of the residents here, yet he liked the way she'd held off Scott at dinner. She gave off the image of a lioness defending the pride, but Fletcher was beginning to wonder if that wasn't as much a front as Lily's self-projected image. *What else are you hiding, Maggie?*

Lily stood up. "Sit up, dear, and have some soup. You haven't eaten since you lost your supper at the hospital. And it'll break through that fog you're meandering in."

Maggie pushed up weakly on her elbows. "Don't tell me you cooked."

Lily grinned. "No. Cookie made it."

"Does it have cabbage in it?"

"Did the sun rise?"

Maggie let Lily plump up her pillows and stack them behind her. "I need to challenge her sometime to make an entire meal without cabbage. Think she can do it?"

"Even Cookie can buy a cookbook, Mitten."

"But old instincts die hard. I think she buys cabbages by the truckload. If I'd been her kid, and she'd told me I'd been found under a cabbage leaf, I'd have believed her."

Lily handed Maggie the soup. "Careful. It's hot."

"Probably in more ways than one."

"Well, she did say something about clearing your sinuses."

Fletcher watched the rapid-fire dialogue for a few more moments, as Lily straightened out the bed around Maggie, poured the soda into the glass and opened the pack of crackers. Their movements were comfortable and familiar, even when Lily reached out and peeked under one of the bandages, only to have Maggie swat at her hand.

"With this act, how can anyone *not* see that you two are sisters?" he asked finally.

Both women sat very still, looking at each other. Then Lily straightened and tossed her hair back over her shoulder. "Fletcher, the drunk 'act' wasn't always an act. I perfected the act through experience with the real thing." Her mouth twisted. "I don't even have a driver's license anymore. Maggie only lets me stay here because I promise to work on being sober more, but she knows I've not been able to give it up completely. It's easier to *not* be her sister when I'm drunk. Or pretending to be. And, right now, that's very important."

He nodded. "Maggie told me."

Maggie set the soup aside and looked questioningly at Lily, who hesitated, then nodded. Maggie took a deep breath. "We think her stalker is close by."

Fletcher felt his face flush. "Why didn't you tell me?"

Lily stood up and went to his side. "Because we don't know for sure. He sends me letters, to my agent. I never see them. But they keep track of them and turn them over to the police. The last two were postmarked from Portsmouth, New Hampshire."

"So he *is* close."

"It could be coincidence," said Maggie. "He's mailed letters from all over the country."

Lily winced. "Usually from places where I've been on location. The police think he's probably from L.A. but is following me whenever I leave."

"Shouldn't you be someplace more secure?" Fletcher asked.

Lily and Maggie exchanged looks again, and Lily's voice dropped so low he almost didn't hear her. "I was more afraid in L.A. and New York, in the crowds. No place is truly secure."

"No one knows she's here," Maggie continued. "And, even if they did, we're not exactly easy to find. There's no mailbox or address. You have to *know* where that little driveway is. We always have to meet the residents in town and have them follow us here."

"Which, of course," Fletcher said, "makes it all the more likely that whoever killed Aaron—and tried to kill you—is still here with us." Maggie and Lily sat in silence as he went to the door. "Tyler was here this morning, and two of his men are still out there, looking for any kind of evidence. I'm going into town to talk to him, and I'll see if one of his men can stay here in the guest room. You two be careful. I want you here when I get back."

"I'll be here," said Maggie.

"And I'll be drunk," answered Lily. "Sort of."

Fletcher shook his head as he left, closing the door behind him. But the girlish laughter that echoed into the hall made him smile.

"I like her laugh," Aaron said, as he gave Fletcher the grand tour of the new retreat, which was then two years old. Fletcher was seeing it for the first time.

"You also like Elvis, vintage Corvettes, and Chicago-style pizza. Fun, but that's not why you hired her."

Aaron shrugged, then led the way down to the game room. "She's a good manager." He paused. "And a good friend. I trust her. She's mature for her age. She knows books and their authors. She can handle the egos that stream in here."

"Including yours?"

Aaron responded by going to a humidor on the bar and lighting up an imported cigar, filling the air with a woodsy, slightly cherry-scented smoke. "Including mine. I have no family, so this will be my only legacy. She's the right person to run it." He saluted Fletcher and took a drag on the cigar. "But in terms of egos, the one Maggie should watch her back about is my lovely and dearest Korie."

Fletcher pulled out a bar stool and half sat on it. "Tell me again why it is that you don't divorce Korie."

"One amazing pre-nup, my dear Judson. She leaves me, she gets nothing. I divorce her and she gets, oh, about sixty to seventy percent of everything I own."

"And you signed this why?"

"I was drunk, and it seemed like a good idea at the time. Thought it would settle me down."

"Did it?"

Aaron laughed and nodded at the cigar. *"Well, I am trying to do this more than the Jack."* He paused. *"You're still a young man, Fletcher. You're what? Thirty-eight?"*

"Thirty-seven."

"Whatever. On August sixteenth, I'll be fifty-four. And I don't have—" Aaron stopped abruptly, then came around from behind the bar and sat on the stool next to Fletcher. *"I've been a drunk for a long time, me boyo, and that stuff will kill you faster than just about anything but a speeding bus. My liver's swimming toward the great beyond even as we speak, and my heart's not far behind."* He took a deep breath, looking somber. *"It changes when you get older. You change. I was mostly meeting women who liked my name, my fame, my money or my bed, so I thought, why not? Korie may even be the worst of the lot, by far. But I didn't want to die alone."*

Aaron stubbed out the cigar, then slapped the bar. *"Enough self-pity. It's boring. Let's look at the rest of my legacy before dark sets in."*

But he had died alone, thought Fletcher, as he drove through the winding country roads into town. That meeting from two years before had been oddly prophetic: His short marriage to Korie had to be the worst of Aaron's three, and Fletcher had finally realized how little Aaron really understood about women. Maggie had been right to keep him at arm's distance.

He also realized that Maggie was right about one other

thing: Jackson's Retreat was not easy to find. When Aaron had first described the town to Fletcher, he thought it was one of those overphotographed hamlets with a few houses and a white church at a dead-end road. Instead, Mercer was a livable little town bordered by a tranquil mill pond at one end, a sturdy granite city hall at the other and a grid of tree-lined side streets in between that had turned into an artisans' haven. Mercer had more artists per capita than almost any town in New Hampshire, which was part of the reason that, when Aaron had come here years ago to get away for a while, he had fallen in love with the town, the land and the honesty and good hearts of the people. There weren't a lot of rebels here, even among the artsy crowd. The people, in turn, had adopted Aaron as their own, taking pride in his books, his love of the town and his retreat.

Fletcher slowed down as he entered the curving main street section of town, with its 250-year-old homes, clapboard stores and a history that dated back before the Revolution. Except for the cluster of "outsider" artists who'd moved in, many of the 2,500 residents were descendants of the town founders, and "change" was almost a vile word.

He understood why Maggie felt safe in hiding her sister here. The retreat was only about a mile or so out of town, but a stranger could ask for details on the retreat, or on Lily's presence, for days, and be met only with noncommittal stares. He hoped he wouldn't meet the same reserve as he worked on finding out who had killed Aaron.

Fletcher pulled up in front of the converted storefront that housed the police department, but he sat behind the wheel a few moments before getting out. Tyler Madison was a good man, but he was young and still somewhat inexperienced. He was also proud, both of his town and his position. And Korie had been right—he'd treated Maggie as if she were a queen, giving her clear deference over Korie. Fletcher grinned wryly.

Having seen both women in action recently, he was beginning to understand why.

Tyler had been forthcoming with his information on Aaron; it wasn't his fault that Fletcher found room for suspicions in it that Tyler had overlooked. That was a matter of experience. Still, Fletcher wanted to tread lightly. Tyler could easily shut him out if he wanted to.

Fletcher got out and went in, nodding at the receptionist. Her name tag read Peg Madison, marking her as Tyler's mom. She smiled. "Hey, Fletcher. He's been expecting you. Said if you didn't come in before lunch to call you." She nodded toward Tyler's office, and Fletcher knocked once before entering.

Tyler was on the phone, pacing. He pointed at Fletcher, then motioned for him to come in. "Yes," he said into the receiver. "Yes, I got it. That's all?" He nodded. "Good. Thanks." He hung up and leaned forward, putting both hands on the desk. "The blood is Aaron's type, but they still have to wait on the DNA results. And that bottle is a mass of prints, but they aren't going to be any help. They found eight sets of prints, six they could identify. Maggie and Scott showed up from the elimination prints. A delivery guy bonded by the liquor store. Aaron, Lily, and Tim were in the system. Aaron had a DUI about twelve years ago, when he 'borrowed' a friend's motorcycle and ran it into the East River. Lily, from an altercation on a show a few years ago. And Tim had that trespassing charge."

Fletcher frowned. "So it could be any one of them or the two they are missing."

Tyler shrugged. "Or none of them, if the killer wore gloves. The lab did say they are doing a DNA workup on anything from the mouth and the labels, just in case anything got snagged."

Fletcher nodded. "Good. Anything else?"

Tyler sat. "Yeah. I need your help with something."

"Name it."

The young police chief crossed his arms. "Korie. She wanted this investigation, now she's demanding we release the body for some fancy New York memorial service. She's driving the M.E. crazy. He covers four counties and has seven open cases, including two murders. He doesn't need some crazy lady screaming on his phone every two hours."

Fletcher stood, his lips pursed as he held back his real thoughts about Aaron's widow. "I'll talk to her."

"Thank you. She and I don't exactly…" His words trailed off as he thought of the best phrasing.

"See eye-to-eye?" Fletcher finished euphemistically.

Tyler laughed. "Yeah. How's Maggie?"

Fletcher stood. "As well as can be expected. Lily is staying with her. I don't like them being in the lodge alone, however. Any chance one of your guys could camp out there for a few days?"

"Sure. The two out there now are married, and their wives wouldn't like me much if I left them in the same house with Lily. But I'll get one of the single guys out this afternoon."

"Thanks."

The two men walked toward the front of the office, and through the storefront window Fletcher noticed an older woman loading two bags of groceries into baskets that hung on either side of the back wheel of a bicycle. Two cabbages poked out of the top of one bag. He nudged Tyler. "Is that by any chance—"

"Ciotka Cookie. Yeah. You probably need to talk to her. She knows what goes on at the retreat pretty well. But good luck." Behind them, Peg laughed.

Fletcher looked both of them over. "Am I missing something?"

Tyler shook his head. "Not yet."

FIVE

Control, Judson insisted, was the key to any investigation. To stay in control of the evidence, the process, the interviews. As the suspects in his cases discovered, Judson was not a man to be fooled, lied to or led astray by wild tales. His ability to stay on target and on topic was legendary, much to the dismay of criminals who thought themselves more clever than the distinguished lieutenant.

Fletcher crossed the empty street with a few long strides. "Excuse me—"

Cookie finished settling her groceries on the bike. "Hello, Mr. MacAllister. I was wondering when I'd see you," she said, without looking up.

Fletcher stopped.

Cookie grinned up at him. "Well, don't look so surprised. It's not like you blend in. Do you like tea, hot chocolate or cider?"

Fletcher found his feet and his tongue. "Is that cider mulled?"

The old woman's blue eyes sparkled. "Absolutely. Wouldn't have it any other way. Give me about thirty minutes to get all this settled, then come on by. It's the logging road that branches off to the left just before you get to the retreat." She fingered the end of her bright red-and-blue knit scarf. "I'll tie this to a tree at the end so you won't miss it. Stop and bring it with you, would you?"

Fletcher nodded. "Yes, ma'am, I will."

"Good." With a slow move that revealed both her age and her arthritis, Cookie mounted the bike and kicked up the stand. "Thirty minutes. Don't be late."

Fletcher suppressed the smile that was begging to come out. "Yes, ma'am. I won't."

With a nod, she was off, and Fletcher looked back at the police department to see Tyler giving him an amused thumbs-up. With a wave, Fletcher returned to his car. He drove about halfway to the retreat, then took a side road, which he knew crossed one of New Hampshire's covered bridges and led to a small picnic area and ball field.

He parked, looking out at the color-dappled trees that edged the field. Most of the leaves had already turned and fallen, making the remaining ones stand out like dots of dark color on a white canvas. A teenager and his dad who were engaging in a little late-season batting practice were alone in the park. Fletcher rolled down the window for a bit of fresh air, and realized the only sounds he could hear were the pops of the bat and an occasional bird. He felt a far distance from New York.

Korie answered her cell on the first ring.

"Korie? This is Fletcher."

There was a brief silence, then a dramatic sob. "Oh, Fletcher! I'm so glad you called! They won't let me take Aaron back to New York."

Fletcher rubbed the back of his neck. It had been a long time since he'd met a woman who made him feel so tired. "His body is evidence in a crime, Korie. After all, you're the one who wanted this—"

"I didn't want *this!*" she screeched. "Holding him hostage—"

"Stop holding court, Korie. *Now.* I'm not one of your subjects."

Silence. "I'm a widow," she said, an edge of tears in her voice. "You shouldn't talk to me like that."

"Yes, but I know more about you and Aaron than most people. Just stop the act with me. And let Tyler do his job. We'll get you the body as soon as possible."

"I need it by Friday." There were no tears. Her voice was even, back to business. "There's going to be a memorial service Saturday night at his publishers', and they're doing a spread in the *New York Times.* This is important."

Fletcher closed his eyes. "I understand. We'll do the best we can. But you screeching at Tyler and the M.E. does not make the process go any faster. In fact, the constant interruptions probably make it worse. Do you get my drift?"

Silence. Then, "Yes."

"Good. I'll keep you posted on any progress. And call me. Not them."

"Fletcher."

"Yes?"

"You're even more of a jerk than Judson."

Fletcher sighed, but the connection had broken. "I'm not Judson."

"I'm not."

"Who cares, me boyo?" Aaron laughed. "I gave them a name because you gave me information. Now they love you because they love Judson. You're famous."

"I don't want to be famous. This work is hard enough without that."

Aaron shrugged. "Enjoy the perks while you can. It's fleeting. Fame is a flash-flame. Searing and brief."

"Yours has lasted."

"That's partly inertia, and that I keep feeding the flame. But it's not real."

"So what is real?"

Aaron looked into his ever-present glass of Jack, then swallowed the last of it, ice and all. "The writing. The people." He got up suddenly and walked out of the restaurant.

Dropping a twenty on the table, Fletcher followed him into a misty Lower East Side night. Aaron preferred this part of town, and often dragged Fletcher down to a dive off East Houston. Now the famous bestselling author walked into the still-busy traffic of North First. "This!" he screamed back at Fletcher. "This is real!" He opened his arms wide and spun around, in the midst of horn blasts from two taxis and a motorcycle.

"Were you ever with Aaron when he thought he was invincible?" Cookie asked, bringing in cider and gingersnaps on a battered wooden tray.

Fletcher sniffed. "More than once." He looked around at the eclectic collection of photos and knickknacks as Pepper whimpered once, then lay down on Fletcher's feet. Fletcher patted the old dog a couple of times, then leaned back in his chair. He tried to sit still, ignoring the fact that the horsehair poked through the fabric of his pants. It itched.

Cookie nodded, then set the tray on a table near his chair. She handed Fletcher a cup of steaming liquid with a clove and spice fragrance that brought back memories of Vermont snowfalls and sleigh rides. He took a snap. Then two.

Cookie settled into one of her horsehair chairs and smoothed her apron over her lap. "He reminded me of my son," she said quietly, gesturing at one photo among the cluster on the piano. The elegant gold frame surrounded a fresh, young soldier with a sly grin and bright eyes. Cookie shook her head. "Laos."

"I'm sorry."

The old woman took a deep breath. "You never get over some of them, y'know? He was harder than my husband, who was harder than my parents were. Aaron will be hard for Maggie, but not as hard as some in her life. She loved him, but not in the way she will the man she marries."

Fletcher tilted his head, puzzled for a moment, then he recognized her implication. He grinned. "I doubt that Maggie would see me as marriage material."

Cookie laughed. "I knew you'd catch it. You're good! I like that!"

The former New York policeman suddenly felt a bit less calloused. "I have a grandmother or two," he said.

She slapped the arm of her chair. "Good for you! Good for them!" She shook her finger at him. "And you never know." She picked up her cider and took a sip. "Now, what's on your mind?"

"How long had Aaron been sleeping with Lily?"

Cookie leaned over and took a snap off the tray. "You don't waste time, either. Good. Good!" She bit into the cookie. "My question for you is why do you think I would know?"

"Experience." Fletcher nodded again at the piano, his focus on a photo to the far left, of a very young Cordelia Holokaj and her husband, who wore the dress blues of a New York City police lieutenant.

Cookie nodded in approval.

"How did he die?"

She took a deep breath. "Cancer, after all those years. Only fired his weapon twice in the line of duty."

"Once. So far." The warmth of the room and the cider had spread to Fletcher's stomach.

"And?"

He set the cider aside and changed the subject. "So you also gave Aaron information about police work?"

She grinned. "You should have stayed on the force."

"Mrs. Holokaj—"

"Cookie."

"Cookie—"

"Yes. My Stanley talked to me a lot about the work. I listened. I remembered."

"And?"

"And the first time I met Aaron, I told him his first book was all wrong. That the procedure was not right, the language. Told him if he knew any cops, he'd better start having a sit-down with them."

Fletcher leaned back in his chair. "So you're responsible for me becoming Judson."

Cookie saluted him with her cider. "The next book was better."

Fletcher cleared his throat. "Aaron and Lily?"

"He was a dog, wasn't he?"

"Cookie—"

"About six months ago, Aaron and Lily started spending much more time together. Scott was going into New York a lot, supposedly to meet with his agent."

"Supposedly?"

She grinned. "How many authors do you know who meet with their agents two or three times a month?"

"I'm not sure—"

"It's unusual. We all knew it."

"Another woman?"

Cookie shrugged. "It wouldn't be the first time a man went hunting for scrawny squirrels when a banquet waited for him at home."

"Lily and Aaron were retaliating?"

Cookie shook her head. "Maybe. Maybe not. Maggie knew they spent time together alone. Didn't like it, but there's a lot about Lily that Maggie doesn't like right now. Still, she's family."

"So I gathered."

Pausing, Cookie took a sip of her cider, watching Fletcher over the rim of the cup. As she lowered it, she cleared her throat. "You know you can trust that one to do the right thing in the long run."

"Maggie?"

"She's too close to God not to. Even if she tries to stray, He yanks her back."

Fletcher pursed his lips, unwilling to comment, his mind wandering to the auburn hair, the blue eyes, the Bible on her desk.

"What about you?"

He looked up. "What about me?"

"What about you and God?"

Fletcher shook his head. "That's personal, Cookie. I'm not going there."

"Does it have anything to do with the one time you fired your gun?"

Fletcher sat perfectly still, determined not to provide her information at all, not even from his body language.

Cookie shifted suddenly in her chair. "Have you heard the old story about the husband and wife who were driving one day when she suddenly started yelling at him?"

Fletcher waited.

"She was ranting about how distant they'd become since the kids had come along. They didn't even sit close to each other in the car anymore. He was patient, didn't speak till she finished. Then he just said, 'I'm not the one who moved over.'"

Fletcher remained silent.

"God's not the one who moved away, you know. He's still right where He was."

The tug he'd felt when he'd seen Maggie glancing at her

Bible strengthened, but he was not about to give up how close to the mark she'd hit.

She watched him a moment, then nodded. She knew. She bit a cookie and wiped her mouth, blithely returning to the case at hand. "I don't think Scott knows that Aaron was sniffing around his wife. I think Lily'd be a lot worse off than she is if he did."

"Could he know and be hiding it?"

Cookie shrugged. "Have you met Scott?" Fletcher nodded. "He's not much of one to keep his feelings to himself, unfortunately."

Fletcher wiped his mouth with his hand. "Did Korie know?"

Cookie coughed out a Polish curse, then spit on the floor. Fletcher sat straighter in his chair. "Like her that much, do you?" he said.

She shook her head, looking exactly like the old grandmother that she was. "Poison. Always was, always will be, unless God grasps her heart in one hand and hangs on for dear life."

"Well, you know what they say…"

"There's hope for everyone, I know. Korie should be thankful for that."

"Did she know?"

Cookie sniffed. "Not that I know of."

"And you would know."

She laughed. "Mr. MacAllister, you can learn a great deal just by paying attention."

"Fletcher. And, yes, ma'am, you can."

Cookie set aside her cup and smoothed her apron again. Her gravelly voice softened some as she asked, "Have you started following the money yet?"

Fletcher returned his cup to the tray and leaned forward, bracing his elbows on his knees. He put his hands together and met her gaze straight on. "Cookie, what is it that you're not telling me? What is it that you don't *want* to tell me?"

She pushed her glasses up on her nose and sniffed. "Aaron had been trying to give up drinking lately. Did you know?"

"I'd noticed. I didn't ask why."

She sniffed, her eyes glassy. "You should have. But before he did, he drank. A lot."

Fletcher nodded. "And when he drank, he talked."

Cookie's eyes grew a little brighter, a little wetter. "I know you'll talk to everyone over there, Fletcher, all the baby writers, and they'll tell you a lot. And there's Lily, and Maggie." She hesitated and clutched her fingers together. They were trembling.

Fletcher reached over and took her hands, grasping them firmly. "I know you don't want to say this. But it's for Aaron. And I know you loved him just as much as the rest of us."

She looked away for a moment, at the pictures on top of the piano. "I think you'll find this has nothing to do with love—or who was in whose bed."

"Money."

She looked back at him, her expression solemn. "And a lot of it. And it's not going to the one you think it is."

"Korie doesn't inherit?"

Cookie shook her head. "Some, but not all. Not the bulk."

"Then who?"

Cookie bit her lip, and Fletcher felt his chest tighten. She didn't have to say. As he stared at the old woman's face, he knew.

Maggie.

SIX

Maggie slid her legs over the edge of the bed and sat up. The room spun a bit, so she grabbed the edge of the mattress and braced herself. Her face ached and there was a dull throb at the back of her skull, but the painkillers kept most of the agony at bay. Of course, they were also the reason she was dizzy.

She could hear Lily in the kitchen, banging drawers and overseeing the arrival of the food for the evening meal. Maggie was grateful for her sister's assistance, but the hovering was beginning to make her feel claustrophobic. And now one of Tyler's men was going to camp out in the spare room, right across the hall from the one Tim used. The walls were closing in.

Help me, God. Please. Show me what to do. She closed her eyes, once again letting all she knew play out in her mind. Aaron's murder. Lily's bottle. Wouldn't the same person who killed him have planted the bottle? She'd been flippant about answering Fletcher's question, but the truth was she didn't know anyone who'd really want to kill Aaron. Hurt him, yes. She probably could have done *that* herself.

Maggie smiled, then grimaced. Obviously, smiling was out of the question for a bit. Feeling steadier, she stood up and shuffled to the bathroom. Her whole body felt stiff, and she rolled her shoulders, trying to ease out some of the kinks. The floor tile felt almost refreshingly cool to her feet, and she paused at the mirror...and groaned.

Her face was swollen, with dark splotches edging out from under each bandage. She pressed gently on the puffy areas; they weren't sore, but the closer to the wounds she pressed, the more painful it was. *No wonder my head hurts. Why would anyone want to do this?*

The obvious answer is that he or she thinks I know who killed Aaron. But why would I? Do they think I saw something? Or that I know—

"Why are you out of bed?"

Maggie cringed. She hadn't heard Lily come in. She shifted slightly so she could see her indignant sister in the mirror. "Because I'm not about to start using a bedpan," she replied.

Lily grinned and held up her hands. "Okay, okay. I just came in to see if you wanted turkey or beef."

"Beef," Maggie replied, then shut the bathroom door.

After supper, Maggie lay on her bed, staring at the ceiling. She had switched from the prescribed painkillers to ibuprofen, which meant that her face still ached, but the pain was manageable. The grogginess had worn off, however, leaving her awake, her mind buzzing. At first she'd just listened to the sounds of the evening drifting through her open door and a window that was raised slightly. Her bedroom was one door down the hall from the dining room, and she heard the snippets of subdued conversation, counterpointed by sounds of the night outside. No one stayed very long afterward, although they had all popped in to see how she was doing. Except Fletcher.

After cleanup, Lily had brought her dessert, wanting to chat. She said that Fletcher had eaten with them, but didn't say much and had left right afterward. Maggie wasn't in the mood to talk and had gently asked her sister to leave. Lily insisted on sleeping on the couch, and now Maggie could hear her gentle snore, something she'd done since she was a child.

Maggie was disappointed, and she didn't like that she was. She'd actually hoped to see Fletcher that evening, to find out if he'd discovered anything else about Aaron. She fidgeted with the sheet, running the edge of it back and forth through her fingers, as she told herself that's all it was. A desire for information.

She let go of the sheet and pressed her hands flat against the mattress. She pushed down, her breath coming a bit more rapidly as she thought about waking up earlier that day, realizing he was in the room. He'd been watching her. Lily had said he had sat in the chair in the corner almost from the time the ambulance had brought her home.

Why? Why wasn't he out trying to catch the bad guys? Maggie closed her eyes.

Because he feels it just like you do.

Maggie opened her eyes and sat up. Impossible. Absolutely impossible.

All things are possible....

Maggie laughed softly, as her memory was jogged by one of her favorite Bible verses. She glanced at her nightstand, then frowned. Where was her Bible? She looked around the room, but it wasn't in sight. Focusing a bit, she remembered that she'd left it in her office. She stood up, fighting only a touch of dizziness, and reached for a robe.

The office was at the end of the hall on the same wing, so she padded quietly down, then shut the door before turning on the light. She sat at her desk and pulled the Bible close, folding her hands on top of it, closing her eyes. *Lord,* she prayed, *give me peace about this, no matter what happens now. Help me with my feelings about Aaron. And Fletcher. And show me the wisest thing to do.*

There was a twinge in her gut as she realized that what was

wisest might not be what was best for Lily or the retreat. A wave of stubbornness went through her, her desire for what was right in torment with the behavior of her sister and her longings to keep the retreat safe and intact.

"Trust God."

Maggie's eyes opened slowly, one of her mother's most repeated phrases echoing in her head. She'd heard it all her life, so often that when she and Lily had taken a detour through another faith in their teens, this one phrase stuck with them, eventually bringing Maggie back to the church. Maggie crossed her arms and tucked her hands in tight, trying to stop their trembling.

Trust Him.

A warmth flowed over her, and Maggie began to relax. A peace. She looked up at the ceiling. "I will," she said aloud, "but this may take more guts than I've got."

Trust Him.

She nodded and looked down at her Bible. Unfolding her arms, she reached for the cover, then stopped, her attention suddenly caught by the light beige filing cabinet in one corner of her office.

It was Aaron's, a storage spot for whenever he decided to work here at the retreat. He kept it locked, but the spare keys were taped to the back of the cabinet. He kept one set on his key ring, and she'd asked him about the other set. He'd told her to do whatever she wanted with them.

"You're the only one who knows, and I trust you. I know you're not going to open that without my permission. It's one reason I hired you."

Maggie could still hear his voice in her head. At the time, she'd felt flattered. Now she wondered if it wasn't just his way of telling her what a dupe she was. She got up and went to the cabinet. She pushed on it a couple of times to rock it away from the wall, then slid her arm behind it, pulling the tape and keys off the back. She inserted one into the lock and popped it out.

The first drawer held submissions from the retreat's writers. Each file was labeled with the writer's name, a date and a title. She flipped through them idly; everything looked normal. The second drawer held more of the same. The third drawer held mostly office supplies, which she had insisted on after one of his raids on her desk.

"It all comes out of the same pot, Mitten," he said, using *Lily's nickname for her derisively.*

"It's not about money. It's about respect. And expectations. When I leave a binder clip in my *desk, I have a right to expect it to be there when I need it."*

"All right, all right," he said, clearly humoring her. *"I'll keep a stash of my own."*

Aaron had once been so open with her, so sweet to her, that she'd worried if he was being wise. Over the past few months, however, he'd become withdrawn, angry, often ridiculing her for things he'd once found charming, like her attention to detail, her closeness with Lily. What had been going on with him?

Maggie closed the drawer, a scowl tightening her lips. *Why hadn't I seen the changes in his behavior more clearly?*

A flash of light caught her attention and she turned, her breath caught in her throat. A man stood outside her window, glaring at her.

SEVEN

That the man was Fletcher MacAllister was the only thing that kept Maggie from screaming. Relief flooded over her as she recognized that scowl, and she slumped in the closest chair, grasping her throat. Relief...followed by anger.

She got up and went to the window. Unlocking it, she lowered the upper sash, which put her at eye level with the tall detective. "What are you doing?" she demanded. "Are you seriously trying to scare me to death?"

He spoke at almost the same time. "Are you insane? What are you doing sitting here with the lights on and the blinds up?"

They stared at each other, anger radiating between them.

Maggie blinked first. "I always have my blinds up. Who would see?"

Fletcher's shoulders slumped a bit. "Maggie, you've got to get over the idea that this place is safe. It's *not*. You have no alarms, no secure locks. And just over twenty-four hours ago, someone tried to kill you. Most women wouldn't even be venturing out of their bedrooms."

Her eyes narrowed. "If you're not Judson," she said evenly, "then I'm not most women."

He stared at her, his voice softening. "Just be careful. All right?"

She nodded, and he glanced over her shoulder. "Find anything interesting?" he asked.

How long had he been watching me?

She crossed her arms over the tight feeling in her stomach. "It's mostly just the writers' stuff. Aaron kept all the weekly submissions here."

Fletcher's eyes locked onto hers, his face smooth, blank. "Are you sure? Sometimes something that looks innocent—"

"I'm sure," she insisted.

"Will you keep looking? Let me know if you find anything?"

She nodded, and he stepped away from the window.

"Close the blinds," he said softly. "And go back to bed." He turned and slipped into the dark.

Maggie closed the blinds but didn't go back to bed. There was no way she could sleep. Her nerves were raw from Fletcher's unexpected visit. Instead, she turned back to the filing cabinet. Sitting on the floor next to it, she reached for the handle on the fourth drawer, her mind still on the man at the window. Her mind kept turning over and over one thought: She'd never lied to Aaron, but he still had not truly trusted her. Fletcher did, and it was a trust he had purposely, intentionally, extended.

Why?

Understanding hit her with a sharp blow, and her body sagged, her hand dropping away from the drawer handle. Fletcher wanted her to be innocent. She leaned against the cabinet and closed her eyes. *"Lord,"* she said aloud, *"show me how to honor that trust. How do I do what's right by him? By Lily?"* Her breath eased out of her in a long sigh. *"And Aaron?"*

She was innocent. So was Lily. It would come out. She had to trust in the truth.

With a new resolve, Maggie inhaled deeply and pulled open

the fourth drawer. It held only a file, a white business envelope and a bulky nine-by-twelve-inch envelope. She lifted out the file, which held notes in Aaron's own peculiar shorthand, what looked like a list of dates and times, and an airline ticket to Aruba. The ticket was in the name of someone she'd never heard of: Chris Taylor. *Does Korie have a brother? Or a sister?* She put the file back and grabbed the white envelope. The return addressed was from the U.S. Department of State and it was addressed to Chris Taylor at a post office box in New York.

It was a passport. With *her* picture.

Maggie's hands were shaking as she replaced it and pulled out the bulky envelope. Somewhere down deep, she already knew what it held. Pinching open the clasp, she peered in.

Cash. And a lot of it. Six bundles of hundreds. A quick count showed it was sixty thousand dollars, an airline ticket out of the country…and a passport. *With my picture. In my office.*

A hysterical rasp of laughter escaped from Maggie as her eyes stung from fresh tears. The truth? *"What's the truth in this?"* She felt lost all over again. Surely, surely there was some way to prove that it wasn't hers. That she was not the one preparing to flee the country. *Why would Aaron have those things?* She turned to look at the Bible on the corner of her desk, knowing she'd have to tell Fletcher about the passport and the money. "You got any ideas, Lord? Help!"

Fear and anger still clutched Fletcher's gut as he walked away from Maggie's window. It wired him, and he clenched and unclenched his fists as he headed back to his cabin. *How could she be so stupid?*

A night owl by nature, Fletcher had been walking the woods, going over in his mind all he had learned, when he'd seen the light snap on in her office. Thinking her attacker might be responsible, he'd crossed through the woods at a trot until he was close enough to see that it was Maggie. Furious, he'd planned to rap hard on the window, intending to scare her as much as possible. She had to understand her danger.

Then he'd seen her sit, her eyes closed, hands folded over what was clearly a Bible. Was she praying?

"And she prays, too."

Fletcher looked at Aaron over the top of his coffee mug. Aaron always insisted on a morning after at the local coffee shop, at a time when most men would have been in bed, nursing the remnants of a hangover. "Come again?"

Aaron stirred his latte, grinning. "A new one on me, huh? All the lovelies in the world want to crawl up in my bed, and I fall for one who prays."

"Yeah, that could explain it."

Aaron cut his eyes toward his old friend. "Explain what?"

Fletcher couldn't help but smirk. "Why this one is under your skin when the others barely manage to get under your covers."

"Bah!" Aaron took a swig, grimacing at the burn. "If they dress like tarts, they'd better get used to being treated like tarts."

"The feminists must love that one."

Aaron sipped this time, then shook his head. "They don't know. I could say it out loud and they'd think I was just parroting something from the books. These women, they all think they know me. They have this image of me they've made up based on the stuff I've written, as if my fiction were me." *He shifted in his chair and leaned closer to Fletcher.* "Do you remember when I had Judson investigating Buddhism to help him with the murder of the girl over on East 42nd?"

Fletcher didn't.

"Mandala Mayhem? *Number fiv—" Aaron stopped and waved his hand.* "Never mind. The point is that after it came

*out, I found out I had an entire cadre of fans who thought I had
become some kind of tree-hugging Buddhist."*

*"I guess they haven't seen you sneaking into the back of that
church in Tribeca."*

*Aaron leaned forward conspiratorially. "Shh...you want
me to lose my card-carrying liberal status?"*

*Fletcher almost snorted his coffee. "They just don't know
how you vote."*

*Aaron sat up straight. "Which is a good thing, but that's not
the point. These women...they make it up as they go along. They
have this image of me...all I do is go along sometimes. They
get what they want.*

"And you get..."

"All I can handle," Aaron said.

"I hope you're not expecting sympathy."

Aaron laughed. "Hardly. But maybe a few prayers."

Fletcher set his coffee aside. "For you or Maggie?"

*Aaron saluted Fletcher. "Both. Maggie...no tart, that one.
But she also trusts me, and we both know that's not always a
good thing."*

Fletcher stopped, and looked around at the darkened woods
as if coming out of a trance. He'd been so lost in the memory
that he'd passed by the cabin, and he glanced up at the moon
through the splotched canopy of leaves. At the time, he'd
thought Aaron was talking about fidelity. Now he wasn't so sure.

"Mr. MacAllister?"

Fletcher whirled, his knees bent, his gun drawn in an instant.

Tim, the young groundskeeper, threw up his hands. "Whoa!
Sir, it's just me."

Fletcher let out a long breath and straightened. "Tim. What
are you doing out here?"

"My rounds."

Fletcher frowned. "What?"

"You know. For security. Every night about this time, I make a round of the property, make sure everything is okay."

"I'm glad you told me. I'd hate to hear you for the first time outside my window."

Tim laughed. "No, sir. I'm pretty quiet. Comes from hunting a lot as a kid, I guess. You learn to step so you don't let them know you're around."

Fletcher's eyes narrowed. "A handy skill."

"Yep. And it's good to know you have that gun. Didn't know if you had one."

Fletcher straightened. "The gun was mine, not department-issued. I also still carry my handcuffs along with my PI license, and some pepper spray. Never know when you'll need them."

The younger man nodded. "I can understand. In your line of work, I guess you have to be prepared." He gestured to the cast. "Did you get lost? Your cabin is that way."

"Thank you," Fletcher said, his eyes still on Tim. "I appreciate the help."

Tim shrugged. "No problem, sir. But I need to move on. Miss Maggie likes me back in the house before midnight."

"I can understand," Fletcher murmured as the young man saluted him, then loped off.

Fletcher looked at his watch—11:45 p.m. Tim had interrupted his train of thought, but he still knew what he needed to do. He pulled out his cell phone. Yes, it was late, but someone should be at the police station. He needed Aaron's keys.

Maggie fell asleep at her desk, her head resting on the Bible, on the side of her face not hit by flying splinters. A white-gold ray of sun through a crack in the blinds awoke her, and she rubbed her neck as she straightened up. Standing brought an involuntary groan as stiffened muscles tingled and clenched. She shuffled toward her room, toward her ibuprofen. She could hear Lily in the kitchen, humming and banging pots. She got the drug, then stood and watched her sister a few moments.

"Has anyone ever told you that you would make a great mom?"

Lily jumped and almost dropped the butter. "What are you doing out of bed?"

Maggie frowned. "Why do people keep asking me that? I'm not an invalid. What are *you* doing up?"

Lily grabbed a skillet and gestured toward the other wing of the lodge. "Since we have a guest, I thought I'd make breakfast. How are you feeling?"

Maggie shuffled over and sat down on one of the bar stools. "Rough. But there." Lily poured her a glass of juice, and Maggie drank it quickly. The sugar boost began to brighten her almost immediately.

"Coffee?"

Lily slid her a cup and pointed at the coffeemaker. "So what brings you out if you feel that bad?"

Maggie poured the coffee, then stared at the dark brown liquid. "Can I ask you a strange question?"

Lily broke several eggs into a bowl, then picked it up and started scrambling with a whisk. "Sure."

"Do you know a Chris Taylor?"

Lily set down the bowl and stared at her sister. "Where did you hear that name?"

"So you know her?"

"Aaron, right? You got it from him."

Maggie cleared her throat and drank. "More or less."

Lily shook her head. "I knew that old man couldn't keep a secret."

Maggie raised her eyebrows, waiting, and Lily let out a

deep breath. "Chris Taylor is a part I'm considering." She shrugged. "You know, maybe to get back on my feet a bit. Small part, big film. My agent sent it over a few weeks ago."

Maggie grinned, wincing slightly from the effort. "Lily, that's great! When will you know?"

Lily resumed breakfast prep. "I called him, you know, just after…" She gestured toward the back deck. "All of this has sort of woken me up, I guess. Anyway, he's going to set up a meeting, and we'll see."

"So tell me about the part."

"Small, keep that in mind. She's a socialite, pretty well-known, but in a horrid marriage."

"Art reflecting life?"

"Hush. Anyway, she plots to get away, fake passport, all that, and disappears to some Caribbean island. It's a key element in a mystery, and I'll be seen mostly in flashbacks." Lily bounced as she slid a pan of biscuits into the oven. "I told Aaron about it, but swore him to secrecy, since I hadn't decided. I didn't want anyone to know, especially Scott. I can't believe he told you." She stopped, then sighed. "Or maybe I can. You guys were close."

"I won't tell anyone. Promise. It'll be our secret."

Lily grinned, then turned to the stove, sending up a sizzle and column of steam as she poured the eggs into the hot skillet.

Our secret, Maggie thought, *and Aaron's twisted sense of humor.* Maggie took a deep breath, a new resolve settling over her. Maybe Aaron hadn't been killed because he was disliked. Maybe he'd been killed because he'd been hiding far too many secrets. Time to find out exactly what those secrets were.

EIGHT

Judson and his new partner, Lee, stood near a makeshift tent and cardboard box structure in a wooded section of Central Park. "The weapon is in there," Lee said. "I can just smell it." He started forward.

Judson grabbed his arm. "Not without a warrant."

Lee was startled. "It's a box in the park."

"Not according to a recent ruling. Another search was thrown out, saying that this same kind of camp was a residence, thus protected. If we're going to do this, we'll do it by the book."

Fletcher toyed with calling Korie for permission or asking Tyler to get a warrant to search the house, then decided that he wouldn't waste the time. After all, this was for Aaron's benefit, not the killer's. He also made a mental note to get the lock fixed on Aaron's office door before Korie returned. When none of the keys from Aaron's effects fit it, Fletcher simply kicked it in.

The room smelled like stale cigars and cologne, a combination that had always been a winner with Aaron's mostly female fans. Fletcher's nose wrinkled at the odor, wondering why. He stood in the door for a moment, feeling awkward about invading Aaron's private space, alone, for the first time. *He should be here,* Fletcher thought, a twinge of sorrow lingering.

He pushed the thought away and stepped into the room, flicking on the light. The office was lined with bookshelves containing volumes on crime and writing, novels by some of the best writers of the past, and piles of manuscripts. The desk sat at an angle in one corner, giving Aaron a perfect view of the landscape outside the window and the door to the hall at the same time.

Fletcher's cell phone rang, and he pulled it out, fumbling a bit to open it. The second ring echoed hollowly through the empty house. "MacAllister."

"Hey, I'm sorry we couldn't get you those keys until today," Tyler said.

"It's fine," Fletcher replied. "What's up?"

"The M.E. is finished," Tyler continued. "And he found something I thought you'd want to know."

"Tell me."

"He compared an impression of the bottle with the impression on Aaron's skull. The tapering indicates he was hit from behind."

"So maybe there was no confrontation, just a sneak attack. And the assailant was right-handed."

"Maybe," Tyler said. "Remember that left-handed people usually drink with their left hand. Lily always carries the bottle in her right, the glass in her left."

Fletcher nodded. "True, but she'd have to reverse it to swing it like a club, and would probably do it with her left."

Tyler sighed. "So we still don't know."

"Not from this alone, but it's a good start."

"There's more. He was also hit from above."

Fletcher scowled. Aaron was almost six-four. "So he was on the steps after all or just at the bottom. With his attacker standing above him."

"Looks like."

"So is the body ready for release?"

Tyler hesitated, then said, "Yes."

Fletcher grinned. "Do you want to call Korie?" Fletcher could almost hear the young man struggling between emotion and duty. Papers shuffled in the background.

Finally, Tyler said, "Would you do it, since you know her and all?"

He almost laughed, but Fletcher kept his voice straight as he replied, "Don't worry about it, Tyler. I'll take care of it."

"Thanks. See you in a bit."

Fletcher tucked the phone away and resumed his survey of the room. Nothing leaped out at him, so he sat and turned on the computer, shifting in the chair to face the screen.

The system was password protected, and Fletcher prowled a bit among Aaron's notepads and phone messages to see if the password was written down somewhere. Probably not. Aaron was a touch paranoid and he had a good memory. Taking a deep breath, Fletcher typed in Aaron's birth date, with no success. Looking around the room, Fletcher saw nothing to give him a hint, so he tried again, drawing on his own memory. "jackdaniels."

Nothing. Fletcher licked his lips, knowing a third try might lock him out of the system.

"Try greenlabel."

Payback is rough. Fletcher whirled and stood, slamming the chair into the wall and tipping it over. His breath was still caught in his throat, his left hand on his gun, when he realized it was Maggie.

She threw up her hands. "Yow! It's just me!" Then she started to grin. "Not much fun, is it?"

Fletcher's shoulders slumped even as his temper rose. "Don't ever sneak up on a cop. It's a good way to get shot."

Maggie pointed over her shoulder. "You left the door open. I didn't exactly tiptoe up the stairs. I thought you heard me."

Fletcher righted the chair. "Obviously not."

She giggled. "I'm sorry. I *am* glad you didn't shoot me. Twice in two days is a bit much, even for me."

His mouth twisted. "Me, too. Would have played havoc with the case." He sat down and typed in "Green Label." The hard drive whirled, paused and stopped: access denied. Fletcher let out a long sigh. There would be no more attempts right now; he was locked out.

Maggie shrugged. "Sorry. Aaron once mentioned that to guess his password, someone would have to know all his preferences. I took a chance that it wasn't his cigar brand." She walked over to stand behind him. "What were you looking for?"

Fletcher drummed his fingers lightly on the keyboard without actually pressing the keys, as if he could still get into Aaron's records. "Not sure. I was hoping some of the file names would give me a clue."

"I wouldn't count on it. If Aaron was hiding something, the files would be hidden deep in other folders and wouldn't have clue-in names."

"What makes you think he was hiding something?"

Maggie gasped a little, and Fletcher waited. He knew she'd found something in her office and was hoping she'd tell him. He didn't like having her in his head as a prime suspect and wished she'd open up to him. He also wished that the smell of sandalwood had not suddenly become more prominent than Aaron's tobacco.

She let out her breath. "Don't you? Isn't that why you're accessing his computer?"

He turned to face her. "No. I was hoping to find some sort of journal or notes on a book or on the residents here, to see if he had problems with them, maybe that he hadn't mentioned

to you. To see what I could learn before I went to talk to them."
He stood up and moved closer. Maggie backed up against the
desk, bracing herself with her hands behind her. "What are you
doing here?"

Maggie met his gaze defiantly for a brief second, then her
eyes softened. "Please don't do this," she whispered. "I
didn't kill him."

Fletcher closed his eyes briefly, pushing away the desire to
take her in his arms and apologize. He couldn't. Not yet. He
opened them again and started to speak, to find Maggie staring
at the wall over his shoulder.

"What is that?" she asked.

He turned. Thumbtacked to a corkboard behind Aaron's
desk was a window envelope, with a red stamp declaring
"OVERDUE NOTICE." Fletcher pulled it down and opened
it.

Maggie read over his arm. "A mortgage?" She stepped
back and stared at him. "He paid cash for this house, up-front
and in total."

Fletcher frowned. "Must be a second mortgage. Looks like
the balance is close to five hundred thousand."

"That's almost seventy-five percent of the value," Maggie
replied. "I don't understand this. Aaron's income was over
seven figures last year. I saw the statements!"

"Something's not right." He dropped the bill on the desk
and started to prowl through stacks of mail on the desk.
"There're bills here that arrived two, three months ago." He
ripped open the electric bill. It held a cut-off notice and a six-
month-past-due amount. "It looks like he's not paid anything
in almost six months."

"It's even worse than it looks," she said, her voice low.

He turned, watching and waiting.

She glanced toward the hallway, as if expecting Aaron to

walk through the door. "His money manager paid all the bills. Edward took care of all the finances, bills, investments, the lot of it. So either Aaron demanded them back, or…"

"Or he fired Edward and didn't tell anyone."

She nodded and looked at him. "Why would he do that?"

Fletcher looked around at the piles of work, the bills, a half-smoked cigar in the ashtray. A humidor filled with cigars, the use of which had left a fragrance that would linger in the office for a long time. "I don't know," he said. He glanced down at the computer. "But I think I need to go to New York and have a talk with Edward before I do anything else here."

He turned to her. Reaching up, he let one finger stroke gently under the two stitches near her left eye. "Tyler says the M.E. has released the body. It'll make a good excuse to leave for a couple of days, and Korie says there's this memorial service planned at his publisher's office. Do you want to go?"

Maggie reached up and pressed his hand against her cheek. Fletcher's gut tightened as she held it there briefly, then let go. "No. Not yet. I need to stay here. Look out for things. I'll be fine. Tyler's guy is at the house, and Lily—"

"That's not why I asked."

She stopped. "I know."

They looked at each other a moment, and Fletcher wanted to say something, anything, to explain how he felt. And what he couldn't let himself feel. Not until he cleared her as a suspect. Instead, he reached over and shut down the computer again. "Let me give you a ride back to the lodge," he said quietly.

NINE

Judson took Lee into the interrogation room and shut the door. He didn't want anyone else in the squad to hear this. Lee turned to face him; Judson's voice was like steel. "Never show your emotions to a suspect again. Never. Not if you want to stay my partner."

Lee protested, "But that guy molested his own—"

"I don't care," Judson interrupted, closing in on the younger man. "Emotions are not part of the job. Ever. Hunches, instinct, yes. Emotions? Never. And you especially never reveal yourself to a suspect. Understand? Do you get it?"

Lee got it.

The mile-long ride back was silent. Maggie spent it staring out the window at the woods, and Fletcher dropped her off at the lodge before easing his rental car down the narrow grated ruts that passed for a driveway to the cabin. Inside, he emptied his pockets onto the desk, then sat on the bed and leaned back against the headboard. He didn't like the way the investigation was going. Too sloppy, and he didn't have the drive that he usually had about finding a clear suspect and eliminating the red herrings. He knew that, in part, his grief over Aaron and his increasing feelings for Maggie were clouding his judgment.

He got up and took his coat off, sliding it down over the back of the desk chair. He picked up his pen and his notebook, flipping through it again, trying to clear up the muddy picture in his head. The pen clicked repeatedly as he tried to work out his frustration.

Too much was pointing directly at Maggie as the killer; yet, he wanted to look at anyone but her. *Click. Click.* Yet no one, including Maggie, had a clear, unique motive. Korie stood to gain the most financially, but Maggie was the one with the most opportunity. *Click. Click. Click.*

The murder itself looked like a crime of passion, but everything that had happened afterward pointed to a premeditated act. Maggie had removed the bottle, tampering with evidence. However, if she was telling the truth, she didn't put the bottle under the deck in the first place, and she only removed it because she thought it was misleading. *Click. Click.*

Then there was Lily. Had she really been sleeping with Aaron? Even if she had been, would she have had reason to murder him? *Click.*

Fletcher suddenly found himself picturing his friend with each of the three women, how he was with each. Fletcher felt stuck, frustrated—and furious. His emotional control was slipping away again. He growled and threw the notebook and pen down on the desk and went out. Letting the door slam behind him, he stood on the porch, looking out. Dusk surrounded the trees. The day had been unseasonably warm, and an autumn fog was beginning to rise off the ground. He knew he should head to the lodge for supper, but he wasn't hungry. Food just wasn't first on his mind.

Aaron was. He truly missed Aaron. Fletcher's breathing deepened as he thought about Aaron, a dull ache echoing through him. He gripped the porch rail, trying to push down the grief and anger that was almost strangling him.

They had been friends for more than fifteen years, since Fletcher was just a rookie and Aaron was still a photographer trying to get a scoop on a New York murder. Fletcher often downplayed the friendship, especially after the Judson stuff started, but the truth was that Aaron was the one he could call any time of day, any day of the week. To vent. To get an objective opinion on a case. To get a laugh.

"Old Mr. Norman Cousins was right about that, me boyo."
Aaron was drinking the rare bottle of water, cooling off after a gym workout. Fletcher had convinced Aaron that weight training would be good for his writing as well as his health. "If you can't laugh, you might as well be dead."

"That's pretty harsh," Fletcher replied, wiping his face on a towel. They worked out together every time Aaron was in town.

The writer shrugged, pausing to catch his breath. Fletcher looked closer at him. Aaron was pale and clammy as well as sweaty. "You okay?"

Aaron nodded and swigged from the bottle again. "I need to drink more water, less Jack," he said, then grinned and clapped the younger man on the back. "Now that we've sweated out the poisons, how about replenishing some of them?"

Fletcher shook his head. "Can't tonight. Have to work. This case is driving me nuts. I need to put in a few hours with the files, see what I missed."

Aaron perked up. "Take me with you."

"Oh, no—"

"I'll be objective. I promise. And I won't put anything in a book until after the trial."

"I can't—"

"You just need a new point of view. You know how it is when you look at the same facts over and over...."

Fletcher did know. Aaron's enthusiasm for it won him over and the two of them had spent six hours going over every scrap of paper, every clue. And Aaron *had* helped. He had a passion for the work; it was the only thing that kept him away from the bars, away from the women.

"Wish you could help now," Fletcher said to the trees, which were stirring in a sudden stiff breeze.

A crack to his right startled Fletcher, and he turned, watching as a large branch broke free from an ancient oak and dropped to the ground. It hit on one end and bounced, the small twigs on it snapping off and scattering over the ground. Fletcher stepped off the porch and waded through the graying ferns that covered the ground. He picked up the branch and hefted it, relishing the feel of the rough bark on his palms. It was shaped like an oversize baseball bat, with the larger end about six or seven inches in diameter, tapering to about three or four.

Fletcher wrapped his hands around the smaller end, checking his grip. He swung a couple of times, then two more, faster, Joe DiMaggio warming up behind the plate. A fifth almost spun him around, and he grinned, emotions surging through him. "Yeah," he called out. His breath came faster and he felt exhilarated. The sixth connected with the tree, the impact thudding through his muscles and joints.

The bark scraped on his palms, but he relished it all. The rush of blood, the pulls on the muscles. He swung again, the anger, the frustration, the confusion—and the grief—of the past two days suddenly focused on the tree.

Bark shattered off the tree and the branch alike, and loose twigs showered down from the branches above him. Dust flew, clinging to his shirt and the bits of sweat that were starting to pop out on his neck. The sound of each impact filled his ears, and he roared as his anger flushed out of him. He was shaking, his palms starting to bleed, but he didn't stop, landing blow after blow on the old tree, which shook but still stood, impervious.

The branch finally splintered, the larger half flying away on the far side of the tree. A chunk of bark flew back, catching Fletcher on the cheek. He staggered backward, released the rest of the branch and sank to the ground. He draped his arms over his knees and dropped his head forward, tears slipping down his cheeks, a last bit of cleansing.

After a moment, he caught his breath and looked at the sky. "Thank You," he said quietly.

Maggie walked into the lodge, her mind a mess, scrambled by the simple touch of one finger on her face. She had planned to tell him about the passport, but his very nearness had locked her down. Now a scream lurked at the back of her throat.

There was no sound, however, as she stopped, watching as Lily darted about, coolly efficient as she unwrapped the food trays that had been delivered and set out the dishes and flatware.

"Nice of you to join us," Lily said. Too cool.

Maggie looked around. They were the only ones in the lodge. "What's going on, Lily?"

Lily's expression was frozen, her eyes hard. "Nothing. I was just wondering if you were going to return home anytime soon, or if you were going to ignore the fact that someone tried to kill you." She went back to the kitchen and started making coffee, each motion precise and quick.

Maggie leaned up against the couch. "I'm only going to say this once, sweet sister. You can lie to your agent, your husband, and the police. But not to me."

Lily stopped and stared at Maggie. Finally, she reached out and grabbed a stack of letters from the end of the bar and flung them at Maggie. They scattered, with two of them dropping to the floor.

Maggie picked them up and read the first one. The block lettering on it looked like a child's:

YOU SHOULD NOT BE AFRAID! I'M ALWAYS WITH YOU. GOD HAS PUT US TOGETHER. WHY ARE YOU HIDING? IT WON'T WORK. I KNOW YOU ARE IN THE WOODS. COME OUT, MY DAR-LING. GO BACK TO THE LIGHT FOR ME.

Maggie's gaze jerked up. Lily crossed her arms, biting her lower lip. "They came today," she said, her voice trembling. "My agent sent them so I would either be more careful or come back to L.A."

"Oh, no. How many?"

Lily shook her head. "I don't know. Six or seven. He sounds crazier than ever. Says we're meant to be together, the usual stuff."

Maggie took her sister in her arms. Lily sagged against her. "Did he threaten you?"

Lily's voice was muffled. "Not unless you count that line about 'I'm the only man on the planet who can please you.' I just wish they could make him leave me alone!"

The back door opened, and Lily stepped away, wiping her face. She smiled at Fletcher, then turned and opened the fridge.

The detective wasn't fooled. "What's wrong?" he asked Maggie.

She nodded at the letters. He gathered them up to read as Maggie looked him over. His hair was wet from a shower, and there was a red mark on his cheek that was beginning to turn dark. "What happened to you?" she asked.

"Wayward branch," he said. "Where were these mailed from?"

"Manchester," Lily said, scrounging around in the back of the fridge and pulling out a bottle of champagne she had obviously stored there earlier.

Maggie heart sank. "Lily, when did you—"

Lily's eyes were cold. "Don't. Just *don't*." She worked on the cork with a fury Maggie had not seen in a long time. It popped, and her elegant-looking sister drank straight from the bottle.

"It won't help," Maggie said softly.

"Maybe not," Lily replied, pulling down a flute from the overhead rack. "But I won't care as much." She poured, then took both toward the back door. "I'm going for a walk. Maybe he'll pop out from behind a tree and I can whack *him* with a bottle."

"Lily!"

Her sister responded only with a slamming of the door. Maggie looked up at Fletcher, a tight feeling in her stomach. "She didn't mean—"

"I don't think Lily killed Aaron," Fletcher said flatly, still looking over the letters. "I'm assuming these are copies."

"Yes, I think her agent always gives the originals to the police. What do you mean you don't think—"

"Why do they think these are different from any other obsessed fan who just spends too much time in the basement with the DVD player?"

"The frequency. Some have been threatening, just not to the point the cops can act. They also have come from places close to wherever she's been on location, so they think he's following her. Why don't you think she's the killer?"

Fletcher put down the letters and looked at Maggie. "Mostly because someone tried too hard to make it look like she did it. Her only motive is weak, and she'd gain nothing by his death. Probably. I'm thinking clearer, but I won't know anything for certain until the will is read and I've followed the money. You understand that, right?"

Maggie nodded, surprised by his renewed fervor about the case. "When are you going to New York?"

"Tonight."

"Tonight!"

"I'm going to catch the train about midnight, be at Edward's office in the morning. I called him a little bit ago, and he's agreed to see me." He looked around at the lodge. "Do you think Scott would agree to let Lily move in here with you? I think you'd both be safer, especially with Tyler's guy still around."

"I think so. He was in a better mood after she stayed on the couch last night. Fletcher, what's going on? What happened after you dropped me off?"

Fletcher reached out and took her hand, a gesture that made Maggie's throat constrict. "Nothing I want to talk about," he said softly, pulling her a bit closer.

Maggie realized she was focusing solely on him, his eyes, his words.

"Maggie, I realize that there's something between us, some connection. But it can't be. Not right now. Because unlike your sister, you *are* a suspect in this."

A wave of cold washed over Maggie. "What? But what about the attempt—"

"The attempt is not evidence. They could have been aiming at me or Tyler and missed. I have to follow the evidence, and right now it's pointing to a number of people, including you."

Maggie stepped back, pulling her hand away. She felt numb. This is what she wanted, wasn't it? To distract from Lily? To muddy…

"Listen to me," Fletcher insisted. "Listen!"

Maggie returned her focus to him.

"I've got to clear some things up, which I hope to in New York. You're a strong woman, Maggie, and I don't want you to give up on this."

A small glimpse of hope came out of his words, but there was still a nagging in her heart. "I won't. But we need to talk."

"We will, later. Right now, I'm still listening to the evidence. Not my feelings. I have to."

"No, I mean about—"

"And I want you to come to Aaron's service."

Maggie snapped out of her fog. "You want me in New York?"

He nodded.

"What happened to 'Don't leave town, stranger'?"

"Extradition laws."

A burst of laughter escaped Maggie, and she covered her mouth. "Sorry."

He grinned. "Don't be." He glanced over her shoulder, then stepped away from her. She heard the back door open, and the sounds of her writers piling in.

Her writers?

She turned to greet them. Some things had to go on.

Her writers.

After dinner, Fletcher walked back toward his cabin with confidence. The conversation over the table had flowed smoothly. The writers were getting used to his presence, his sense of humor. Good. He would need that if he finally had to sit down to talk to them. He was waiting. His instincts told him that they needed time to think, to absorb fully the impact of Aaron's death. And that was if they knew anything at all about the murder, which he doubted. Most seemed to be caught up in their own world and wouldn't have realized it if a bomb had dropped on Portsmouth. He was beginning to believe that his best clues would be found outside of the retreat.

He pushed open the cabin door, his mind on packing the few things he would need to take with him and wondering how his apartment would smell after so long away. As the door shut behind him, he stopped, all thoughts leaving him.

Lily Dunne was asleep in his bed.

TEN

Scott surprised her.

When Maggie knocked on his cabin door, he let her in without a word. He walked in front of her to the little kitchenette and poured a cup of coffee. "Want one?" he asked.

Maggie shook her head, and he returned to the chair by his desk. Unlike the other cabins, this one was older and had a bedroom that was separate from the living area. Maggie perched uneasily on the edge of a low love seat, glancing around at the room. Everything was spotless, as she knew it would be, except for Scott's desk. His computer was surrounded by stacks of paper and history books focusing on the first part of the twentieth century. One of his novels was set in 1920.

Scott glanced at the closed bedroom door. "If you're looking for Lily, she isn't here. Again."

Maggie crossed her arms and took a deep breath. "Actually, I came to ask a favor of you."

Scott was silent, waiting. He sipped.

Maggie fought the urge to stand up and fidget. Scott had been at the retreat almost from the time it opened, yet she had never gotten comfortable with him. "I was wondering if you would mind if Lily stayed at the lodge house a few more nights."

Scott's eyebrows arched for a moment, then he pushed a stack of papers away from the edge of his desk and set the cup on it. "That's it? That's the favor?"

Maggie nodded.

Scott looked at his computer, then back to her. "Last night, I did some of my best work in weeks."

After a pause, Maggie asked quietly, "Does that mean yes?"

Scott stood up suddenly, causing Maggie to jump. He turned his back on her and started tossing books on the floor, letting them land with loud plops. As he moved things around on the desk, clearing a workspace, he spoke, his voice clipped. "Yes. You need her right now. I don't. It might be better for everyone involved if she stayed with you for a while."

"Thank you," Maggie said. She waited, but Scott didn't continue. She started to leave, then hesitated.

"You can go now," Scott said. "Small talk doesn't become either one of us, and I have work to do."

Maggie left, walking back down the narrow, well-worn path to the lodge. The cabin was original to the land, and when Aaron had the lodge built, the construction foreman had used it as his office. Maggie had stayed in it while the lodge was being decorated, overseeing all the interior design. She knew this path so well she didn't even think about where she was putting her feet. Instead, she pulled her light sweater tighter around her as she walked, her mind wandering.

Her whole world felt like it was spinning away from her. Life had been so good, with the retreat under control and everything in her life settled. She'd been content to stay here, grow old here. She'd certainly had the same deep longings most women have for a home and family, but she'd always thought there would be time for that later. She'd been settled and ready for things to move along, one day the same as the next, for a long time to come.

Now, nothing is the same. She stepped over a fallen log and around a moonlit birch tree, letting her hand slide over the smooth trunk. *I can't even tell how people I've known for years are going to act.* Maggie had truly thought Scott would object to Lily moving into the lodge house.

She looked up at the stars through a break in some low-hanging clouds. "Nothing is ever truly under our control, is it?" she asked, wishing once again that God would drop a neon sign on the lawn with ready-made instructions.

But that wasn't going to happen. Maggie avoided the bottom tread of the deck stairs, then slowly entered the house, grateful for its fragrant warmth. She stood by the fire a moment, warming her feet and hands, then slipped out of her sweater. She went to her room, fighting the urge to get into a snug gown and curl up under her comforter. Dropping the sweater on her bed, she headed for her office, her mind still locked on Scott and Lily. Her chest ached with love for her sister, and she longed once again for a panacea for all Lily's pain.

Pain. Scott. *Maybe he needed a break from her as much as she needed a divorce from him.* Maggie cringed at the thought. As she settled in her office, blinds down, to do some paperwork and wait for Lily, she hated thinking about Lily and Scott breaking up. But he hit her. Only once, according to Lily, but in Maggie's mind, even once was too much. It was only a promise to her sister that kept Maggie from siccing Tyler on Scott.

Now what?

Is divorce ever in Your plans, God? Maggie looked at the Bible on the corner of her desk. *Doesn't it say that divorce is never allowed, except for adultery?*

Well, there was Lily and Aaron. That qualifies.

No! Maggie squeezed her eyes shut and clenched her fists until the nails bit into her palms. Tears burned her eyes. It was all going so wrong. All wrong! She'd had everything in place—

her life, her world, even her sister—here so she could get help, but it just got worse. The drinking, the time she had spent with Aaron…

"You know what your problem is, Little Maggie?" Aaron asked, half teasing, half not. "It's not that you're a control freak. That title would go to my darling wife. No, babe, you just have this illusion that you already have everything under control."

"It looks pretty good from here," Maggie responded, grinning. They were standing in front of the lodge's fireplace after a cold walk through the woods from Cookie's, who had invited them for tea and gingersnaps.

Aaron reached out and took her hand. "So it does."

It was a move that had so often led her into his arms. This time, she didn't feel even a tiny draw toward him. She pulled her hand back and shook her head. "It was your decision, Aaron. You know how I feel. You're married. I don't even want you flirting with me."

Aaron looked her over, head to toe, then nodded. "Okay, babe." He backed up, then stopped. "I blew it, didn't I?"

*She had loved him so much. If only he hadn't pushed….
"Yes, you did."*

He shrugged, then smiled. "I usually do." He stepped backward again, then broke into a quick two-step. "But I'm a writer. I'll write my way out of it." He tipped an imaginary hat to her, then left.

Maggie opened her eyes. "Write your way out?" Her attention turned to the bottom drawer of his filing cabinet. She walked over, but as she bent to open the drawer, she hesitated. There was something else, something she'd seen but that hadn't quite registered.

Instead, she jerked open the top drawer and flipped through the folders of manuscripts. Carter, Mick, Dan, Scott, Tonya.

Several weeks' worth. Maggie stopped and backed up, pulling out Scott's folders. Two of them were empty.

She put the folders back and closed the drawer. Where would they be? She propped her elbow on the cabinet and closed her eyes, trying to envision when and where Aaron would work.

Here, in this office, obviously. At night, downstairs, after everyone had left. Sometimes, in the bedroom that he used.

She tried to remember if he'd ever taken manuscripts back to his house. He was not someone who usually carried any kind of case or notebook. He didn't like the burden of anything, although he would carry a briefcase to meetings. So they had to be here somewhere, right?

Maggie left her office and went to the bedroom across the hall from hers, which was the one where Aaron usually stayed. Stopping in the hallway, she peered through the main room and down the opposing hall. All was quiet. Tim's door was shut, as usual, but his light was still on. She smiled affectionately. Her groundskeeper fit in well here because he was good at his job and a bit of a night owl, so the late prowlings of the other residents didn't disturb him. In fact, the late-night rounds he always made around the property had added to Maggie's sense of safety and security. He kept to himself, and she knew he loved online chatrooms. She'd given him a laptop last Christmas, and she didn't think he'd have reacted more strongly if she'd made him President.

Tyler's officer, a soft-spoken giant of a man named Ray Carpenter, slept in the other bedroom, and his door was open, light on. Maggie still wasn't used to him being here. He ate with them and was a nice enough fellow, but it was just strange to hear sounds in the house. Tonya's door was closed, light off.

Stepping into Aaron's room, Maggie stopped, looking around. It wasn't really "his" room…but it was. She'd decorated it, and he had not used it often at first—only when he worked late on the submissions or had fought with Korie. In the past eight months, however, he'd been there almost every night, and the room had his presence, his smell—tobacco, whiskey, cologne. It was hard to believe he'd only been dead three days.

Dead. Maggie weaved from the unexpected wave of grief that washed over her, and a low moan echoed in the room. She backed up, holding on to the door frame. *Why hadn't this happened at the house? Why now?* She blinked away the sting of tears. "I can't do this."

"Yes, you can," Aaron said, as somber as she'd ever seen him. "I need you to do this."

Maggie leaned back in her chair, glad that they'd met on the neutral turf of a sushi bar down on Second Avenue. They'd eaten well; now was time for the proposal and the questions. "Writers can have pretty strong personalities," she said. "I'm not sure I can enforce the rules you're proposing."

"Yes, you can," he replied, and motioned to the waitress for another pot of tea.

She raised her eyebrows. "No beer? Not even a sake or plum wine?"

He grinned. "Not tonight." He reached over and took her hand. "I'm serious about this, babe. I want to leave more behind in my life than a few trashy novels about an emotionally dead detective. I have no family. This is my only legacy. I want you in charge. You can do this."

Maggie closed her eyes and took a deep breath. Letting it out slowly, she looked around the room again. "I can do this." *For Aaron.*

The room was decorated in muted earth tones, with furniture that had clean, elegant lines—a bed, narrow dresser, two bedside tables with lamps. Aaron's favorite chair was here, a

Stickley he'd rescued when Korie had redone their penthouse in New York. He would turn it toward the window and prop his feet on the sill while he worked on a manuscript.

Maggie squared her shoulders and started with one of the bedside tables, but found only a few books and a notebook filled with story notes and character sketches. And a Bible. Picking it up slowly, Maggie turned it over and realized it was a study Bible she had given him during the first month of their romance. She smiled, then flipped through a few pages, pausing when she saw notes in the margin. She stared, turning more pages. Lots of notes.

"I can't believe you read it," she said softly, then put it back in the drawer, her mind awhirl with the contradictions that were Aaron. He was an alcoholic womanizer who read the Bible, went to church and had encouraged his writers to explore their own faiths, saying it would help inform their hearts as well as their talents. Somewhere buried in that mix was the real Aaron Jackson.

The closet held nothing spectacular either, only more boxes of books, old magazines and a few clothes. Maggie started to leave, then turned and took one last look around. Where she'd sat on the bed had rumpled the spread, and she went back to smooth it down, then realized that she needed to change the sheets in case Lily wanted to stay in here instead of on the couch. She turned back the spread and reached to pull the sheets off. As she yanked the bottom fitted sheet off, the mattress shifted and Maggie grabbed the corner to pull it back into place. As she looked down to make sure they were aligned, the tip of something beige caught her eye.

The edge of a file folder stuck out between the mattress and the springs. Maggie lifted the corner of the mattress and pulled out two more folders of manuscript. Maggie sat down on the floor and spread them in front of her, turning through the pages, one by one.

Scott's submissions, with Aaron's editorial markings.

She frowned. A lot of markings. Too many. Maggie stopped, staring at one page that was almost completely crossed out, with Aaron's angular but clear handwriting filling every clear space on the page and running over to the back. Her chest tightened. Aaron had not been editing Scott's manuscripts.

He had been rewriting them.

ELEVEN

"I don't like surprises," Judson said to his young partner. "I never talk to a suspect without a clear plan. Most of the time, I can even tell you what they are going to say."

"Then why do you even ask them?" Lee questioned.

"Because it's important for it to come from them," Judson explained. "But it's also vital that you maintain control and that you don't get caught off guard."

Fletcher stared at his bed, not entirely sure what to do next. Lily looked like a tiny china doll, curled on her side and snuggled beneath his covers, although her light snore ruined the picture of the perfect sleeping beauty. The Dom Perignon was on the desk, and he walked over, turning it around in the dim light of the cabin and testing its weight. It was almost full, and the flute she'd filled before leaving the lodge was only half empty. He pulled out the desk chair and sat down.

The workout with the branch had cleared his mind and renewed his energy. He'd let his emotions, especially about Maggie, about Aaron, drag him down too far. He saw a lot of things clearer now, especially where this one was concerned. He looked at the delicate curve of her jaw, the lacey frill of her eyelashes against her cheek. She was not the lightweight she'd like to have people believe, that much was certain.

"Lily," he called softly.

One leg stretched and she snored harder.

"Lily," he said, a shade louder.

Her eyes fluttered, and he waited. She stirred and the green eyes opened, blinked, then widened, as did her mouth. "Oops," she whispered, staring at him.

Fletcher laughed. "Oops?" he asked. "You wake up in a strange bed and the first thing that comes to your mind is 'Oops?'"

She pouted and pushed herself up on her elbows. "Don't be mean. I didn't intend to fall asleep."

Fletcher raised his eyebrows. "So you crawled beneath my covers because…?"

"I was cold," she finished, sitting up and bracing herself against the headboard. "I'm still dressed."

Fletcher turned the Dom bottle around so that the label faced front again. "It's going flat."

Twin spots of red tinged her cheeks. "I wanted to drink it, believe me. It just didn't seem right this time. I didn't…" Her voiced faded.

Fletcher gave her a break. "So why did you come here?"

She rubbed the corner of her eyes carefully, trying not to smudge her makeup any more than it already was. "I thought of something this afternoon, and I don't know if it means anything. But I thought you ought to know. And I wanted to ask you something."

Fletcher leaned forward, bracing his elbows on his knees, his hands steepling beneath his chin. "Tell me."

She met his gaze steadily. "I didn't kill him."

"I know."

She looked startled. "You do?"

"Talk to me, Lily."

Her shoulders drooped a bit. "You know about Aaron and me, that we were…"

"That you were sleeping together, yes."

Lily sat up straighter. "What did you say?"

Fletcher's head tilted to one side. "Why don't you tell me about it?"

The young actress didn't relent, her cheeks pinking. "Does everyone think we were sleeping together?"

"I'm not in a position to know what everyone else thinks. At least, not yet."

She looked away, out the front window of the cabin. "I didn't cheat on my husband," she said softly. "No matter what *everyone* might believe. Aaron and I were… Aaron was very sympathetic. The whole fame thing. Scott doesn't get it, didn't understand. He's very temperamental, my husband. Which I liked." She winced. "But he didn't like it when I drank. Didn't know how to deal with it."

"Is that when he hit you?"

Her eyes flashed back to him. "Scott's not abusive."

"Lily—"

"He's not!" she insisted. "He doesn't… It's not a pattern." Her voice softened. "Maggie says we both need a lot of prayer and even more therapy."

Fletcher gritted his teeth and stuck one hand down in his jacket pocket. It closed around his pen.

"Scott knows that if he hits me again, I'll call a lawyer. It's not that."

"Did he *think* that you and Aaron were—"

She shook her head. "I don't think so." She paused, then continued, more determined to get all the details out now. "Although we only saw each other alone when Scott was gone. The first was when Scott was in New York with his agent, and I got a call about the stalker. I was so scared…." She hugged her knees to her chest. "Aaron listened. Just listened at first. Korie was gone, too, and when I was finished, he talked. We talked for hours. It felt good." Lily's eyes were turned toward the floor, but her focus was distant, in another time and place. "I thought it was just sympathy on his part. That we had something in common. That he even maybe liked me a little. I never thought… I never realized that he'd use me."

Fletcher's eyes narrowed. "What happened, Lily?"

She was still for a moment, remaining in that far distant place. Slowly, she took a deep breath and returned. She looked up at Fletcher, her eyes hard. "After a while, he asked me to help him with a practical joke. A tease on Scott."

Lily got up and walked to the desk. She picked up the bottle and the flute and went to the sink, where she emptied both into the drain. Fletcher waited, and Lily was silent as she watched the liquid disappear. She then turned to him.

"My husband had been working on two novels, rotating them, depending on how he felt that week or that day. He'd turned the majority of both over to Aaron. They'd been fighting over them, with Aaron telling him that his quality was going downhill."

"What did Aaron ask you to do?"

"Scott's notorious for depending on his hard drive. He hardly ever backs anything up to a disk."

Fletcher sat up straight. "You deleted his novels?"

She nodded. "I reformatted the hard drive. It wiped out everything. Aaron had the only copies. He said he wanted Scott to beg him for—"

Lily's knees buckled and she turned, grabbing the sink. Fletcher was there before she started to retch, and he snatched a dishcloth off a rack and flipped on the water, soaking the cloth. He held her, bathing her face and neck, as her shoulders shook with sobs. "I'm sorry," she cried. "I'm so sorry."

Fletcher pressed the cloth into her hands, then he picked her up and carried her back to the bed, sitting her gently on the edge of it. He brushed her hair away from her face. She was still trembling as she crossed her arms, tucking her hands into her armpits. "I don't know what to do."

Fletcher pulled no punches. "Take back your life."

She looked up at him, confused. "What?"

He stood up and went to the sink. He finished cleaning as he spoke, his voice hard. "Stop doing things you don't intend to do. Stop hiding out in your sister's backyard."

"You don't under—"

He turned. "What don't I understand, Lily? That you decided you weren't strong enough to handle what life handed you? That you loved success but not the downsides that come with it? That you can excuse your husband's abuse because 'it's not a pattern'? That you can regret destroying your husband's work when you realized it gave him a motive for killing Aaron? You love playing the victim, Lily, and that I *do* understand."

Her eyes flashed and she stood up. "I am *not* a victim!"

"Then prove it. Take responsibility. Take back your life."

She blinked, her resolve faltering. "You mean, tell Scott."

"Yes. And stop drinking. Stop joking around about stopping and just do it. Call that lawyer, so Scott will know you're serious. Take the precautions you need to and tell your stalker to go fly a kite. Live your life. Stop hiding in the shadows."

Lily sank back down on the bed, and Fletcher watched as a dozen emotions flashed over her face. Fear. Worry. Anger. And plain old-fashioned weariness. There was a reason she had fallen asleep in his bed. He walked over and reached out his hand. "Let me walk you over to the lodge," he said softly. "You need to get some rest."

She was silent for a moment, then took his hand and stood up. "No," she said. "I'm going back to my cabin and see my husband."

Fletcher nodded, then offered her a stick of peppermint gum. She laughed and took it.

They walked silently back to her cabin, her hand curled lightly around his arm. The gesture sent an odd feeling through him, one that told him that having a lady on his arm was normal and comforting. Yet he didn't think about Lily—his mind went immediately to the woman with the auburn curls and hint of sandalwood. Maggie. He pushed the thought—and the feeling—away, and he and Lily paused near her cabin's front porch. "Do you want me to wait and see if I should call 911?" he asked.

She grinned. "No. I'm not going to hit him with everything tonight. Just enough to get things started." She tiptoed up and kissed his cheek. "I'll keep you posted."

Fletcher watched her go in, then turned toward the lodge, to let Maggie know that Lily wouldn't be spending the night. He was lost in thought as he approached the back deck, wondering if Scott Jonas really was temperamental enough to kill Aaron over a couple of lost manuscripts. It was weak. After all, they were still in existence, and all Scott would have to do was pay someone to type them into the computer again. Still, he'd seen people kill over much less.

Fletcher stepped over the stained bottom step, as he'd seen everyone else do, before climbing the stairs. He stopped on the deck, looking into the main room of the house. The overhead lights were out, but lights in both wings were still on, casting elongated shadows into the central area of the A-frame. Fletcher's breath fogged around his face as he watched Tim Miller pacing back and forth in front of the fireplace, the last of the embers on the hearth casting a soft red backlight on the young groundskeeper. Tim had several sheets of paper in one hand. The other hand flicked nervously, and he occasionally ran it through his hair.

Fletcher frowned. Tim had always been soft-spoken and laid-back; now, he acted as if someone had dropped hot coals in his shoes. Fletcher backed away from the door, into the shadows, and waited. Finally, Tim walked to the bar and dropped the papers on it, then went down the hall toward his room.

After a moment, Maggie came into the room and looked around, as if checking on something. She turned the light on, and Fletcher sighed. He left the shadows and tapped on the door. Maggie jumped slightly, then walked over and opened it.

"You're making a habit of this," she said quietly.

He shook his head and nodded toward the light. "So are you."

She shrugged. "Thought I heard something."

"Mind if I come in a second?"

She stepped back, and Fletcher entered, rubbing his hands together. He headed for the fire. "It's getting colder out there."

She tilted her head. "What are you doing here? I thought you were catching a train."

Fletcher glanced at his watch. "I just wanted to let you know that Lily went back to her cabin. She decided to stay there tonight."

Maggie looked worried.

"What's wrong?"

"Nothing," she said. "I just hope Scott's agreeable with it. He seemed really happy to have her gone."

"I think they'll be okay."

Maggie looked closely at him. "I hope so." She paused. "I think we need to talk…." Her voice faded as she realized he wasn't really listening.

He nodded, looking around on the floor, which was dry. Tim had apparently not been outside, but his previous tramps around the grounds still left their mark: a faint outline of soil and crushed leaves, in a smudged, wafflelike pattern on the hardwood floor near the fireplace.

Fletcher then wandered over to the bar, where he glanced down at the papers Tim had left on the bar. Lily's stalker letters.

"What?" Maggie asked.

He looked up at her. "What?" he asked.

She crossed her arms and leaned on the counter. "You're in detective mode. What's going on?"

Fletcher froze, staring at her.

"Yeah, detective mode," Aaron said. "It's when you get so focused on the facts that you forget anyone else can see you. You walk around with your thoughts on the outside of your head, and you wander about as if your brain and your feet weren't quite on speaking terms. I'm surprised you don't run into walls."

Fletcher's face grew warm. "I have."

"Ha! I knew it! I'd steal it for Judson, but he's too classy to go about banging into things."

"Aaron used to say that," he said.

Maggie nodded. "I know. He knew you pretty well, didn't he?"

"I guess so, although he didn't put much of me into Judson."

Maggie snorted a laugh. "You're joking, right?"

Fletcher shook his head. "I'm not Judson."

Maggie grinned. "Friends for fifteen years and you still don't know how writers work." She moved closer and lightly touched the arm of his coat. "You don't look like Judson and you don't act like Judson, but all the things that make you…well…*you* are the same things that make Judson who he is. The way you think, work a case. Your ethics, the determination. The way you follow the evidence and treat people with respect…" Her voice trailed off and she looked away from him.

Fletcher crossed his arms. "You like Judson."

She nodded, and the reddish curls slid forward to frame her face. Fletcher fought the urge to brush them back, to caress her cheek, to check her wounds. "As much as you can like a fictional character…" she said, then looked up at him. "I like the reality better."

He felt his chest tighten, and he was suddenly as warm as he wanted to be. Swallowing hard, he stepped back. He wasn't ready for this, for her to know this much about him. "I'd better go. We'll talk when we get back."

Maggie blushed, and she reached out toward him again. "I'm sorry. I didn't mean—"

He took her hand and kissed the back of it. "No. It's all right." He let it go and backed away again. "But I do need to go."

She nodded, looking away.

"I'll call you with the details about the memorial service."

"Okay." She looked away.

He wanted to hug her and tell her that everything would be fine. Instead, he turned his back on her and left the house.

TWELVE

Maggie couldn't sleep. *This is getting to be a habit,* she thought. After Fletcher had left, she'd put on her nightgown and stretched out in the bed, but closing her eyes seemed to be a wasted effort. Tentatively, she touched the wounds on her face, halfway hoping they were no longer there, even though her head still ached with a dull throb that the pills barely kept at bay. She knew the drug the doctor had given her for pain would knock her out, but the grogginess she'd felt most of Wednesday was still a strong memory and not one she particularly wanted to relive.

What she *was* going over and over in her mind was the way Fletcher had acted, just before he left, this strange mix of boyish curiosity and fear.

Fear?

That didn't make sense. But then, none of this made sense. With the release of a long breath, Maggie sat up and reached for her robe at the foot of the bed. *Might as well get some work done.*

She closed her door and padded to the office, where lightning from a late-night storm reminded her to close the blinds. Behind the desk, she snapped on her computer and pulled a stack of bills and the retreat's checkbook from the right-hand drawer. Aaron had suggested turning this task over to Edward, just as he had his own finances, but Maggie liked keeping control of where the money went. *Now,* she thought wryly, *I'm glad I did.* Still, she found that she was writing out the checks almost automatically, her mind still caught on the man in the wrinkled suit.

He *was* Judson—and he was not. Fletcher had moved about the room with an excitement very much akin to the fictional detective, but then froze with her tentative affection, completely unlike the sophisticated Judson. The hero of more than fifteen novels had enchanted her at one point, moreso when she was still in love with his author.

"He's more the me I thought I'd grow up to be when I was seventeen," Aaron said. "Smooth, urbane, intelligent. The love child of Edward R. Murrow and James Bond. I couldn't be that, so I wrote about it. Amazing how witty you can be when you've got five months to write a comeback." He laughed. "No wonder the women love him."

They were walking in Central Park, which they did almost every Sunday afternoon. Maggie's idea, but Aaron loved it; and they even explored some areas that were normally avoided. "Murder fodder," according to Aaron. It was one of those New York autumn days that Maggie adored, almost as much as the man next to her. She loved feeling his hand gripping hers in a way that was both protective and affectionate, as if suddenly pulling her into a hug would keep her safe from the world.

Without warning, Aaron tugged on her hand, and turned his loose-jointed lope into a trot, then a jog. She laughed as they ran until breathless, collapsing on the ground with giggles. This was the Aaron she loved, playful and challenging. It was only when they got around the gold diggers of the world that he treated her as if she were a provincial child, as if he were embarrassed that she wouldn't sleep with him, even though no one knew that about them. It bothered her almost as much that people assumed they did.

Aaron lay on his back and pointed at a cluster of cumulus clouds. "What do you see?"

Maggie studied them. "A group of mean old men."

Aaron snickered. "Must be book critics."

She laughed. "Not yours, then. They loved your last Judson."

Aaron was silent a few moments. "Do you love Judson?"

Maggie turned on her side and rested one hand on his chest. "Yes. But I don't think you're him."

"Are you sure?"

Maggie's pen paused over the checkbook, and she frowned.

Aaron as Judson. Fletcher as Judson. Was she blurring the lines? Was she assuming things about Fletcher based on what she knew of Judson? She'd certainly studied Aaron's novels as if they were part of life itself, a part of him. She'd even used them in a paper on modern heroes during her senior year at college. Were even her memories of Aaron colored by his fictional hero? Had she placed her trust in Fletcher blindly because of Judson? Because of Aaron?

"I'm not Judson." He'd said it a dozen times this week. So who was he, really? She stared down at the bills in front of her. "For that matter," she whispered, "who was Aaron? Really?"

Someone, she thought suddenly, *who had hidden sixty thousand dollars in my office.* She pushed her chair back a bit and pulled open the two bottom drawers of her desk. She rarely used them, and most of the files were old records for the retreat that she would eventually put in storage. She kept as much as possible on the computer, and some of the papers dated back to the start of the retreat. Past applications, records of past residents, old receipts from the caterers, details on the escrow account.

She ran her fingers across the tabs in the right-hand drawer, but saw nothing unusual. In the one on the left, a file near the back had no label, and she pulled it out. She opened it with a snap, then stopped, paging slowly through the papers it held. They were copies of letters canceling Aaron's magazine subscriptions and closing his credit card accounts. Each letter had a note in Aaron's handwriting on it: "Keep until 12/15," or "Destroy after 12/1." Toward the back was a slip of paper with a shipping address in Vermont and the paperwork for setting up a corporation in Toronto. As Maggie flipped through it, a small card fell, facedown, out on the desk. She turned it over.

It was her Social Security card.

Maggie froze, staring at the card. A thick weight settled on her chest, and she forced herself to breathe. "No," she whispered. "No." The papers slid from her hands as she pushed away from the desk and ran back to her bedroom. Scrabbling furiously, she dug boxes from the bottom of her closet until she got to the fireproof container where she kept all her personal papers. Sitting on the floor, she pulled the box into her lap. Her hands shook as she dialed through the combination on the lock and snapped open the top.

She rustled through everything. Hers and Lily's wills, their birth certificates, the death certificates of their parents, insurance policies, her real passport...but her Social Security card was missing.

What had he done? All the paperwork pointed toward a man who was planning to disappear, but then there was that passport with her picture. *Why? Why bring me into it? Was he going to ask me to join him?*

Or was he framing me?

Maggie dropped the lid shut, and it locked with a solid click. Then she heard a second click, more distant. Then footsteps.

Shoving the box aside, Maggie got up and went to her door. "Tim?" she called out.

The footsteps started to run.

Screaming Ray's name, Maggie flew toward the main room, her feet slipping when they met water on the hardwood floor. Her rear hit the floor hard as the officer and Tim bounded into the room. She pointed toward the back door, which was banging open with the wind. Spray from the storm had spread over the floor.

Ray went to the door, peering out, then securing it. Tim rushed to help Maggie up. She looked wildly at both of them. "Didn't you hear someone running?"

They looked at each other. Tim stroked her arm. "No, ma'am. I had just gone out before it started raining. I'm sorry. I must not have latched the door good."

"I heard someone running!" she insisted.

Tim shook his head. "You must have just heard me and the door. I've been kinda antsy tonight. Been up walking about some."

Maggie's shoulders drooped. "I called your name."

He shook his head. "I didn't hear you. Sorry."

Maggie rubbed her eyes, then brushed her hair back. "I don't believe this."

Tim squeezed her hand. "Miss Maggie, you've been through a lot. I don't wonder that you're a bit on edge. You need to get some rest and not be wandering about so."

She nodded, then shivered as a chill settled in her bones. Maybe she hadn't heard the running footsteps. The house had always made funny noises, especially at night as the temperature dropped. She turned back toward the hall. Between that and Fletcher sneaking up on her so much lately, maybe she was just being skitt—

Maggie stopped, her head tilting sideways as she studied the bar. The room was streaked with long shadows. With the storm outside, the only lights came from the two hallways, but this time, Maggie knew she was not imagining things.

The letters from Lily's stalker were gone.

THIRTEEN

"People don't always know what they know," Judson explained.

They were on their way to interview the best friend of the victim's neighbor. Lee thought it was a waste of time.

Judson disagreed. "Most civilians aren't trained as detectives. They have no idea what's important and what isn't. Yet they see and take in some of the most amazing things. I've broken a lot of cases on tidbits that people didn't even know were tidbits."

Fletcher stepped away from the train, rolling his shoulders as he threaded his way through the crowd in Penn Station, glad to get his feet on the ground again. He'd slept little on the long trip through the darkness. Fifteen years in New York and he still hated the train, which amazed the few friends he had. He never tried to explain it, figuring it was pretty much no one's business anyway, and knowing that if he did, Judson might suddenly develop a fear of rail travel as an explanation for his need of well-kept cars.

He sniffed and stretched his neck again as he waved down a cab. Once inside, Fletcher sat back, watching the street scenes flash by as he organized his thoughts, deciding on which questioning tactic to take with Edward. The meeting with the manager was at ten, which gave Fletcher time to go to his apartment, shower and find one of the few suits that had been recently dry-cleaned. Fletcher grinned, remembering the look that Maggie had given him and his suit when he'd plopped down on the ground beside her that first day. And a few times since. It wasn't his intention to come off as slovenly, but he'd discovered over the past few days that he liked surprising her, in whatever way that happened.

His apartment smelled like soured Moo Shu Pork. Gagging, Fletcher opened several windows and turned on the air-conditioner fan. Finding the offending carton, he dumped it in the hallway incinerator, then spritzed his cologne throughout the four small rooms where he lived. The odor was less eye-watering by the time he had finished his shower and shave, but he was glad to leave again.

In the second cab, Fletcher focused more on the storefronts that blurred by as the driver dodged his way toward the theater district. Although it wasn't even Thanksgiving yet, Christmas decorations filled the windows, reminding passersby that now was time to buy or layaway, don't wait too long for the latest…whatever. But it was normal for this time of year. Normal for New York.

A New York that would never see Aaron again. Fletcher rubbed the back of his neck, trying to push away the thought.

"Open it," Aaron demanded, a broad, enthusiastic grin on his face. He held out a large, beautifully wrapped box toward the younger man, motioning for him to take it.

Fletcher stepped away from his door and motioned for Aaron to come in. "It's two in the morning, Aaron."

"It's Christmas, me boyo! What are you doing asleep?" Aaron came in, the red-and-white Santa hat on his head tipping

precariously. He grabbed it and shoved it back down over his hair. Passing by Fletcher, he sat the box on a table and dropped a huge stuffed sack into one of the chairs.

"What are you doing upright and walking?" Fletcher asked. "Shouldn't you be passed out under Korie's table, snoozing in wait for Santa?"

Aaron straightened his hat again. "Ah, don't bring my beautiful bride into this. She's not in the giving mood tonight, like most nights." He laughed. "She prefers Valentine's Day, even if she doesn't appreciate what she's given. Besides," he whispered conspiratorially, "I'm not even drunk." He made a broad motion toward the box. "Open it, my dear Judson!"

Fletcher winced. It was not a good memory, of Aaron or Christmas, and Fletcher now realized it was when he'd first noticed that Aaron wasn't his usual self. The giving, laughing Aaron he knew so well had developed a vengeful streak. The sack of gifts, intended for Korie, had later been returned to the stores, and Aaron had canceled her accounts at four major department stores. The fight had been minor; Aaron had escalated it into a two-week battle.

So what did Edward do to get fired? Fletcher checked the knot on his tie as he entered the polished lobby. Fletcher knew all too well that being neater didn't improve the quality of his suit, but he wanted Edward to focus on his questions, not his image. He'd met the wiry manager at a couple of gatherings Aaron had dragged him to, and Fletcher's impression was that Edward was a straightforward professional who gave "efficiency" a new definition. This was confirmed by Edward's greeting of "I'm ready to get to the bottom of this," as he ushered Fletcher into an office that was well organized and masculine, with a heavy cherry desk and coordinating credenza and shelves and a lingering smell of cigars and imported French Roast. "Coffee?" he asked.

Fletcher shook his head and sat in a chair with clean lines and polished leather. He reached for his pad and pen as Edward pushed aside the one sign that he worked here, a thin notebook and several sheets of paper. Edward leaned forward, his hands folded on the desk. "Aaron fired me about six months ago, to answer your first question."

Fletcher's eyebrows arched. That was not his first question, but he let it ride. "Did he give you a good reason?"

Edward hesitated. "A reason, yes. A good one, no." He sat a bit straighter. "He told me he wanted to take over the management of his finances, wanted more control of where everything was going."

"You didn't consider that a good reason?"

"How long have you known Aaron, Fletcher?"

"Fifteen years."

"Ever known him to be smart with money?"

"Only when it came to the retreat."

"Exactly." Edward leaned back in his chair. "He was an idiot. That's why he hired me in the first place. I did everything for him, in terms of his finances. Investments, shelters, I even paid his household bills."

"So why do you think he did it?"

Edward stood up suddenly and went to the credenza, pouring himself more coffee. Fletcher was silent. The money manager drank, staring out his window at the Manhattan skyline. After a moment, he set the cup back on its silver tray and went to a wooden filing cabinet behind his desk. He removed a folder, then sat back at the desk. He pushed the folder at Fletcher, who opened it slowly.

"About seven months ago," Edward said quietly, "Aaron asked me to set up an offshore account for him. I've seen his prenuptial. I assumed it was to hide money from Korie, who was beginning to seriously drain his resources. Late last year, she had brought me a notarized statement from Aaron, authorizing me to close out one of his mutual fund portfolios and give her the money."

Fletcher remained calm. "For what?"

"She wanted to open a gallery."

"Did you?"

Edward shook his head. "Aaron had already been complaining to me about how much money she'd pulled from their liquid accounts. I told her I'd have to verify it with Aaron in person, and she stormed out. That girl can make quite a scene."

Fletcher sniffed. *Click.* "Is that when Aaron wanted the offshore account?"

"Yes. He had already set up a direct deposit system with his publisher for the royalty payments. He simply changed the bank to the one in the islands."

"Did you know anything about him mortgaging his house?"

Edward nodded. "He told me that Korie had tried the same thing with the bank—to get a mortgage—that she had with me. So Aaron mortgaged everything he had—his apartment here, his house, the place in L.A.—everything but the retreat, which is run by a trust and not part of the personal finances or covered by the prenuptial."

"So only the trustees have access to the money in escrow."

"Yes. If it were set up as a business, Korie would still be eligible to inherit half. As a trust, it's protected."

"Who are the trustees?"

"Originally, Aaron, me, his lawyer and Maggie." Edward paused and threaded his fingers together. "Maggie doesn't know this, or I'm fairly sure she doesn't. Aaron took steps to protect the retreat, during his life and after. He consulted with me about the financial end of it, and he and his lawyer set it up so that it's specifically excluded from the prenup and handled separately from the rest of his property in the will. In addition, everything he has, except for monthly operating expenses, will now be channeled into the retreat's trust, with enough legal beagling to make sure Korie won't be able to touch it, even if she decides to contest his will. He put the operating money offshore, and set up with the bank there to make direct payments to the mortgage companies. His plan was to keep her away from as much money as he could."

"Why didn't he just sell the properties?"

"He couldn't without violating the prenup. As long as they were married, he couldn't sell without her permission. He could, however, get a mortgage on them without her signature. And he really didn't want to give them up. He just wanted to keep her from getting the money that was invested in them."

"Why couldn't she get a mortgage?"

"Because she's a ditz. She had no idea he'd mortgaged the property, so she went to their local back in Mercer, trying to get one. He'd already warned them that she might try. They were his friends, not hers, but they did tell her they wouldn't risk a mortgage on a house already deep in debt. Aaron's mortgage is with a private lender in Arkansas."

"How did she take it?"

Edward was silent, but the message in his eyes was clear.

Fletcher nodded. "Got it. So why do you think he fired you?"

The older man cleared his throat. "I didn't just work for Aaron. I have a roster of clients that would make a tabloid reporter salivate. But we were also friends, and had been for more than twenty years. I don't think he wanted me involved."

"Why?"

Edward shifted in his chair and his voice dropped, marking the shift from business to personal. "I don't know if you had noticed, but Aaron's behavior had become a little…odd lately."

"Odd how?"

Edward's silence stretched out, but Fletcher had been a cop many years. He waited. Edward finally sniffed. "I need to make some calls before I explain what I know. But I can tell you that Aaron was about to take actions that were not going to be exactly legal, and he no longer cared about his own risks." He took a deep breath. "Aaron Jackson was getting ready to disappear."

Fletcher believed him. Edward was a good man; Aaron had always spoken highly of his old friend, and Fletcher knew that Edward had bailed the gnarly author out of more than one financial scrape. It gave Korie a clear motive for murder, and Fletcher knew she was quite capable of whacking Aaron upside the head with a champagne bottle. But it gnawed at him that no one had heard anything that night. Not Maggie, who was in the kitchen, nor Tim, who was in a bedroom that overlooked the backyard. Korie *could* make a scene, and she was loud when she did it. Quietly murdering her husband didn't seem her style.

Still, Fletcher knew all too well that anything was possible when passion and money were involved. Especially passion *for* money.

Pausing in the lobby, Fletcher took out his cell phone. Korie answered on the second ring, and Fletcher winced at the noise in the background. "When's Aaron's service?" he asked, without preamble.

Korie had to shout. "Fletcher? Is that you?"

"Yes."

"Sorry, I'm at O'Toole's. Lunch. What did you say?"

"Service. When? Where?"

"Oh. Tomorrow. Saturday. Around eight in the evening. At his publisher's. They have a huge reception area for company functions. There'll be a guard to let everyone in. It's going to be huge. The *Times* is paying for part of it, and I called the *Daily News*. They are even sending some people to cover it."

Of course she had. As Fletcher hung up, he thought he could hear Aaron laughing.

FOURTEEN

"Are you going?" Maggie asked Lily, handing her a cup of Earl Grey. She plopped down on the couch next to her sister and drew her feet up under her, then sipped from her own cup.

Since Lily's arrival at the retreat, they had spent a lot of mornings like this, curled together on the large, comfy sofa, sharing one afghan, drinking tea, and firming up the sister-bond between them. For Maggie, it was the perfect location and the perfect time of day, with the morning sun beginning to heat the room and illuminating it with long steaks of dusty, glowing rays. Some days, when she was busy watering the houseplants, Maggie would spritz the rays with water, watching as tiny rainbows danced for a second or two in the air.

Maggie also found Lily to be the perfect companion. Rediscovering their friendship had been a true joy. She only wished this morning's topic was not so joy*less*.

Holding the tea out away from her, Lily spread a throw over their legs. "No. Scott and I have reached a tentative truce. Getting Aaron out of our lives is going to be part of that."

Maggie frowned. "Does that mean you're leaving?"

Lily stared into the cup for a moment. "Not just yet, although it won't be too long. I'll probably go first, open up the house in L.A. My agent thinks I'll get that part, and I may need to go talk to the producers, convince them I'll stay sober, among other things. And Scott needs to finish some things up." Swirling the tea gently, Lily told Maggie about the deleted manuscripts. "So we need to get those back from Aaron's files, too. Get them retyped."

Maggie's stomach tightened, and she sniffed, staring out the back glass. Her heart ached as she was torn between her loyalty to Lily and her desire to do what was right. All of her instincts told her those manuscripts had played a role in Aaron's death and that she needed to talk to Fletcher first. *Lord,* she thought desperately. *What's right?*

She took a deep breath as a sense of peace settled on her. Finding Aaron's killer had to come first, and Maggie's body and mind seemed to relax as she felt her mind shifting its priorities. *Fletcher* had to come first.

Fletcher.

Maggie cleared her throat. "Lily, Scott's manuscripts are not in the filing cabinet."

Lily put down her cup. "What?"

"They're not there. I was looking through some of Aaron's files to see if anything looked…odd. Scott's files are empty."

Lily uncurled and dropped her feet to the floor. She took a deep breath, then folded her arms over her stomach. "Scott's going to kill me."

Maggie set aside her tea and slid over to her sister. "No, he won't. They're here somewhere. No one had access to those files but Aaron and me, so it had to be Aaron. He probably took them somewhere to work on them. They're here somewhere."

Lily looked at the fire for a second. "You think she did it?"

Maggie hesitated, and picked up her tea again. "I honestly don't know, Lil. I guess…I guess maybe I did before. She was pretty horrid to him at times."

"And now?"

Maggie shook her head. "I'm just confused. It feels like half the world had a reason to kill him."

"Even you?"

Maggie squirmed underneath the throw, thinking of all she'd found over the past three days. Before, no, no reason. Now?

"Yeah," she said softly. "Even me. I think that's what's making all this so crazy, especially with Fletcher."

"You like him, don't you?"

Maggie shrugged, unable to meet her sister's eyes. "Yes. But..."

"He's not what you expected."

Maggie shook her head. She shifted, turning to face Lily. "Can I ask you something?"

"Sure."

"Did a lot of people, fans, think you were Cathy after *Ramsey Place?* I mean, it was your first big role and all."

Lily set her cup on the floor and drew her knees up, wrapping her arms around her legs. She studied her sister a moment. "Some. Most people are more savvy these days than to think actors are actually their characters. I got a few crazies, but not many. Why?" She paused, a look of recognition on her face. "Oh, girl. Are you having a problem distinguishing Fletcher from Judson?"

Maggie suddenly felt hot as well as foolish. She pushed the throw aside. "I don't think so. I don't know. Really. I guess..."

Lily laughed. A real one, from her gut, like Maggie had not heard in a long time. Still... "Lily. Come on, now."

The laugh settled into a few giggles hidden behind her hand. Lily's eyes were bright with joy and tears. "You're really falling for him, aren't you?"

Maggie's eyes widened. "No! I mean...no. I don't think so." She stood up and headed for the kitchen. "Just forget I said anything, okay?"

Lily grabbed her tea and followed her. "Absolutely not.

You've got to be kidding." She set her cup in the sink and grabbed her sister's wrists. "Look. Listen to me."

Maggie took a deep breath and tried to look composed.

Lily was still smiling. "I love you. You're my best friend and big sister. And I know you. You're not some weepy little girl who can't distinguish fantasy from reality. You may have liked Judson a lot, and Aaron. But when push comes to shove, you'll know the difference between the man in the room and the one in the book."

"How can you be so sure?"

"Because I know you. Trust me." She released Maggie's hands and stood up straighter, taking a deep breath. "I had a long talk with Fletcher last night, and I've been watching him. Believe me. You won't be confused long, if at all. Fletcher is a very distinct personality."

"Like you." Maggie finally grinned.

"Like me. I'm not Cathy. He's not Judson."

Maggie shook her head. "But he is a detective. And I'm a suspect."

Lily tilted her head to one side. "Then you just need to prove to him you're not."

"Obviously. Got any ideas?"

After a moment's hesitation, Lily asked softly, "Have you prayed about this?"

Her older sister was speechless, but only for a few seconds. "You're asking me about prayer?"

Lily scowled. "I know how important it is to you even if I've walked away from it."

"Why did you?"

Lily's casual shrug was cautiously noncommittal.

"Well, that's a solid answer."

Lily stepped away. "I don't want to talk about this. Bottom-line—your faith is solid. Mine is not."

Maggie followed her back into the main room. "Don't walk

away from me, Lily. Please. We were apart for so long, and I know we've taken different paths, but we came from the same place. I want to know what happened."

The young actress turned suddenly. "Nothing happened! Okay? I had no great tragedy or epiphany that turned me away from the church. Okay? I just woke up one morning and saw that I had no place there. I moved on. So let's drop it. I don't want to be preached to."

Maggie stopped. "Okay. On one condition. You do this and I'll never mention it again."

"It doesn't involve Job-like suffering, does it?"

Maggie suppressed a grin. "Not exactly. It does involve a foolish husband."

Lily perked up. "Yeah?"

"Read First Samuel, chapter twenty-five."

Her sister was dubious. "Just one chapter?"

"Just one. Then come talk to me about the place women can have in the faith."

"Just talk. No preaching?"

"No preaching. I promise. Then you can help me figure out how to show Fletcher I'm innocent. Any ideas?"

Lily grinned. "Ask a writer?"

The Victorian was cold, much more than when she and Fletcher had been here before. At first Maggie thought that the electricity might be off, but everything was in working order. The thermostat was set lower than usual, probably Korie's doing before she left for New York, and the colder temps of the last two nights had settled in, ridding the house of any residual heat it may have had. Thanksgiving was only a week away, and their mild fall had ended abruptly over the past forty-eight hours. If the temperature held steady, she expected the first heavy snowfall within a few days.

Maggie shivered as she adjusted the setting, but she knew it was from more than just the cold. The house still felt hollow, surreal in its emptiness. She ached, longing to hear Aaron's gravelly baritone call out at her from his office. She climbed the stairs slowly, feeling heavy but without the same level of grief that she'd felt at the lodge house. She still wondered why it was much stronger there—her only sense was that it was there she had been with him the most.

Maggie bit her lip, fighting back a wave of tears. Aaron had been a presence in her life for almost ten years. Going on without him was going to be hard, even feeling the anger with him that she did. She stood in the office door a moment, reaching in to turn on the light. She was the intruder, even though he was gone.

But she had to know.

Slipping into his chair, she looked around, getting her bearings. *Ask a writer, indeed,* she thought, a little annoyed that her smart-aleck sister may have been more right than she had guessed. She turned on the computer, and as it booted, she closed her eyes, trying to slip into Aaron's skin.

"I want to set a password."

She grinned. Maggie liked being right. When he first un-packed his new computer, Maggie had told him to call her if he needed help. Nope, he'd insisted. He'd be fine. Now she held the phone with her shoulder as she sat in her office, trying not to gloat. "What kind? For online or the computer itself?"

"The computer. One that's just me, babe. I don't want prying eyes on my files. Tell me what to do."

She walked him through the steps and heard him typing in his slow, deliberate way.

"No more than eight letters," she reminded him.

"It has seven, dear Maggie. The number of perfection."

"So it's the perfect password?"

"Only if you know me well, babe. Only if you know my secret dreams."

Maggie opened her eyes. "Seven. Secret dreams." She looked around the office. Cigars, dictionaries, reference books. A poster from an Ansel Adams show in San Francisco. A poster of ancient Ireland. A stereo with a rack of CDs. Piles of manuscripts. A tray holding tumblers and an unopened bottle of Green Label.

She sighed. Nothing. No clicks, no hints. She closed her eyes again, letting memories of Aaron flash across her mind. His total lack of seriousness about anything but writing. His raving parties with Celtic musicians of all ranks and talent, in all kinds of venues, from Boston to New York.

One stood out, and she let her mind drift.

They were leaving a surprise party he'd thrown for a friend, which had been held in an apartment in lower Manhattan; Aaron could barely stand. Disgusted and angry with him, she'd poured him into a cab, but he'd grabbed her at the last minute, pulling her in. She'd resisted at first, but Aaron wrapped her in his arms, laughing and teasing her. "We need to do this more often."

She gave up and snuggled against him. "You don't do it enough?"

He shook his head. "Nope. Not near enough. And they come close, but no cigar."

Maggie looked up at him, curious. "Close enough to what?"

Aaron hadn't answered right away, and she saw the pain cross his eyes. "The real thing. County Mayo. Da. He could throw a party like no other. He was the king." He turned away to stare out the window.

Maggie opened her eyes and stood, crossing quickly to the shelf holding his collection of Judson novels. Pulling down the second one, she flipped it open to see if her memory was correct about the dedication.

There it was. "To Da. The ceilidh king."

Maggie smiled. Aaron, the sentimental romantic. His father had been Aaron's greatest hero. That he had not been able to make it to Ireland when the old man died had been one of his greatest regrets, his greatest haunting.

Returning to the computer, she typed in *C-E-I-L-I-D-H*.

The hard drive whirled, and she saluted it. "Here's to you, my Irish party boy." She scanned a list of his files and clicked open one bearing her name. As she read, her color, as well as her joy, began to fade.

FIFTEEN

"Do killers often come to the funerals?" Lee asked.

"In crimes of passion, more often than not," Judson replied. "If they haven't already been caught."

"Why?"

"Who knows? Remorse. Guilt. Gloating. I always have someone take pictures, especially if we have a witness. You never know what will happen."

Fletcher stood near the back of the reception hall, not too far from the food. He'd been there since the caterers arrived, having talked to the *New York Times* and the *New York Daily News* photographers earlier in the day. They promised him copies of any pictures, and the *Times* reporter explained that, in a slight deference to good taste, Aaron's coffin had been left at the funeral home, despite Korie's insistence that it be present. Apparently, neither the *Times,* who was co-sponsoring the service, nor the publisher thought it appropriate, and this time Korie's wailing-widow act had no impact. Fletcher found himself thankful for people with far more taste than his best friend's bride.

There was a smattering of tables and chairs around the room, but most people chose to stand and mingle. The hall was classier than he'd expected, with dark, draped walls and muted lighting. Yet the one touch of kitsch still annoyed Fletcher: Stand-ups of Aaron's most recent novels dotted the room like cardboard headstones.

The rest of the guests began arriving just after seven, showing off a glittery mix of furs, diamonds and jeans. *Both sides of his personality,* Fletcher decided. *The celebrity versus the writer.* On the writer side, Fletcher recognized and acknowledged Aaron's editor, Bill Davis, along with a few writers and students from Aaron's occasional stint as a writer in-residence at a local university. He'd spoken briefly with Bill early, and now he made a mental note to talk to the editor later that evening, to get his impressions of tonight's to-do. Edward was also there, standing off to himself.

On the celebrity side was a syndicated gossip columnist and a number of Tony-winning actors here to do readings from Aaron's books later in the evening. And, of course, Korie and her entourage, who arrived at a fashionably appropriate 8:05 p.m. The grieving widow was wearing black, but the dress was a design and fabric that was more magnetic than mournful. The high-profile pastor on her arm had eulogized more celebrities than the evening news, and the brooding young man who followed her clearly had more on his mind than grief.

The crowd grew, people circulated and hugged. Some shed polite tears. The writers from the retreat showed up in a group, but they dispersed quickly as Fletcher counted heads. Scott and Lily were missing. Tim was there, looking awkward, underdressed and out of place. But no Maggie.

Fletcher frowned and scanned the crowd again. She wasn't there. He paused, looking around a group of mourners, spotting a movement of auburn curls. *Was that her?* The height and shape were right, and as the woman turned, he took a step forward.

Then he stopped. It wasn't Maggie, although she looked a great deal like the manager of Aaron's retreat. His attention lingered on her as he noticed that she was carefully avoiding Korie and her group. She spoke quietly to Bill, then skirted wide around the widow's show. She nodded at Edward, then headed for the table of champagne, glancing over her shoulder at Korie.

Fletcher cut straight through the crowd and met her just as she turned away from the table. "Friend or foe?" he asked quietly.

The woman paused and looked Fletcher over carefully. She was tall and slender, and Fletcher was again caught by how much she resembled Maggie, even more so up close. Her makeup was carefully and professionally applied, but her eyes were swollen, with red streaks that no eyedrops were going to relieve. "Are you Judson?" she asked softly.

Fletcher pursed his lips. "I'm not—" She was wearing Aaron's cologne. "Yes," he said. "I'm Fletcher MacAllister."

She nodded, then looked over the crowd, her eyes lingering on Korie. "I was his—" She stopped. Her voice was low, choked. She pulled a business card out of her pocket and slipped it into his hand. "Publicist. I was hoping you'd be here. Please call me."

"I will." He put the card in his coat pocket without looking at it.

She stepped away, melting into the crowd.

Fletcher closed his eyes for a second, wondering if this one would have disappeared with Aaron, or would have just been another abandoned dalliance. Publicist. "You never did stray too far from home, did you?" Fletcher murmured.

"Why should I, me boyo? The girls here are smart, sassy and beautiful.

They were holed up in Aaron's apartment, going over the plot details of the book he wrote just before meeting Korie. They huddled over the kitchen table, surrounded by books, stacks of manuscript, cups of stale coffee, and the remains of cold and congealing reubens.

"Speaking of," Fletcher said, without looking up from the plot template in front of him. "Where is Maggie these days?"

A gargling sound rumbled deep in Aaron's throat. "I have no idea."

Fletcher's brows met in the middle as he glanced up. "She got away?"

Aaron ran his hand through his hair. "God got to her long before I could."

"Ladies and gentlemen, please." The pastor's voice echoed over the room, and Fletcher scanned the crowd again as they quieted and gave the cleric their attention. Koric moaned loudly and was comforted by the dark-haired young man, whose touches were more affectionate than consoling.

Fletcher grimaced, then noticed Maggie slipping in at the back. She stayed close to the wall, her arms wrapped tightly around her body. Her hair was windblown, the curls wild, and her face was still reddened by the cold. With her makeup streaked and her eyes as bloodshot and puffy as her look-alike's, she was the picture of misery. Something deep in Fletcher's gut twisted, and he ached to hold her, let her cry it out on his shoulder. She saw him and quickly wiped at her eyes, succeeding only in smearing what remained of her mascara. Her face still somber, she shook her head, hugged herself a bit closer then turned her attention to the pastor.

Fletcher stood a bit straighter, a small alarm triggering in his head. This wasn't grief. Something had happened.

"In accordance with Aaron's wishes," the pastor said, "there will not be a traditional funeral. In fact, I've been told he didn't want anything at all, that he said he'd done enough partying for everyone when he was still alive." A smattering of laughter interrupted the preacher, and Fletcher couldn't tell if he was startled or pleased. He plunged gamely on. "I will turn the floor over to a few people for comments, then we will have a few readings from Aaron's books, then close with a prayer."

A quiet murmur echoed uncomfortably around the crowd. Maggie pressed harder into the wall at her back. Korie turned her face into the neck of the young man, whose shoulders stiffened as he whispered something into her ear. She nodded, then held her head up, taking a deep breath and wiping one eye dramatically.

Fletcher refrained from sneering. Instead, he looked around, taking in the faces of the celebrants, noting how easy it was to spot the genuine mourners from those who were there from a sense of duty or the scent of free food—or free press. The writers from the retreat seemed sad, but honest about their lack of true grief. Tim just looked lost. Edward and the others who had worked either for or with Aaron were the most affected.

"Aaron's beloved bride, Korie, doesn't think she's up to speaking, so I've asked his editor, William Davis, to start with a few words about Aaron, the writer."

Bill set a glass of water on a nearby table and stepped up next to the pastor. He cleared his throat, then took off his glasses and wiped them with a handkerchief as he began.

"I've been Aaron's editor for the past ten novels. But I was also his friend. We hit it off on the first day we met, which started with a story conference about ten in the morning and ended somewhere near Orchard Street just after midnight. My wife even started dreading my meetings with Aaron, knowing she'd not see me for at least twenty-four hours. I'm convinced Aaron is the real reason she bought me a cell phone."

Modest bits of mirth rewarded him. Fletcher watched him for a moment before returning to his scanning. He liked Bill. A lot. The man was a true lover of books and as honest as anyone Aaron had around him. Aaron had also adored Bill, claiming that if the work was junk, Bill wouldn't pull any punches or flatter him to death. But Bill had catered to Aaron some, going to bat for him when the publisher had wanted to drop Aaron, just because of his behavior.

Bill replaced his glasses and tugged on his graying beard. "Aaron could definitely party. But he was also a professional, caring a great deal about his craft. He was constantly studying other writers and their work, absorbing techniques, trying things out. He never wanted to stop growing. There was going to be a huge announcement when the next Judson book came out. It was going to be his last, although I didn't think of that prophetically when he told me."

The room was still for a moment, except for the flashes of the cameras. Bill took a deep breath. "Aaron had brought me two proposals for other novels. Other *types* of novels. We'd contracted the first one, and he is scheduled to finish early next—" Bill's voice broke, and he swallowed hard. As he did, there was a slow undercurrent of chatter in the crowd. This was obviously a surprise.

It wasn't to Fletcher, since Aaron had told him about it the day before he died. They'd talked about the loss of Judson— something Fletcher was actually relieved about—and the new, more literary direction Aaron wanted to take. He'd even mentioned using a pseudonym, since he wasn't sure that "Aaron Jackson" would be taken seriously.

Bill cleared his throat again and continued. "At first, I kidded Aaron about the whole midlife crisis. I mean, why not do another Judson book and just buy the Porsche?" He paused for a few laughs to die away. "But he was serious about staying on top while he could. Getting better instead of just older. I think that's why he wanted to start the retreat. I see that some of the current residents are here, and we're glad. I'm in the process of contracting two books from this group. Incredible stuff. But the person who probably knows more about his work there is Margaret Weston, who runs the retreat. I've asked her to say—"

"No!" Korie's screech echoed, followed by a wave of murmuring.

Bill looked stunned. "What? Korie—"

Korie stepped away from her young man, every bit the incensed, grieving widow. "No! I won't have her speaking. I don't even want her here!" Her voice rose with the last words, ending in a hysterical scream. She looked around wildly. "You don't know what she's done!" Spotting Maggie against the back wall, she pointed at her, her hand quivering in a crazed palsy. "You! Get out!" She stalked toward Maggie, her arm still outstretched. "You've ruined everything! You took it all! You killed him! You killed—" Color drained from Korie's face, and she went down in a quiet slump to the floor.

Her young man rushed to her side, pulling her over on her back and patting her cheeks lightly. He helped her sit up as a crowd gathered around her, chattering. Finally he swooped her up in his arms and carried her out, led by one of the publishing house employees.

Maggie still stood against the back wall, motionless. Not a muscle had moved during Korie's accusations, although her eyes lost all alertness, as if she were staring into a spot far beyond the walls of the room.

"Ladies and gentlemen, please. Please!" The pastor raised his arms as well as his voice, in hopes of restoring order. Bill stood at his side, his mouth slightly open. "Please. Remember why we are here. We're here to remember Aaron and celebrate the life that he lived and the people he loved."

Some of the chatter settled down, and Bill tried to resume. "I don't really know what happened," he said, his hands shaking as he pulled down on his beard. "I had told Korie that Maggie would speak. I don't know what happened, what she was referring to—"

"What she's referring to," Edward said loudly as he stepped forward and took command of the room, "is that Aaron left her bereft. Nothing."

This time, the silence in the room was complete. Edward took Bill's place beside the pastor. "For the past two days, Korie has been pressuring Aaron's lawyer to reveal the contents of the will. He wouldn't, so she came to me. Aaron had told me about it, and I'm aware he told a number of his closer friends the same thing.

"So it shouldn't be any surprise to some of you to hear that Aaron recently changed his will completely. All of his assets will go into the trust that supports the retreat, and Korie is not a trustee. The retreat gets everything." He paused, almost as if he relished the drama of the moment.

"So who gets the retreat?" one of the reporters called out.

Edward cleared his throat. "No one. The trust will be self-sustaining, administered by a board of trustees."

"Who's the head trustee?"

Edward hesitated, and Fletcher saw him focus on Maggie's face. Neither of them moved, but Fletcher watched as all eyes turned to Maggie. Edward shook his head and came back to earth, quickly, however, and his voice boomed out over the crowd. "Doesn't matter. I say we forget the readings and send Aaron off with a bang, because he, once again, had the greatest last word." He raised his glass. "May you rest in peace, Aaron, wherever you are!"

The room seemed to explode with salutes, cheers and startled conversation. The pastor gave up, said a quick prayer, then blended into a group of businessmen. The two reporters made a beeline for Maggie, but Fletcher got there first, trying to ward off their questions.

"Maggie—"

"No!" She moved for the first time, shaking her hands in front of her as if trying to throw off the grief. "I can't do this. I can't." She looked up at Fletcher, her eyes flooded with tears. "I'm sorry." She turned and fled.

The reporters started to follow her, but Fletcher grabbed them by the coats. "Don't," he said firmly. "You both know her number. Call her later."

One started to protest, but a good look at Fletcher's face stopped any words, and they slipped away from him.

He followed Maggie into the long hallway, but she was just disappearing around a corner toward the front of the building. He didn't know much about women, but he sensed that this one was not up to a chase tonight. He stuck his hands in his pockets, wishing it were different. Wishing that he did not have to follow up on Korie's accusations. Maggie had not seemed surprised by the news of her inheritance. This was not a good thing....

His fingers searched for his pen but curled around the business card instead, and he pulled it out. The woman, Susan Thomas, worked for the PR firm that handled most of Aaron's press. She'd written her home phone on the back of the card. He'd call her later, too. For now...he took a deep breath and turned.

Bill Davis was walking down the hall in front of him, deeper into the building and away from what had turned into a party.

Fletcher followed him, his long strides soon overtaking Bill's slow shuffle. He caught up just as Aaron's editor turned into his office. "Bill?"

He turned, looking only a bit startled, then motioned toward a chair. "Greetings, Fletcher. Come in, have a seat."

Fletcher watched the older man sit carefully, cough, then run his hand through his thinning strands of hair that were still mostly black. "You okay?" Fletcher asked.

Bill nodded. "For the most part. I couldn't stay after all that. The whole money business depresses me, and I thought Edward was out of place to bring it up, especially in front of the reporters. It was unseemly. It takes away from why we were really there."

"You miss him."

Bill tilted his head to one side, his expression clearly indicating that he thought that was a statement of the obvious. "Oh, yeah. More than most people will ever realize. Aaron was a friend. Crazed...but still a good friend." He started to fiddle with a small paperweight on his desk. "Did you know that he was the godfather to two of my kids?"

Fletcher shook his head, though he wasn't surprised. Aaron had a serious tender spot for children, even though he couldn't have any. He'd seen Aaron with kids on occasion. They brought something special out in him. "He must have had a blast with them."

Bill nodded. He stared down at the desk.

"What is it, Bill?" Fletcher asked gently.

Bill shook his head, then wiped one eye. "I knew things were bad with him and Korie. Knew that when he changed the deposits to a different bank." He stopped and stared at a shelf of books, as if searching the titles for help.

Fletcher leaned back in his chair and waited. As much as he wanted to yank the information out of Bill with a hook, he knew the editor was more savvy than he acted, and more careful about people's reputations. He knew something. So Fletcher waited.

Bill cleared his throat. "Did you read his new book?"

"Yes, I did." Fletcher nodded. "I thought it was good."

Bill sniffed. "Possibly great. Award-winning great. He worried about it. That it wouldn't be taken seriously coming from him. We talked about a pseudonym, but finally rejected it. Talked to the marketing people about making a big splash of it instead. The new Aaron Jackson. The first feedback on the novel was extremely positive."

Bill stopped again, running his finger up and down the edge of a manuscript.

"Bill, I know Aaron was thinking about disappearing."

"Ah. Yes. I thought he might confide in you. He loved you like a brother. Talked about you a lot, even when he was sober."

Fletcher wiped his mouth with one hand. "He also talked about Elvis as if they were brothers."

"Yes," Bill replied, "but only when he was *not* sober." They both grinned, and after a moment Bill's shoulders slumped a bit. "I don't want people to misunderstand what he was going through. This wasn't sour grapes. We'd made him famous, and he didn't regret that. Couldn't. He cherished the dream too much. I think it was more that he wished he had been able to handle it better when the dream *did* come true."

Bill paused. "That's one reason he built the retreat. Did you know that?"

Fletcher shook his head, not wanting to interrupt.

"He wanted to guide other writers through it. Make sure they made choices that would help, not hurt. But things had gotten so bad with Korie that he just wanted to start over. He'd made a mess of it, but he thought he'd finally found someone to start over with. I'm not sure who, but he sat in my office and talked about getting away."

"How serious do you really think he was?"

Bill sighed. "Very. At first I thought…maybe not. He was all over the place, as if he were brainstorming a story. Talked about adopting a couple of kids, finding a new place of his own. Then he sat down in that chair, the one you're in, and asked me to help him." Bill leaned back in his chair. "I couldn't, of course, but I wasn't surprised he'd asked. As much as Aaron thought of himself as 'regular people,' he'd gotten used to other people doing things for him without question."

"The perks of fame."

Bill nodded. "He wasn't happy I'd refused. Told me that I had no idea what it was like to have someone willing to do anything for me. That he'd found that. That loyalty was priceless."

Fletcher frowned. "What did he mean by anything?"

The office was silent for a moment, then Bill swallowed hard. "He asked me if my wife would be willing to die for me."

Fletcher sat up straight. "Say what?"

Bill finally met Fletcher's eyes. "I didn't know what to make of the question. I still don't," he said quietly. "But he said that he knew at least one person who would be willing to die for him."

"Who?"

"Maggie."

Fletcher returned to the hall in a daze, trying to process all that Bill had told him.

The party was now in full swing, and Edward brought him a club soda, which Fletcher accepted but did not sip. Edward munched on hors d'oeuvres. "Did you go see what happened to our drama queen?"

Fletcher blinked, coming back to the present. He grinned at Edward. "You enjoyed that, didn't you?"

Edward laughed. "It showed that much, huh?" Fletcher raised his eyebrows, and Edward laughed. "Yes, I did. You should have seen the fit she threw in my office yesterday after you left. She fainted then, too, but she woke up in a hurry when I told her that if she didn't, I was going to pour a pot of coffee on her silk dress."

"So who's the guy—"

"Artist, probably of the starving variety, probably in it for the money as well. I doubt you'll see much of him after tonight."

"I can understand Aaron wanting to protect the Retreat, as you said yesterday, but he really left her nothing at all?"

Edward shrugged and popped an olive in his mouth. "A small allowance, which will end in six months. Something to help her until she finds another man or—shockers!—a job."

"I've seen her art, Edward. She really is talented."

"Then she'd better find a patron...or a sugar daddy. I'm sure she's got a heart, too. Let's hope she remembers where she put it." Edward paused and rested his hand on Fletcher's arm. "Look, I know you want to find out who killed him, and I'd like nothing better than to hand you Korie on a silver platter. Truth is, I'm not sure she could do it and then hide it. You'd probably find her standing over the body claiming 'He deserved it' as her defense."

Fletcher coughed a laugh into his hand.

"See? You know I'm right."

"What about Maggie?"

Edward paused. "I don't know." He dropped a piece of cheese back on his plate. "If she did, it wasn't for the money. Aaron only signed that will last week. There's no way Maggie could have known she'd inherit. What other motive could she have?"

"Do you think she still loved Aaron?"

Edward resumed eating. "Only as a friend. I think that if he believed he had another shot with her, he wouldn't have been skirting around all over the place. You know he was seeing another woman? Have you seen her?"

Fletcher nodded, slipping one hand into his pocket.

"She looks like Maggie. But she's not Maggie. Not by a long shot. Anyway, Maggie doesn't seem like the type who would kill, does she?"

Fletcher had to admit, "No."

"Still…" Edward leaned a little closer to him. "Aren't those the ones that usually do?"

Fletcher turned and looked out over the room. "Usually. Yes, they are."

SIXTEEN

Lee flipped through his notebook again, then shut it with a frustrated grunt.

Judson looked up from the report he was reading. "This much emotion is never good. What's going on?"

Lee shrugged and tossed the notebook to one side. "I think I have too much information. It's all a jumble. I can't see a clear pattern of evidence in any of it."

Judson flipped over another sheet of paper and began to read again. "Then I suggest that the problem is not too much information. It's too little of the right information. Keep digging. And get some rest. You may be foggy in the head simply because you haven't slept enough."

The person Fletcher most wanted to interview—Susan Thomas—was gone, so he circulated, chatting a bit with people he knew, and taking the opportunity to speak briefly with the writers from the retreat. Most had similar stories about Monday night—a tense meal, after which they had gone back to the cabins. Only Dan and Patrick had more to add.

They had gone downstairs to play air hockey, when two fights broke out—first Maggie, Lily and Aaron upstairs, then another one in the yard.

Dan grimaced. "We were afraid to leave the room or the house. We weren't surprised to hear that Maggie and Aaron were into it. They did that a lot."

Patrick agreed. "They fought quite a bit in the last few months. If I didn't know better, I'd say they were married."

Inside his coat pocket, Fletcher's hand closed around his pen. "What about the one outside?"

Dan shook his head. "Aaron, without a doubt. I think the other one was a man, but I couldn't say it in court."

"Me either," Patrick said. "It didn't last long."

"But that's not when he was killed."

Dan put up one hand. "Oh, no. When everything got quiet, we snuck out the downstairs door. There wasn't anyone out there, on the deck or the steps."

"Maggie was still in the kitchen. We could hear her doing dishes. But we didn't want to take a chance that Aaron would come back."

"Thanks, guys." Fletcher shook hands with both of the young writers, then looked around the room again, not wanting to be any more obvious than he already felt. The noise of the crowd was starting to make casual conversations more difficult. It was definitely turning into an Aaron kind of party— boisterous and fun.

Fletcher spotted Tim sitting alone, staring at the floor. Fletcher pulled up a chair next to the young groundskeeper, who looked up. There were tears in his eyes.

"Are you all right?" Fletcher asked.

Tim shook his head. "We should all be here. Out of respect." He paused and crossed his arms. "I'm a fan, y'know? It's why I took the job."

Fletcher nodded. "It must have been hard finding him like that—"

Tim's head snapped around. "She didn't do it. Miss Maggie.

She couldn't have." Fletcher had never heard him sound quite so Southern. "Miss Korie," Tim started, his voice choked. "Miss Korie had no right to say stuff like that. Both those ladies, Miss Lily and Miss Maggie, they loved Mr. Jackson. They was like his only family. Like they was his sisters. You don't go about hurting family."

"Tim, how did you wind up in New Hampshire?"

Tim wiped his eyes with the heels of his hands and sniffed. He ran his left hand through his limp light brown hair. "You mean, how did I get from Tennessee to New England?"

Fletcher nodded.

"A girl. Isn't that always the way it is?"

"Sometimes."

"I followed a girl."

"Is she still around?"

Tim shrugged. "Yes and no. She's still around, but she's married. I have no right to her. But Mr. Jackson was good to me so I stayed on."

Click. Fletcher took a deep breath and leaned forward. "Tim, Dan and Patrick heard someone arguing that night. Did you hear it?"

Tim shook his head. "I usually take a walk after dinner, kind of a security thing, like the one I do later, if you know what I mean."

Fletcher did.

"Anyways," Tim went on, "I get pretty far from the house at times. I didn't hear anything. When I got back, it was just Miss Maggie, so I got a cup of coffee and went to my room."

The detective frowned. *Click.* "Aaron was already gone?"

"Yes, sir. And he wasn't dead yet, neither, 'cause I came in the back way, up those steps, so Miss Maggie would know I was in my room."

"So he came back."

Tim nodded. "Must have."

Fletcher sat up straight and patted Tim on the arm. "Thank you, Tim. And I'm sorry."

Tim looked closely at him. "You'll find who did this, won't you?"

Fletcher's jaw tightened. "I will, Tim, I promise." Fletcher walked away from the publishing house, needing some fresh air, his feet pounding the sidewalk. It helped, the motion, the cold. He'd been a fool, had gotten too close to Maggie. She had to have heard that fight outside the back door, yet she never mentioned it. Edward didn't think she knew about the will, but her reaction was one of numbness, not surprise. No one gets told they're going to unexpectedly inherit millions of dollars without showing *some* reaction. She already knew; everything in his gut told him she did.

It was not quite ten o'clock, but he had no urge to spend any more time out, and he had no desire to go back to New Hampshire. He needed to talk all this over, lay it out before someone who was objective. But his main sounding board, the one man he'd talked to for almost fifteen years, was dead.

After a moment, Fletcher dug out his cell phone and dialed a number. A short conversation later, Fletcher waved down a cab and gave the driver an address in Brooklyn.

Maggie stood at the window of her darkened bedroom, staring out into the night. She hadn't bothered to undress; she knew sleep would be impossible tonight. She had planned to stay in the city with an old friend, but after the service, all she wanted to do was come home. She was glad she'd decided at the last minute to drive; yet, the trip back to New Hampshire had been five of the most miserable hours of her life. Her stomach cramped, and the grief of the past week seemed to be a living beast clawing through her chest. She'd tried to keep the tears to a minimum but hadn't always succeeded. She'd had to pull off the road several times.

The long drive did help some, even though her mind continued to replay memories faster than she could process them. Aaron's body. Talks with Lily. The strange feelings she felt whenever she tried to talk to Fletcher. Her discoveries about Aaron, here and at his house.

Her torn loyalties lay like a hot weight on her chest. "God, please help me," she whispered. Maggie stood a little straighter and tried to slow down her breathing; she was almost panting. *Must not hyperventilate.* But the very act of holding her breath released another wave of tears, and Maggie's knees gave way. She slid down the window, sobbing. Leaning her head against the windowsill, she let the waves flow over her, the tears flooding her entire being. Her heart felt shredded.

And not just by Aaron's death. There was so much more. Bank records, falsified credit cards. The copy of his will on the computer. The manuscripts that were clearly Scott's, but with Aaron's extensive edits; the versions of those on Aaron's computer, already typed in. He had stolen them. Them, and so much more. Her identity. Her future.

What was wrong with him?

Maggie's nose clogged hard, and she started to choke. Making herself stand up, she stumbled into her bathroom for a tissue. She blew her nose, the sobbing finally easing up. Taking another handful of tissues, she went back to the window, wishing the dark would simply surround her, absorb her.

"Lord," she whispered. "Please help me. Heal my heart. Open my mind and lead me to see what happened more clearly. Please give me the wisdom to know what to do next."

Maggie sighed. She knew what the answer to that prayer was, even as she whispered it. It was common sense. The right thing to do. Tell Fletcher. But she couldn't. Not him. Not now.

"I do need to tell someone, though, don't I?"

Taking a deep breath, Maggie pushed away from the window and picked up her coat off the bedside chair. She dug her largest flashlight out from under the bed and left the room, the tissues clutched in the other hand.

She needed to be in the fresh air. To be in her refuge. Most of all, she needed Cookie.

Jason MacAllister loved Brooklyn, which was something Fletcher had never understood. To him, Brooklyn must have been dropped onto earth from some other planet. Still…here he was in the middle of it. His cell phone rang, and Fletcher jumped, annoyed by the interruption. He checked the numbers, thinking it might be Maggie. But Korie's number glowed under his finger. Muttering something rude, he turned the phone off and dropped it in his pocket, then looked back up at the ancient brownstone, thinking about the man who'd lived in the same third-floor walk-up for more than twenty-five years. He'd married there, raised three kids in the same five rooms he'd rented when first landing in New York. Cousins that Fletcher never saw.

"How are they?" he asked, as his uncle brought him a cup of coffee. They settled into comfy, overstuffed chairs that had seen much better days. His aunt's carefully tatted doilies still decorated the arms and backs of the chairs, while one, starched and permanently shaped like a tiny doll's hat, hung on the wall behind Jason's head.

Jason snorted. "Do I know?" He waved his hand dismissively. "Since Alice died, they don't come around like they used to. One's in Atlanta, two in California. They don't like flying, so they say."

Fletcher glanced at the wall of family photos near the front door, lovingly collected, framed and hung by his aunt Alice.

Most were several years old. One was of him in his police blues, at his academy graduation. His uncle was the reason he had become a cop, the reason he was in New York.

"So what brings you back after all this time, and this late at night?"

"Sorry about that. A case."

"What else is there. Aaron Jackson?"

Fletcher shifted in his chair. "You heard?"

"My nephew is one of the most famous literary figures in the world. I pay attention."

"I'm not—"

"Don't start. Tell me what happened. I assume you've fully retired off the force."

Fletcher nodded. "Official the first of this month."

"Can't say I'm thrilled, but I understand." The older man sniffed, then pinched his nose with his left hand. "So, fill me in."

Fletcher took out his notebook and pen. He flipped through the pages and explained everything he knew so far, starting with Aaron's death and ending with the memorial service. Just the facts.

But his uncle was no fool. "So you think the fact that you care for this woman is clouding your judgment?"

Fletcher paused. "That's outside what I—"

"Answer the question."

The younger detective leaned back in his chair, his left hand absentmindedly clicking the pen. "Maybe. I don't know."

"And that's what's driving you nuts. That you don't know."

Fletcher shifted in the chair. "Yeah." *Click.*

The older man took a long drink of his coffee, then let out a long breath from the heat of it. "Would you hesitate to cuff her if you thought she had killed the man?"

"No. Of course not." *Click.*

"Then don't worry about it."

Fletcher was silent, and Jason grinned at him. "Look, boy, your hormones are going to do weird stuff to you all the time. It doesn't stop, not even at my age. And it sounds like this one is special to boot. Hard to deal with, which I think you like. Spunky women always did get your attention. But right now, she's probably as messed up as you are about it. He was her friend, too. So is whoever killed him, if it ain't her. This is driving her nuts. She won't know where her loyalty is. If you can get her to give it to you, this will likely fall into place, and she'll tell you what she knows. If you can't see things clearly, it's not because of her. It's because you haven't finished the investigation. You still need to do some prowling around, but my guess is that she's your key. She knows all the players, and probably more of the secrets than she realizes. You know people always do."

"But if she's the killer, then who took a shot at her? Was it revenge?" *Click.*

"Who says they were trying to kill her? There were three of you on the porch. Maybe they were just a bad shot."

Fletcher thought for a second. "No, I don't think so."

Jason sat back in his chair. "Then you have a woman with no alibi and all the motive, but someone's trying to whack her."

"Yeah." *Click.*

"Then the next attack on her will give you more clues."

"Oh, thanks." *Click.*

Jason grinned. "You know how it works. You know if she's the target, they won't give up." At Fletcher's silence, he leaned forward. "Look, Fletcher. You've done a good job so far, but there's still too much to learn to make a guess right now. In the morning call that girl, the one on the business card, then call Korie. Then get yourself back up to New Hampshire.

You're wrong about where the answers are. You may find clues here in New York, but whatever you really need to know is there, not here."

Fletcher nodded. "I know."

Jason paused for a second. "Who else have you talked to about this?"

Shaking his head, Fletcher clicked the pen.

"What about God?"

The clicking stopped abruptly. "What?" Fletcher said.

"Have you prayed about this?"

"I don't—"

"You should."

"Jason—"

"Don't talk back to me, boy." Jason's voice softened a bit. "You came here for advice, didn't you?"

"Yes, but—"

"So I'm giving it. You need to think about this. You're letting that shooting go too deep, if you let it get between you and God."

Fletcher stood up suddenly and turned for the door.

"Don't walk away from me!" Jason stood, sounding like the precinct commander he'd once been.

Fletcher pivoted slowly. "This is none of your business."

Jason didn't relent. "You are my business, ever since your mother died. Don't backtalk me on this. You're too young to know everything, even about yourself."

Crossing his arms, Fletcher leaned all his weight on his left leg.

His uncle nodded, taking that as assent. "Sit down, drink your coffee. I'm not going to pry. I just want you to think about some things."

Fletcher hesitated, then stepped forward and sat, his thumb finding its home again. *Click.*

"And stop clicking that pen!"

Fletcher laughed, slipped the pen back into his pocket and finally took a sip of his coffee.

"It was a mistake, Fletcher," Aaron said, his voice somber and even. "There was no intent in what you did. Internal Affairs cleared you. You have to find a way to let this go."

"Yeah, right. No one blames me."

"Except yourself."

Fletcher jerked out of the chair, pacing the same ten steps over his apartment carpet he had every day for a week. "Don't lecture me, Aaron. You don't know."

"I know that you are harder on yourself than anyone else is. You didn't know that guy was a cop. He was undercover."

"He was a kid!"

"He was dirty!"

"I didn't know that!"

"You also didn't know he was reaching for a badge. You saw a perp reaching for a gun. He should have known better."

"I should have waited."

"And if it had been a gun? Would you have let him kill you?"

"I should have followed procedure." Fletcher shoved his hands in his pockets, his left one closing around a pen he'd forgotten was there.

"So should he. He should have identified himself, told you where the badge was. Right?"

Silence reigned.

"Have you talked to anyone about this besides me?"

"They want me to talk to a counselor. Never."

Aaron shifted in his chair. "I meant Someone a little higher up."

Fletcher stopped pacing. "You mean God?"

"It could help."

An involuntary snort escaped Fletcher, and he wiped his eyes, then his mouth. "God wasn't there," he pronounced. "Don't talk to me about God ever again. God doesn't hang out in the back alleys of New York."

Aaron leaned back, his gaze distant. Silent.

It was the first night Fletcher had clicked his pen.

It was the last time Aaron had ever mentioned God to him.

After about twenty yards into the woods, Maggie shut off the flashlight. The final leaves of the season had been ripped out of the trees by last night's storm and now gathered in wet clumps on the mushy ground. The moon was full and there were enough clouds that the reflective light illuminated the woods in silvery shades that were broken up by the dark, spidery image of the empty branches overhead. She'd walked this path hundreds of times, and the flashlight was more a distraction than a help. Without it, she looked ahead, far beyond where its beam could reach, and she let her feet find their way.

She inhaled deeply, relishing the cold air. It made her feel more alive, as if she were intimately aware of everything around her. Her fingers buzzed with the chill, but she didn't care. This…*this*…had always helped. The movement of the air, the smells of the trees and plants, the feel of the earth beneath her boots. It grounded her, and right now she craved that.

She knew it was late; she also knew Cookie wouldn't mind. Not now. Not with all this going on. Still, she was surprised to see the porch light on, and the smell of ginger oozing from the cottage. She knocked lightly, and Cookie opened the door, her robe wrapped tightly around her and a cup of hot chocolate in one hand. Pepper waited behind her, a shaggy tail wagging a slow greeting.

"Ah," Cookie said, a few extra gravels clogging her throat, "there you are."

Maggie stared at her as she stepped into the cottage. "How did you know?"

Cookie grinned and handed her the cup. "Because I know you. Because I know the memorial service was tonight. Still, I wasn't too far from giving up on you. I was watching a talk show but it was annoying, so I'd switched to an old rerun of *Speed*."

"Speed?" Maggie couldn't believe it.

"Hey," Cookie explained as she went into the kitchen. "It's good for keeping me awake, and they're both fun to watch jump around."

Maggie smiled, infinitely pleased that she'd come. Cookie came out carrying her own cup of chocolate and a plate of steaming, chewy cookies.

"If I keep coming over here, I'm going to get fat," Maggie said, taking a cookie.

"There are worse things in life than getting fat, I can tell you that," her friend said. She settled in a chair, wriggling her broad behind back into the cushions. "All right. Talk. I want to hear it all. Start with what Korie did at the service."

Maggie's mouth fell open, and Cookie looked at her over the glasses. "Baby, I didn't get this old by being stupid. The announcement of the memorial service was in the *New York Times*. It was getting press coverage. I could smell a drama-queen fit in the making. Tell me."

Maggie took a deep breath. "I need to start with yesterday. I went over to the house, and I figured out what Aaron's password was…." Maggie covered it all, the documents, the manuscripts, the accusations Korie had made. Cookie's frown deepened as she went on. "I couldn't stay, Cookie. I couldn't. Not with him there and all that—" Maggie's voice broke, and she pulled her tissues out of her sleeve, where she'd tucked them during the walk over.

Cookie was silent. Finally, she asked softly, "Do you realize how many laws Aaron has broken?"

Maggie nodded, sniffing.

"Do you realize it could mean that you won't inherit after all?"

Maggie stopped sniffing. "What?"

Cookie sat up a little straighter. "Depending on what laws he broke and how he broke them, if it involves the way the monies in the will are distributed, it could throw the whole thing into a jumble. And you know Korie is going to contest the will. Even if the trust is secure, it'll be a long time before everything is settled."

Maggie nodded.

Cookie shook her head sadly. "Baby, you've got to get Fletcher involved with this. And you both need to talk to Aaron's lawyer. You are in way over your head."

Maggie's hands went limp in her lap, the cookie hanging loosely from her fingers. Pepper, sensing an opportunity, waddled over and relieved her of it. Maggie didn't protest.

Cookie looked her over carefully. "You really thought Lily might have killed him, didn't you?"

Maggie raised her eyes. She didn't even want to admit it. "That night. When I first saw him. I thought—"

"That she'd had it with him."

Maggie nodded. "There's something else I didn't tell Fletcher. I don't think Aaron was killed as he was leaving. I heard him fighting with Scott on the back steps, and they both stomped off in different directions. I went downstairs to clean up. Aaron had to have been coming back. I don't know why."

"Maybe to apologize?"

"Did you ever know him to apologize for anything?"

"Then what do you think?"

"I think he was coming back to fire me—maybe even hurt me."

Now it was Cookie's turn to look surprised. "Are you serious?"

This hurt, even to say it. "I didn't want to think so, not at first. But after what I found…after the fight. He almost hit me,

Cookie, and he'd never done that, either. He knew Tim was out on his rounds, that everyone had left. And it's pretty clear from what I found that his plan would succeed better if I weren't around."

"Do you really believe this? The man *adored* you, Maggie. More than you realize."

"I knew he hadn't been acting much like Aaron lately. I knew he was desperate— Oh, I don't know what to think anymore!" Maggie put her hands over her face and bent forward, the sobs threatening to come out again. Her body ached and her mind was a mass of confused and whirling images.

"Come here," Cookie demanded.

Maggie looked up.

"Now."

Maggie got up and went to Cookie, kneeling on the floor beside the old woman's chair. Cookie reached for her, and Maggie let Cookie draw her in close. She rested her head on Cookie's shoulder and wrapped her arms around the warm, broad back of the concentration camp survivor. Cookie grabbed the back of her head and hugged her close.

"Maggie," she whispered. "Listen to me. You've not slept. You're not eating. You've been hurt. You're grieving. And you're falling in love."

"Humph," Maggie protested into the soft robe.

Cookie tightened her grip. "Hush. Don't argue. Just listen." Maggie felt her body start to relax as Cookie talked. "It's a wonder you've not completely lost your mind. You ever hear Dr. Phil say that you've got to 'behave your way out' of something?"

Maggie almost laughed, a bit of hysteria slipping over her. Instead, she just nodded.

"Then you know what you have to do. You have to sleep, even if it means taking a sleep aid. You need to drink more water so your brain will work. Eat better. Pray more."

Maggie slipped away from the hug. "You sound as if all I need to get out of this is to be practical."

"And?"

Maggie dropped her head and rocked back on her heels. "I think it's more complex than that."

"Is it? Baby, you've got some hard stuff in front of you. The will. The accusations. All the stuff about the money and Aaron's deceptions are going to come out. Right now, it looks like you're involved. You're not, so you've got to figure out how to make it *not* look like that by solving the puzzle. Clear up the misunderstandings. You think you're going to be up to it if you're a mess of raw nerves, numb ganglia and red eyes?"

Maggie looked away, then down as Pepper came over and nuzzled her hand, wanting a pet. She scratched the old dog behind the ears, and was rewarded with a satisfied series of grunts. She sighed. Cookie's advice had so much "rightness" in it that she felt almost overwhelmed. Finally, she looked up.

"Got any chicken soup?"

Cookie grinned. "Don't I always?"

"It has cabbage in it, too, doesn't it?" Maggie stood up and offered Cookie her hand as the older woman struggled to get out of the chair.

"It wouldn't be the good stuff without it."

An hour later, with her stomach full of chicken and cabbage soup, homemade bread and butter and two cookies, Maggie started back to the lodge. *Maybe Cookie is right,* she thought as she picked her way over some logs on the way to the path. She did feel lighter—despite the food in her tummy—and warmer, ready to slip into sleep. Tonight, she would pray. Tomorrow, she would lay everything out before Fletcher. Be honest with him, Cookie had said.

Maggie rolled her shoulders, trying to stave off her exhaustion, and pulled her coat a little tighter. Her gut still clenched a bit at the idea of opening up to the detective. She'd have to tell him about the suspicions she'd had, true or not. But there was no way she was going to dig her way out of this by herself, and everything would come out anyway, if he kept digging.

If only Aaron hadn't made me look so guilt—

Maggie jumped as a branch to her right broke loose from its tree and slid fifteen feet or so to the ground. She stared at it, vaguely aware of a fog of leaves and dust that were settling with it. She looked around again. The moon had passed beyond its peak and was slipping down behind the trees, and the shadows around her had deepened without her really noticing. She wasn't that far from Cookie's, but the woods had already closed around her.

Too much thinking. She balanced the flashlight in her hand and snapped it on, its sharp yellow beam now oddly comforting. She stepped off again in the direction of the lodge.

The two blows came sharply, barely giving Maggie time to scream in surprise. The first knocked the flashlight clear of her hand, sending it bouncing into the thick carpet of leaves. The pain that shot up her arm was matched when a gloved hand slammed into the side of her head. Maggie crumpled but found her voice. Her shrill scream echoed a second time through the woods before a boot connected with her ribs, shutting off her air and her voice.

The fist landed again, this time between her shoulder blades. Her face went into the debris on the ground, and a knee planted in the middle of her back pinned her. A wave of pure panic surged through Maggie, adrenaline putting every nerve on edge. She planted her hands solidly against the ground and shoved upward, twisting her hips as she did.

It worked, catching her assailant off guard and off balance. He stumbled back, and she rolled over, kicking out with her legs. One toe connected with bone, and he grunted, fighting to keep his balance. He reached down, his hands closing on a branch, which he raised over his head, rushing toward her. Maggie tried to scramble away, to get to her feet, but her heel caught on her long coat and she dropped to the ground. At the last minute, she threw up her arms to protect her head, and he crashed the branch down on her ribs. The pain was like a shot of fire through her body. He threw away the remains of the branch and got his balance, preparing to kick her again.

The shotgun blast scared both of them and caused her attacker to trip and almost fall over her. They both heard the sound of the gun being pumped, and her attacker bounded up and away, racing through the woods and disappearing into the darkness. The gun blasted again, and Maggie could hear pellets raining down in the direction he had run, but there was no sign of him.

Maggie sat up, panting, looking toward the shooter.

Out of the darker shadows slid the short, round bulk of a Polish widow, her sixteen-gauge pump-action shotgun grasped firmly at hip level.

"Cookie!" Maggie gasped.

Cookie's expression was somber. "How bad?"

Maggie fought to get her breath. "I don't know. My ribs—"

"Can you walk?"

Maggie nodded.

"Let's go back to the cottage. I'll call Tyler."

This time it was Maggie who needed help up. She clutched Cookie's arm as they headed back to the cottage. The old woman walked sideways, keeping sharp eyes scanning behind and around them.

SEVENTEEN

Lee found Judson in the gym, soaked in perspiration. He watched as the older detective finished working out with the punching bag, bouncing around it as if he were twenty years younger. Afterward, Lee threw him a towel, and Judson mopped his face and scrubbed his blond hair vigorously. "I'm surprised," Lee said. "I didn't realize you ever broke a sweat."

"Ah, dear partner," Judson replied. "If you haven't learned it yet, you will. Physicality will clear the mind, as will a good night's sleep. Never underestimate the value of taking care of your body. It'll take care of the brain."

Sunday morning, Fletcher woke up without an alarm or sleep-shattering phone call. He stretched and took his time getting out of bed. He dressed in sweats, then stretched and went downstairs for a quick run. Ten blocks out, two over, six back. He slowed then, listening to the bells of a neighborhood church and watching the parishioners trickle in under the arched and carved wooden front doors.

He stopped, thinking about the glimpses he'd seen of Maggie's faith. She'd not said anything about her relationship with God, but there was the Bible on her desk, and he'd seen her pray. That could simply be for show, but he didn't get the feeling it was. It was well used, the spine creased and the pages heavily fingered. And there was her refusal to sleep with Aaron, which mystified him and, he was sure, had frustrated Aaron to no end, as had her opposition to his drinking. Fletcher smiled, remembering her comment that not everyone coming out of New York was a heathen.

Hardly, he thought, watching the smartly dressed worshippers greet each other, mentally comparing their friendly warmth with screeching, maniacal street preachers he'd had to deal with as a beat cop. New Yorkers were about religion the way they were everything else—private yet inclusive. Dedicated to their own but tolerant, for the most part. There were exceptions, always.

His mind drifted to Aaron and his up-and-down spirituality, then to Jason and Cookie and their recent words to him about his own faith. They didn't understand; they'd not been there in that dark alley. Still, he admired that they had stood fast, even in the face of their own life trials.

Yet Fletcher had not met anyone who seemed to live the faith as much as Maggie did, without proselytizing. Just being who she was. It was part of what drew him to her, but he couldn't let it blind him to the facts of the case.

Would this woman kill?

His gut said no.

His head unequivocally reminded him that he'd seen all kinds of people kill, even the unlikely ones.

His heart…

Fletcher turned and resumed his jog. He wasn't ready for whatever his heart had to say just yet. Not yet.

Back at his apartment, he lingered in the shower, letting the hot water scald his back before scrubbing down. He shaved, then made coffee and a breakfast of eggs and toast.

He felt better than he had in more than a week. Rested. The talk with Jason had helped him understand that his confusion was just a lack of information. Sipping on the last of his coffee, he reviewed the notes he'd made on the case and made a few more. He'd decided that Korie's accusations against Maggie were mostly dramatic hysteria, but he'd ask her about them anyway. As Jason said, people don't always know what they know.

Just after ten, Fletcher placed a call from his apartment to Susan Thomas. She answered with a low, soft alto, and Fletcher identified himself. "Do you want to talk now?"

There was a silent pause. "Can you come here? I don't really want to be out."

"Sure."

She gave him the address, which was only a short cab ride away. It was a doorman building, but she'd left his name with the guy on duty, so he entered without a problem and took the elevator to the seventh floor. Susan welcomed him into a stylish, immaculate apartment with a large living room and adjacent dining room. She obviously saw the surprise on his face at the size and luxury of her home.

"My father," she explained simply. "He bought it, not Aaron. He's in banking and likes to think I'm safe." She motioned toward a plush sofa. "Please. Sit."

He did, then waited.

She sat stiffly on the edge of a wingchair opposite him and took a deep breath. "I didn't expect to do this. I'm not even sure what it is I want to tell you."

"Why don't you tell me about the first time you went out with Aaron?"

Her eyes lost their focus. "It was a few months ago. Maybe a year. I'm not sure. We'd been doing a lot of PR for his last book. I'd been squiring him around, making sure he showed up for interviews, stayed sober." She folded her hands primly across her lap. "What happened was very unprofessional. I've never crossed the line before."

"Why did you this time?"

"Aaron is very persuasive." Susan turned her focus on him. "Was."

He nodded. "So you gave in to the affair."

She was silent, still looking at him. He could almost see her processing past events, deciding what to tell him. After a moment, she blinked hard, and he could see the film of tears. "Not exactly." She swallowed. "I fell in love with him. We spent a lot of time together. He told me that he was planning on leaving Korie. That he wanted to be with me, even though we never—" Susan shifted in her chair, clearly uncomfortable with the topic.

"You never slept with him?" Fletcher's surprise showed in his voice, and he cleared his throat to get his emotions back under control.

Susan shook her head. "He...um. At first I thought he was just trying to be honorable. And I think he was, at least in part. He would occasionally mumble something about 'never dishonoring her in kind.'" She sniffed lightly. "I thought he meant me. Now I'm not sure. But he also...couldn't." Her face reddened and she looked away for a moment. "Some medication he was taking." She sat straighter, clearly wanting to move on as she looked back at Fletcher. "I knew about the prenuptial. He'd complained a lot about it, especially when—when he...wasn't quite sober."

"You didn't believe divorce was an option?"

Susan stood up and went to a French Provincial secretary against the far wall. She pulled a disk out of a drawer. She handed it to him. "I saved two of his e-mails to me. He confessed that the prenuptial would take too long to break off legally, and he didn't want to spend what was left of his life shackled to Korie." She stopped to wipe her eyes and take a deep breath. She waited, then her eyes seemed to clear. Her voice was even as she continued, and her shoulders had a firmer set to them. "He told me that he was going to disappear. That he had a plan for, as he called it, 'revenge and glory.' And he wanted me to go away with him."

"Did you want to go?"

"No. Mr. MacAllister, despite this apartment, I've worked very hard to get out from under my father's shadow. I'm thirty-two, and I look to make VP of the firm next year. I have a life. A good one, as you can see. I loved Aaron, but I was not about to leave all this, my family, my friends, cause them grief, just so I could run off to some desert island to be in yet another man's shadow."

"How did he react?"

"He was furious. Called me names I usually hear in the street. Told me I'd ruin everything. Ruin all his plans to get away from Korie. To get even. I don't know what he meant by that." She paused thoughtfully. "He raged, Mr. MacAllister. I had never seen him do that."

"Did he hurt you?"

She shook her head, focusing again on the wall to Fletcher's left. "No. Although I think he wanted to. He left. I didn't see him for a week, then he called, wanting to make up. He was very enthusiastic, said his plans were almost complete. He told me some of them. I was appalled. They would seriously damage the reputations of some people close to him. I realized he was hurting, that he was desperate, but not that much." She returned her gaze to Fletcher. "Mr. MacAllister, he planned to steal other people's work, their identities. This was not the man I had fallen in love with. Over the last few weeks, he had changed dramatically. I have no idea what had happened to him, but everything he said went against what I believe, what I thought he believed. I told him I couldn't see him."

"And that was it?"

She nodded. "That was it. The next thing I knew, my boss called to tell me he'd been murdered. I can't say I was surprised."

"Whose work was he going to steal?"

She looked down at her hands. "I thought you needed to know these things, but I have no proof of anything he told me. It's all hearsay. You couldn't use it in court."

"Let me worry about that."

"Scott Jonas."

EIGHTEEN

Lee nodded. "I can understand where having a clear head could help when deciphering all the work on the investigation. But I've questioned witnesses when I was so tired I could barely stand up."

Judson frowned. "You shouldn't. You never know where questions are going to lead you. Stay on your toes. Listen for fresh clues. Witnesses sometimes drop information that's important, things you never expected. An interview should be fluid, organic."

Lee almost smiled. "Organic."

Judson was not amused. "Pay attention to everything they say, every nuance. And never let them surprise you. Even if they drop a new motive, a new perp, and positive proof right in your lap, never let it show."

Fletcher left Susan's apartment, fighting rage with every step. He paced furiously as he waited on the elevator, thinking that if Aaron were still alive, he might just kill him. A soft *bing* sounded, and Fletcher stepped onto an elevator that suddenly felt claustrophobic.

What was he thinking? How could Aaron turn so cruel, so malicious over the course of just a few weeks? Violating his own personal code of ethics that he'd clung to since he was a cub reporter? What had been wrong with him? Fletcher leaned against the wall of the car, drumming his fingers on the handrail. Just as the doors opened, Susan's voice echoed again in his head.

I realized he was hurting, that he was desperate.

Fletcher froze just outside the car, causing one of the residents passing through the lobby to dodge around him. He stood still, staring at the floor, his mind in a flurry of thoughts.

Desperate.

What did that mean? What would push Aaron to the edge? What would he care about that passionately? Fletcher had known the man for more than fifteen years. Aaron was a survivor. It wasn't the money; he'd taken care of Korie's drain on his finances. It wasn't the work, Aaron was far more talented than his Judson books revealed. Fletcher had read some of his rough drafts of other works and the most recent mainstream novel. Excellent work. He didn't need Scott's manuscripts. And he had the retreat, his own personal lega—

Fletcher looked up. Legacy. Aaron's words echoed in his head.

"I have no family, so this retreat will be my only legacy."

Then Bill's.

"Talked about adopting a couple of kids…"

Then a second line of Susan's.

"Never dishonoring her in kind…revenge and glory…"

Aaron wasn't having an affair with Lily, but he let everyone think he was. He used her to get back at Scott. The manuscript theft was simply revenge.

Scott and Korie.

But he didn't care about Korie, so why would the affair trigger such rage?

There was suddenly a hard, cold rock in the pit of Fletcher's stomach. *Please, God, no.* The unbidden prayer burst into his mind. *Let me be wrong.*

* * *

Maggie remembered the ride to the hospital in Tyler's cruiser, the siren screaming overhead, and the initial exam, but little else. X-rays revealed a broken rib and a bruised right wrist. Fortunately, there was no concussion, but the doctors wanted to keep her overnight for observation, just in case. They gave her something to make her sleep, and her world once again became a drifting existence, in and out of consciousness. Cookie stayed with her. She thought Lily had come, but wasn't sure if it had been a dream, since she also saw her mother and Fletcher. She tried to talk to Fletcher, but he kept waving his hand at her, motioning for her to be quiet. Her mother just stood in the doorway, looking solemn and sweet, as she always had.

The darkness faded for a bit, and her eyes hurt from the light. Her body ached, the pain from the rib and the pressure on her chest from the bindings made it hard to breathe, and she could smell cabbage and perfume. Lily's perfume. Someone helped her sit up and eat something that was hot and spicy. It burned her tongue but was strangely filling and comforting as well. There was the coolness of ice and the sweet sting of soda. She mumbled, but there was lots of shushing, people telling her to be quiet. To rest.

So she did. The darkness came again, softly this time, with the sweetness of drugless sleep but the puzzlement of dreams.

At first she was in a house filled with people. The rooms were small and dimly lit, with people scattered throughout, eating, drinking, lounging on chairs and standing in corners. Everyone was dressed in bright colors—royal-blues, emerald-greens, rich yellows and reds. Maggie wandered through, spotting Fletcher in each room. No matter what corner she turned, he was there. Mostly he was talking to other people, ignoring her, and each time she would start toward him, he would turn and walk into another room, without ever noticing her.

Her heart raced, and a sense of urgency flooded her. She needed him, needed his help. She prowled through one room after another, looking for him, seeing him, only to have him turn away again. Finally, she stopped as a sense of panic threatened to overwhelm her. Why didn't he see her? Why didn't he know she was looking for him?

She took deep breaths, trying to calm herself, and the house slid away, morphing into an open field of wildflowers. She began to run, then fly over the landscape, still searching. There was a calm lake and another house, one dilapidated and wind-worn, made of timbers gray from too much sun and little care.

She stopped and went in. It was an old-fashioned general store, with tin product signs on the walls and a hard-pressed dirt floor. She looked down and her feet were bare and cold. Fletcher was there, behind the counter, and he smiled, brighter than she'd ever seen him. "Babe," he said softly, affectionately. "Let it be. It is what it is."

Maggie snapped awake, a cool sweat clinging to her body. She looked around the gray-shadowed room, unafraid. Despite the emotions in the dream, it had left her feeling reassured.

It is what it is.

It was Aaron's phrase, something he'd picked up some-where. For so long he'd used it as a reflection of his life, his philosophy, his faith. Aaron was a Christian, which was a side of him that few people besides Maggie knew, because she had drawn it out of him with her own sincere love of God and His people.

He had loved God. Maggie knew that. Aaron couldn't follow the path, had found giving up his sins hard to do. But he'd never given up on God.

Maggie closed her eyes. *"Lord,"* she prayed aloud, *"I don't know what was wrong with him, but I hope his faith gave him some peace in the end. He loved You."* She paused and took a deep breath. *"I love You. I hope Fletcher does, too. Please help us. That's all. Just please help."*

Maggie knew He heard. That in itself helped.

Without opening her eyes, Maggie drifted away again, this time to rest without dreams.

Fletcher began to fidget in the cab, and he knew he was close to losing control. He had to stay calm with Korie, or she'd fly into one of her dramatic fits. No accusations, no biases. Just questions, carefully worded. But he hadn't called her, either. He wanted to catch her as unprepared as possible. Fletcher tried to center himself, to breathe slowly and deeply. *Keep the emotions in check and do your job.*

He stood outside the building where she and Aaron had shared an apartment, clenching and unclenching his fists until he thought he could do this. *This one's for Aaron,* he thought as he went in through the front door. He greeted the doorman, a retired cop who knew the detective well, even knew he was the model for Judson, and the man didn't hesitate to buzz the Jackson penthouse. Korie sounded startled, reluctant on the speaker, but she agreed to let him in.

Korie and Aaron had bought the penthouse just after they had married. At the time, it had been furnished in clean, modern lines, with an abundance of Stickley furniture and Mission-style accessories that Aaron had adored. Now it looked like a cross between a fin de siècle salon and Jackson Pollock's studio. Overstuffed chairs, low sofas and textured wall hangings contrasted with canvases filled with bright colors and geometric shapes.

Korie opened the door, a wadded handkerchief in one hand. She'd hesitated about inviting him up, but the touch of common sense she had left had apparently won her over. "I'm sorry," she said quietly as she ushered him into the living room. "I'm just such a mess."

"I understand," he said evenly. "I promise this won't take long. I just need to clarify a few things before I go back."

"So are you close to proving Maggie killed him?"

Fletcher put a lockdown on his emotions. "I do think I'm close to a solution."

Korie flopped down on one of the sofas, spreading her arms wide. "Well, it had to be her. She had the motive—my money—and she was right there with him. She had to!"

Fletcher sat on the edge of a chair. "I'm working on finding all the proof I can, Korie. There're still a lot of unanswered questions."

She leaned back with a sigh. "I know. You have to follow procedure, even though you're just doing this for me."

"That's right."

"Well, you know I'll help any way I can."

"Do you plan to contest the will?"

She smiled. "Not if she's convicted. I won't have to."

Fletcher's jaw clutched. To cover, he pulled out his notebook and a pen. He clicked the pen with his left hand and referred to his notes. "Did you notice any changes in Aaron over the past few weeks?"

She shook her head. "He was Aaron as usual. Mostly drunk. I suppose you know that we didn't see much of each other anymore."

"But you knew he had fired Edward?"

Korie sat up, her face reddening. "As he should have. The man was not a good manager."

"But you went to see Edward on Friday." *Click.*

She sniffed. "Are you going to put me through the third degree? Do I need to brighten the lights?"

"Korie…"

She waved her hand. "Sorry. This is all just very hard."

"I understand. You didn't know Edward had been fired." *Click.*

She shook her head. "Aaron still saw him a lot. How would I know?"

"You had gone with Aaron to New Hampshire this time. Were you putting things back together?"

She sighed deeply. "I had hoped so. I loved Aaron. I didn't like it when he wouldn't speak or was mean." She pouted a little. "He sometimes did that for no reason."

"Did he ever hurt you?"

"You mean physically?"

"Yes."

She hesitated, then looked down. "I don't want to slander a famous man. His fans—"

"Will want to see justice for you both." Fletcher loosened his tie. He felt as if he were choking.

She nodded. "Of course. No, he didn't hit me, if that's what you're asking. I mean, there was only that one time he got rough, but he didn't—"

Fletcher tried to stay calm. "Can you tell me about it?" *Click.*

Korie got up and came to Fletcher, kneeling by his chair. He put his knees together as she laid a hand on his thigh. "I don't want you to think badly about him," she said softly.

"I know, Korie. I won't. I promise. The more I know, the more I can prove."

She paused, then nodded. "I suppose it's all right, since he's gone and all."

"What happened that day? Tell me what you saw, how you felt."

Korie dropped her hand away and sat back, pulling her knees up and wrapping her arms around them. Fletcher focused on his notebook. *Click.*

"I think I was naive, like a lot of girls are, when the marriage started to go sour."

"Naive how?"

She shrugged, and her voice softened. "I thought a baby would help."

Fletcher clutched his notebook, wrinkling the pages. He forced himself to breathe easily. "Are you saying you got pregnant?" *Click.*

She nodded, then dropped her head forward, letting her hair fall over her shoulders. "Stupid, huh?"

"How did Aaron respond?" *Click. Click.*

She sniffed, wiped her eyes with the handkerchief then looked up at him, her eyes wide. "At first he was surprised, and I thought he'd be happy about it. Then he just got cold. You know, not talking, moody. Just sitting around staring."

"What do you think was on his mind?" *Click. Click. Click.*

She looked down and shrugged. "His age, maybe? I mean, I really thought he liked kids. He'd talked about them enough."

"What happened next?"

"It just got worse. He would say things, wouldn't sleep with me, drank a lot more. I thought he'd been trying to quit. I'd had enough, you know?" She looked at him, pleading. "I thought he'd be happy. He wasn't. And I didn't really want a child. I'm too young!"

Fletcher closed his eyes. *Please, no.* "What did you do?" *Click.*

"I got rid of it."

Fletcher's pen snapped in half, smearing ink over his hand.

"Fletcher!" Korie leaped to her feet and rushed out, returning with a rag. "Be careful that you don't get it on—" She stopped, catching the look on his face. "On your suit."

She stood, waiting as Fletcher wrapped his hand and the pen in the rag, clenching everything tightly. He sat up straighter, and his notebook slid off his lap to the floor. Korie reached for it, but he shook his head. "Just leave it."

She stopped.

"Is that when he got rough?"

Tears slid down her cheeks and she sat down on the very edge of the sofa. "Yes. I did it for him, and he shoved me down and just left me! I just wanted him to be happy! I couldn't do anything right!"

Fletcher had stopped caring if the tears were real or not, or whether he kept his cool. "Who was the father, Korie?"

She froze. "What?"

"Who was the father?" he demanded.

Her face hardened. "Aaron, of course. You have no right—"

"Aaron had a vasectomy in 1979."

"No."

"Yes!" He stood up, unable to contain the rage anymore. "After his third paternity suit in three years. That's why he didn't have kids!" He paced back and forth.

She stood up, facing him. "This isn't fair. I'm his widow!"

Fletcher stood as close as he could, his face next to hers. "Who was the father? *Now!*"

She met him, rage for rage. "You can't do this! You're a cop! You can't treat me like this!"

"I'm not on the force anymore, remember? I'll treat you any way I please in order to find out who killed my best friend!"

"Maggie killed him!"

"Who was the father!"

She backed away, breathing heavily. "I won't say."

Fletcher's jaw tightened. "Then I will drop this right here and now and you won't get a penny. Maggie will get it all, just like Aaron wanted. After all this time, she was the one he still loved."

The slap landed across his left cheek, but Fletcher barely winced. He kept talking. "And everyone will know it. I'm under no confidentiality restraints with this, lady. I will tell the reporters all about your fits and your schemes and your infidelity, and those art deals you're trying to work will go out with the wind."

Korie blinked first, dropping her gaze. "He was unfaithful, too."

"Who was the father?"

"Scott."

Fletcher nodded. He'd expected it. He wanted to hear her say it. He bent down and picked up the notebook, then turned for the door.

"Fletcher, wait." She met him there. "You don't think he was killed because I—"

He shook his head. "Nothing is certain yet."

She looked at the floor a moment, then back up at him. "I'm sorry. I really did love him once. What's going to happen now?"

He took a deep breath. "I honestly do not know."

She stepped back, her shoulders drooping, as he reached for the knob. "Oh, by the way," she said, absently. "That old woman is looking for you."

He stopped, his eyes narrowing. "What old woman?"

She waved her hand in a vaguely northern direction. "You know, the one that lives up next to the retreat. She said your phone was off. She said it was urgent that you call the lodge."

Fletcher closed his eyes, digging deep for a reserve of calm. "Thank you."

"Yeah. Whatever," she said, as she closed the door behind him.

NINETEEN

Judson closed his notebook and shut off his desk lamp. Lee looked at him in disbelief. "Are you just leaving? That's it?"

Judson nodded. He stood up and reached for his coat. "There's nothing more to do on this case. You're going to have to let it go."

Lee stood, his face red. "But we know he did it!"

"Yes," Judson said, tucking his PDA into a pocket. "But we can't prove it. And after two months, you should realize we'll never be able to prove it. The evidence is gone. The one witness has gone ex-pat on us and refuses to testify. There's no forensics to back our belief."

"This isn't fair."

Judson slid a scarf around his neck. "No. But that's how it is sometimes. Knowing who's guilty isn't proof. Sometimes, we don't get our man."

Fletcher slumped down in the train seat, the fully rested feeling he'd had that morning completely depleted. There was an odd weariness in his bones he'd not felt since his first year as a detective, when the promotion had opened up a whole new world of depravity to him. It had taken him more than a year to learn to balance the good with the bad, hope with despair, to realize that just as cops are privy to the darkest of human behavior, they can also be witnesses to some of the most golden.

This case. His mind didn't quite want to classify what was happening as "a case," but that's really what it was. It was also a prime example of why doctors shouldn't treat family and detectives shouldn't investigate friends.

Or friends' murders.

When he'd called the lodge, Lily had answered, setting off all his alarms. As she explained the attack on Maggie, his first impulse was to charter a jet; fortunately, common sense prevailed. She was still in the hospital, and Ray had taken up residence outside her room. But clearly, she was going to have to be more wary until this was over. He called Tyler, got his machine and now waited for the return call.

Fletcher stretched in the seat, rolling his shoulders and massaging his scalp. He'd bought a Sunday *Times,* but after reading the story about the memorial service, he'd left it untouched. Nothing he read about world affairs, cultural events or scientific breakthroughs distracted him from the path his mind was going over and over.

No matter how right Jason was, Fletcher was still uncomfortable with what he was feeling about Maggie. She'd never been far from his mind this entire trip, and if he indulged himself, he could imagine how it must feel to have his hands entangled in those dark red curls, to hold her close. It had been a long time since he'd wanted to kiss a woman this much, yet it felt so wrong. Wrong that it was this soon after his friend's death. Wrong that he desperately wanted her to be innocent of everything. Instead of finding ways for her to be guilty, he had been trying to explain away her involvement.

She had tried to mislead him about who was involved with

Aaron and who hated him, trying to draw attention away from Lily—or so he had thought at the time. Fletcher had called Jamie, the writer she'd so politely muddied, only to find out that he had been in California almost from the time Aaron had kicked him out. He was working as a technical writer for a firm near San Francisco, a time to "clear my head and make some money," as he'd put it. His boss had verified his presence at work every day.

The circumstantial evidence against Maggie was strong. She'd found the body. She had motive—the money she'd inherit. Fletcher had also toyed with the idea that the first attack, the shot out of the dark, had been her idea, another distraction. He'd dismissed it quickly—she'd been hurt too badly, and her turning had been impulsive and impossible to synchronize with a long-range shot. And whatever she was going to say had been forgotten.

But that was the only suspicion that he had dismissed, and the attack was the only thing that kept him from pursuing her actively as the killer.

Well…not the only thing. Fletcher wasn't the only one who believed in her.

"I guarantee you, Sir Fletcher, if I were to die tomorrow, that girl would be the only one I'd miss. Or who'd miss me." Aaron stretched out on the leather couch in the downstairs game room, a cigar replacing a glass. He was tall enough that his heels rested on one arm and his head on the other, his frame still lean from years of jogging, too little food and too much booze. He closed his eyes for a moment, and Fletcher thought he might be drifting off.

"Why do you say that? You're not together anymore." Fletcher sat in a matching chair, enjoying the soft comfort of it.

Aaron sniffed. "Maybe because I'm a man and she's the one who really got away."

Fletcher hesitated, wondering if Aaron was serious.

After a moment, the writer grinned. "Okay, so not really. I think it's just because she's the only one who liked me." He opened his eyes. "Not just loved me, but liked *me." Taking a deep breath, he sat up. "When you're in my position, me boyo, you have no idea how intoxicating that can be." He took a sip and grimaced. "She's also fun, and I know there's not a devious bone in her body."*

Fletcher shook his head. "Everyone can be devious if they want to."

Aaron stubbed out the cigar. "Too true. And I guess she could. But I can't imagine what would make her do that."

Actually, that was an easy one. Her sister. Without a doubt, Maggie would even go to jail for Lily.

Fletcher jerked upright. "Lily," he whispered. Well, not Lily. Not as the killer, but because she was someone who would suffer if the killer was caught. A killer who, of all the people at the retreat, was the only one other than Maggie with the clearest motive.

Scott.

Fletcher snatched out his cell phone. He had some calls to make.

Maggie drifted in and out of consciousness over the next twenty-four hours, her body finally claiming the sleep she'd missed during the past week. She had awakened briefly Sunday night, just long enough to eat something and take a pill for her pain. She slept through the night.

She awoke slowly on Monday morning, her grogginess gone, and most of her pain lessened to a dull ache. Except for the rib, which still made it hard to take deep breaths. Other than that, she felt almost blissful from the rest and the gentle waking. As her eyes focused, she realized that Fletcher was standing at the window of her room, looking out toward the airport. Since there was no hospital in Mercer, Tyler had brought her to Portsmouth, where they had treated her after the shooting.

She cleared her throat. "Are you going to hover every time I'm hurt?"

He turned, then smiled. "There's a good possibility of that," he said quietly. Before the meaning of it could register on her, his professionalism returned. "We need to talk, but I want you in full mind before we do. Can I get you something to eat?"

She reached for her console and raised the head of her bed. "No, thank you. But I should probably talk to the doctor and get dressed. Can this wait?"

He paused, then nodded. "I should warn you. This may get intense."

Maggie looked him over carefully. He hadn't shaved and he was more wrinkled than usual. His hair looked as if it had been styled by a wind tunnel. "Something happened in New York, too, didn't it? After I left?"

He nodded.

"Have you slept?"

He tilted his head to the left and looked at her more closely. "A little."

She looked down for a moment, then back up at him. "Fletcher, I'm not going anywhere. I'm going to see this through, no matter what the outcome. No matter who really killed Aaron. Why don't you go back to the cabin and get some rest? It'll take a while for me to be discharged. Plus—" She paused.

"What?"

She met his gaze. "We need to have this talk at Aaron's house. Is that going to be a problem?"

His brows furrowed. "A problem how? I don't think Korie

is coming back anytime soon. It might be if this goes to court, in terms of a search."

She smiled. "Well, even though Aaron owned the house, officially it sits on land owned by the retreat, and I have a key. I oversaw the care of it when they were gone. Doesn't that give me legal access?"

He stepped a bit closer to the bed and crossed his arms. "Probably, but I'll double-check. You're not going to tell me what this is about, are you?"

She shook her head slowly. "It's better that I show you. You need to see it for yourself."

He didn't respond, then Maggie realized he was looking at the side of her face, which was bruised from the blow of her attacker. He stepped forward, reaching out. His fingers traced the edge of it, and Maggie felt her stomach contract. His touch was tender, and Maggie could smell his cologne now that he was near.

Feeling suddenly vulnerable, she pulled the sheet up a bit. Vulnerable, not because she was wearing only a hospital gown but because she didn't want him to stop. She closed her eyes. *I'm not ready for this.*

His fingers lingered, then traced down her cheek. *I shouldn't,* she thought, as she turned her face and pressed it into his palm. She heard the sharp intake of his breath, and his hand curled gently, caressing her skin.

Then he pulled away quickly, whispering, "I'm sorry."

Before she could open her eyes, he was halfway out of the room, and she watched as the door closed behind him with a muffled *whuff.* Letting out a long breath, she pressed her head back into her pillow. "Oh, Lord," she pleaded. "What am I doing?"

TWENTY

Lee was persistent. "I don't want to let this one get away, Judson."

The older man paused at the door. "Then be creative. Just remember the rules about entrapment. Call me when you have an idea."

Lee strode across the room. "Why aren't you doing anything on this?"

Judson looked down on his partner with a slight smile. "What makes you think I'm not? If you want to set a trap that's not a trap, it takes more than footwork." He buttoned his coat. "I'm going to get some rest. I suggest you do, too."

Lee motioned at his desk. "I want to go over the paperwork again. All the notes."

Judson nodded. "Let me know if you find anything." He started out, then paused at the door. "No matter what time it is."

Lee grinned. "You got it."

Tyler had left a message on his cell, so before he even left the hospital, Fletcher returned the call, not only to get an update on what had happened with Maggie, but to distract himself from the sandalwood scent that lingered on his fingers.

"No scrapings or cloth under her nails, although we tried," Tyler explained. "Obviously Maggie connected with his leg or ankle, but not enough for serious damage. We thought Cookie might have hit him, so we carried one of the dogs out there, looking for blood or torn clothing so they could get an air scent, but no luck. There was only one set of footprints on the scene that wasn't Maggie's or Cookie's, but they were too mushed up to get a good impression. Basically, even if we knew who had attacked her, we wouldn't be able to prove it. The scene isn't giving us anything."

"Any clues as to how he knew where she'd be?"

Tyler cleared his throat. "Not really. Maggie said half the retreat's residents are night owls by nature and that she was not a quiet hiker. She mentioned something about a 'moose in passing.'"

Fletcher stifled a snort. "Yeah. She's not that hard to track, and I guess it's pretty obvious that if she's not at the lodge in the middle of the night, she'd be at Cookie's."

"Well, it's not like we have a twenty-four-hour supermarket around for midnight prowlers."

"True," Fletcher said with a chuckle. "Anything else?"

"As a matter of fact…" Tyler paused and Fletcher could hear his chair scoot and papers shuffle. "I had a friendly judge light a fire at the state lab. They faxed me the DNA results on the champagne bottle this morning."

"Anything significant?"

"Yes, but only if we already had a suspect. There were four different samples on the bottle."

"Four?" Even Fletcher was surprised.

"Yep. Aaron's on the main part of the bottle, where the label snagged skin cells when it hit him. One inside the mouth. That was Lily's. Lily's was also on the upper label, where you grip the bottle, along with two others. Maggie's—we matched it to the sample you gave us—and one unknown. Could be the killer, could be just one of the folks who left their prints when moving the bottle around."

Fletcher paused outside the hospital, near his rental, and looked back up at the windows. Maggie's room was on the fourth floor. "Just out of curiosity, why is Lily's DNA on file?"

"Very early in her career, she got involved in a scuffle with another actress, either over a role or a man, it was never made clear which. Lily was the one attacked, and it was just before her first big hit, so they think probably it was professional. Fingernails as well as jealousy were involved, so her DNA and her prints went into the system, even though it was settled out of court. You don't read the tabloids, do you?"

"They dug that up?"

"Oh, yeah. Very juicy."

"Tyler ..."

"Yeah?"

"Do *you* read the tabloids?"

Tyler paused for a long moment. Fletcher could almost see him blushing over the phone. "My mother keeps me informed."

"Gotcha." Fletcher grinned and decided to let the young chief off the hook. "Too bad we can't convince a judge that the retreat is a closed community so we could get a warrant for everyone else's."

"I could always ask. He might laugh, but it never hurts to try."

Fletcher grinned at the young man's innocence and chutzpah. "Go for it. Let me know what you learn."

"Will do. Uh, Fletcher?"

"Yeah?"

"There's one more thing. The lab found traces of Aaron's DNA on the upper label as well. On all sides of the bottle. Not like he'd been hit with it. Like he had been holding it."

"Which is consistent with him taking the bottle away from

Lily, like Maggie described." So she was telling the truth about that much.

"True. I'll get to work on that warrant. The subpoena you asked about as well."

"Thanks."

Fletcher left the hospital, but was distracted enough that he became confused in the early-morning work traffic and wound up wandering the maze of roads and neoclassic office buildings near Pease Tradeport. Irritated, he stopped for a soda, got new directions then drove the twenty minutes or so back to the retreat. Once on the road, he let his mind drift again. Maggie was right. He needed more rest than the one night at his apartment had offered him. Too much was coming at him at once.

He let the automatic scanner on the radio run through the dial, finally choosing a classic rock station. Recognizing a song he loved from the mid-seventies, Fletcher couldn't decide if it was a remnant of his mother's love of music or if he was just getting old. He turned the volume down to the level of a thumpy background score for his thoughts as he drove by fields turned under for the winter and thick groves of trees now bare-limbed and skeletal. Horses were the only signs of life he saw, but he enjoyed the peace of it. After fifteen years in New York, a city he usually loved, he could see the pull this countryside had on Aaron.

And Fletcher realized he missed Vermont. With his parents gone, his one sister in Miami and Jason in New York, he'd only returned to his hometown a handful of times over the years. A funeral. His high-school reunion, which had been a disaster.

But the years he'd lived in the area around Stowe were filled with good memories as well. As Fletcher drove past a blueberry farm, he remembered days when he and his friends would explore every neighbor's backyard, looking for discarded treasures. He crossed over the Lamprey River, thinking of himself as a teenage Huck Finn, lying on the bank of a stream, counting clouds.

Passing by one of the quintessential New England church-yards, complete with a white chapel banked by thick ever-greens, Fletcher's mind also drifted over times he'd sat in one of them, squirming on the hardwood pew. His mother had polished him up every Sunday until he'd left for college. After a while, he hadn't minded, enjoying the youth group and the feeling of belonging, the comfort of the faith. He'd even con-tinued going after arriving in New York. For a few years.

He shifted in the car's bucket seat, also remembering the terror of that alley, the stark realization of what he had done.

"God's not the one who moved away, you know."

Fletcher shook away Cookie's words. He *liked* his life now. He wasn't sure he could imagine any other. Yet the older he got, the more he felt an odd tug on his heart, his mind. A tug that said he was missing out on something vital.

"Why are you still here?" Aaron asked, looking around at Fletcher's functional but tiny apartment. "You could afford to move."

"I like it here. It's just what I need. I had bigger one once. A condo in the Village, remember? I sold it."

Aaron took up his usual position on the lumpy couch. "Why?"

"I didn't like the hassle. I'd prefer to be more mobile, and if I want an investment, I'll look into another mutual fund."

Aaron sighed. "I'm never gonna get you married, me boyo. Women like security. Stability."

Fletcher coughed. "Didn't stop you."

Aaron laughed. "Yes, but I have the big bucks, and they all know it. Makes up for a lot."

"Yeah, but I remember that you didn't have any trouble with the ladies before you had the bucks."

Aaron looked around Fletcher's ceiling, at his walls. "That's the creative spirit. Attracts a certain type of—why is it that you don't even fix this place up? Are you so afraid the IAB will come snooping around that you can't even paint?"

Fletcher growled. "It has nothing to do with Internal Affairs. If I were worried about them, I wouldn't have bought that condo in the first place. I just haven't had the time."

Aaron sat up, looking over his friend closely. Then he grinned. "You haven't told anyone, have you?"

"Told anyone what?" Fletcher tried to pretend he didn't know what Aaron meant.

"Told anyone that I signed over part of the royalties on the last ten books to you."

"Why would I?"

"What are you doing with the money? Other than buying and selling condos other cops couldn't afford?"

Fletcher squirmed. He didn't like talking about money. "Paid off the credit cards, then cut 'em up. Bought into some mutual funds. Gave some to a couple of charities." He got up and went to the kitchen for more coffee. "Am I going to have to give you an accounting for it?"

Aaron laughed. "I can't believe this makes you so uncomfortable. You really don't know what to do with money, do you?"

"Not a habit I've acquired, no."

"How much is there?"

"They're your books. Don't you know?"

"I know the last one sold close to two hundred thousand in hardback. Edward takes care of everything else. Besides, I want to hear you say it."

Fletcher stood in the door to the kitchen, coffee in hand. "With or without interest?"

Aaron grinned. "Just the raw details."

"Just over seven hundred fifty thousand dollars."

Aaron let out an Irish whoop. "Son, you ought to spend some of that."

"It's invested."

"So's your retirement money, but you probably get a better yield."

"No doubt."

"Still, you should never overlook the advantages of a good piece of real estate. Or, even better, a wife."

"I'll think about it."

But he hadn't. Not really. Until now.

Arriving back at the retreat just after eight in the morning, Fletcher took Maggie's advice. He went to his cabin and slept, dreaming of slow-moving rivers, whitewashed churches and children who never seemed to stop running and laughing.

By Monday afternoon, Maggie's discharge was complete and Ray drove her back to the lodge. Fletcher, Lily and Cookie waited on her in the main room and fresh coffee steamed on the coffeemaker's hotplate. After gentle hugs, Cookie and Lily hovered as Maggie settled into a chair, wrapped in her favorite afghan. Fletcher brought her a cup of coffee. Ray stood next to the fireplace, looking ominous.

Maggie took a sip of her coffee, and after a moment of awkward silence, she cleared her throat. "I know it's obvious, but I think someone needs to say it."

They looked at one another, then Fletcher shifted his weight from one foot to the other. "Whoever killed Aaron is still here, still part of the retreat and still very much interested in killing you."

Lily took a deep breath and let it out slowly. "Now what?"

Maggie looked up at Fletcher and nodded. He crossed his arms. "Tyler got a subpoena for Aaron's financial records. He doesn't really have anyone on staff who can help, so he's sending them to Edward. Edward said he'd go through them immediately, so we should have an idea of what's going on there fairly soon."

Cookie coughed, then looked from Maggie to Fletcher. "So you don't think this is personal?"

Fletcher shrugged. "Maybe. Maybe not. But we're not going to know until we have all the pieces." He looked at Lily. "And at least one piece involves some missing manuscripts."

Lily reddened. "I'm sorry I did that. I had no idea that Aaron would take it—" She stopped, staring at Fletcher. "Are you saying that Scott is a suspect?"

Fletcher didn't blink. "Everyone still is, Lily. I'm sorry. We still don't know enough to eliminate anyone."

She looked at her sister. "You don't think—"

Maggie shrugged. "No one knows for sure. Thank about it. If this was a crime of passion, *anything—anyone—*is possible."

"I can't think of Scott like that."

"Then don't," Fletcher said. "He's your husband. You shouldn't, unless you know something."

Lily shook her head. "I don't. I don't remember much of Monday night. The only thing I can remember is the sound of thunder."

Maggie looked at Fletcher, startled. He caught the look, then went to Lily. "Thunder? Where were you?"

Lily wiped at one eye. "At the cabin. We'd fought, as usual. He walked out, said he had to get some air. Sometime later, I woke up, from the thunder, I thought. Then went back to sleep."

Maggie started to speak, but Fletcher motioned for her silence. He took Lily's hand. "You keep that in mind. If you think of anything else, voices, wind, anything, you find me. Okay?"

Lily nodded.

Maggie pushed back the afghan. "I love you all, but I need

to talk to Fletcher alone. Please." She looked at Ray. "Get some rest. He and I will be together for a while. I'll be safe with him."

Cookie hugged her again. "If you need me, I'm here," she whispered.

Maggie hugged her back, as tightly as she dared. "I know. I love you. And thank you."

The three left and she turned to Fletcher, who tilted his head to the left and raised his eyebrow. "You know it was not thundering last Monday," she said.

He pointed to his ear. "She heard something. Let it ferment. Time to go to Aaron's?"

She sighed. "Most definitely."

He walked her to his rental car in silence. They sat as she struggled with the seat belt for a few moments, her sore wrist preventing her from fastening it securely.

"May I?" he finally asked. With a sigh of resignation, she nodded. He clicked it into place, then started the car. As she tightened her seat belt, he said evenly, "You *really* don't like people hovering over you, do you?"

She smiled. "That obvious, huh?"

"Oh, yeah."

"I'm not surprised. It always makes me feel as if I'm inadequate, like I can't take care of myself."

"You know it's not. People care about you."

Maggie nodded. "I know. I just can't—"

"Accepting help is hard. We think we should be able to do it all ourselves."

She looked at him. "Yes, it is hard."

"But that's a myth. We're all dependent on other people in a variety of ways, from the guy who signs our paycheck to the grocer who stocks the shelves." He paused. "Let me ask you something."

"Okay."

"You're a Christian, right?"

"Yes," she answered slowly. Where was he going with this?

"Well, doesn't Christianity preach that you should help others?"

"Yes."

"And don't you get a kind of blessing when you do? It makes you feel good?"

She nodded. "Of course."

"So why deny that feeling, that blessing, to the people who love you?"

She stared at him. "What did you say?"

"You don't think Cookie gets a blessing for bringing you soup and tea?"

"Of course, but she—"

"So why wouldn't you let her help you? Want her to do it, in fact?"

"I don't believe—"

"I mean," he went on, ignoring her interruption, "what if she hadn't been there last night?"

Maggie slumped down in her seat, recognition setting in. She didn't want to think about what would have happened. She glared at him, and he chuckled. "Don't hate me because I'm right."

She sniffed, then gestured royally at her bruised and cut face. "I won't, as long as you don't hate me because I'm beautiful."

Aaron's house was still chilly, although not as bad as before. Maggie adjusted the thermostat up a couple more degrees, then led Fletcher upstairs. He grinned when she told him the password, but his smile faded as they started to work through the layers of files on Aaron's hard drive.

Fletcher stood behind her as Maggie sat in the desk chair, clicking on the file program. "I didn't get a chance to go through everything on Saturday," she said. "But enough that I realized that something had happened to Aaron. I still don't know what. But it was clear that he was getting ready to—"

"Disappear."

Maggie froze, then turned in the chair to look up at him. "You knew?"

He crossed his arms. "Edward told me on Friday. We haven't had a chance to talk."

"Do you know the details?"

He shook his head. "From the way you looked Saturday night, I thought you might have found a few things."

She nodded, then looked down. *I don't want to do this,* she thought.

Fletcher squatted down in front of her, taking one hand in his. "Maggie, look at me."

She did. His expression was tender, and she was caught by the affection she could see in his eyes. Her throat tightened, and she wished he would just hold her. Just for a moment. *Make this go away,* she thought, *if only for a few minutes.*

"Maggie," he said softly. "You can't hurt Aaron anymore. And what he did is going to come out. It's going to hurt. Now. Or later."

"It already hurts," she replied, wishing that she didn't like holding his hand so much. "You have no idea what he's done."

"Then show me. Let's get this out of the way."

She nodded and slipped her hand away, turning her back. Reaching for the mouse, she opened the first layer of files. "Aaron liked games," she said slowly, her eyes bouncing from one file to the other. "And he loved to layer things. He considered it organizing. For instance, here's a file called 'The Vineyard.' Confused me at first, but it also made me curious. When I opened it, I found information he'd researched for one of the novels, the one he set in the wine country in California."

"I remember."

She grinned. "Judson was great in that one."

Fletcher coughed. Maggie cleared her throat and went on, her mind swirling. There was so much to tell, to show, yet none of it made sense, not in regards to the man she knew. Or thought she knew. She took a deep breath and opened a series of folders. Again, the top layer looked like research. The final file contained Scott's manuscripts, as rewritten by Aaron.

"These are Scott's," she said. "Or they were. I found the originals in the bedroom that Aaron uses at the lodge. I wanted to show you all this first before telling you the rest of it." She explained finding the money and the passport in her office. "I thought maybe he was going to disappear and ask me to go with him, or frame me for his disappearance."

He looked puzzled. "Who's Chris Taylor?"

"Another one of Aaron's jokes. She's a character that Lily wants to play in a film. Someone who disappears and takes a lot of money with her."

The color drained from Fletcher's face, and he backed away from the desk. He walked to the window, his mouth over his hand. He stared out over the landscape of the retreat, slowly shaking his head. "No," he said quietly. "You couldn't. Please."

Maggie followed him, a tight, scared feeling in her chest. "Fletcher?" She reached for his arm, but he backed away.

"I don't believe it," he muttered, his gaze moving around the room wildly, from one object to another.

"Tell me!" she insisted.

He froze, looking at her. "I can't. I don't know—"

Maggie grabbed both his wrists. "Fletcher! On Friday I found enough information on that computer to prove that a man who was my friend—a man I had once *loved!*—had made false documents with my information without telling me, and it looks as if he was trying to steal another writer's work! He betrayed his wife and Scott! And *me!* What could be worse?"

Fletcher looked down at her, his face twisted in disbelief. "Aaron wasn't just going to betray you." His low voice was harsh. "He was going to kill you."

TWENTY-ONE

Maggie couldn't breathe. She tried to gasp for air, but nothing moved, as if her lungs were frozen.

"Maggie," Fletcher said. "Breathe."

She shook her head, feeling dizzy. Fletcher grabbed her arms and shook them. "Baby, breathe!" he insisted.

Her body finally took over, desperate for oxygen, and she inhaled sharply, which made her even dizzier. She felt her knees giving way. Fletcher scooped her up and carried her out of the office and down the hall to the bedroom he'd stayed in. He pushed the door open with his foot and stretched her out on the bed, then turned toward the bathroom. "I'll get you some water."

Maggie's eyes took in the pristine elegance of the room, decorated with a slightly masculine flavor and early American furniture, but she felt like a fish suddenly cast upon a dry bank gasping for air. Fletcher returned with the water and slid one arm under her shoulders, helping her to sit up. The coolness of the water finally broke through her senses, and she sipped, once, twice. Then the third sip turned into a choke, followed by a sob.

Fletcher set the water aside and took her in his arms. She clung to him, burying her face against his shoulder. But the tears never came. The gasps of her few sobs were dry, and as she caught her breath again, her senses seemed to move from numb to hypersensitive, as if every nerve were exposed. She felt the cloth of Fletcher's coat as she dug her nails into his arm and shoulder, aware that what felt soft under her hands was slightly rough on her cheek. There was a hint of dry-cleaning fluid in his jacket, but even more powerful was the exotic scent of his cologne.

Slowly, the tension eased away from her.

"Maggie?" he asked softly.

"Please," she whispered. "Just hold me."

She felt him take a deep breath, then close his arms tighter around her. She let go of his arm and shoulder and slid her arms around his back. His chest was firm, and his warmth seemed to envelope her.

After a moment, she pushed back, and he released her easily. She looked up at him. "Thank you."

"Glad I could help."

She released a great breath, then she put one hand on his arm. "I don't want it to be true."

"Neither do I. But I don't seen another reason." He told her about Susan, then Korie and the baby. And Scott. All of it in the name of revenge.

Maggie took it in with a silent prayer. "All that pain," she whispered. "If they had only talked to each other. Do you think Aaron went to Lily because of Korie and Scott?"

Fletcher paused. "I should have told you sooner. I thought Lily would have. Maybe she didn't realize ..."

Maggie's forehead creased. "What?"

"Lily and Aaron weren't sleeping together."

"What?"

He took her hands. "Your sister is struggling, Maggie. All the downsides of fame hit her pretty hard. Aaron helped her with that, listened to her about her marriage. He used her to get back at Scott, but only through the work, not her bed. And I don't think she knows about Scott and Korie."

At that moment, Maggie wanted nothing more than to hug her little sister. And slap Aaron. Or hug him one more time, try to talk some sense into his thick head. She looked down at their hands for a moment, comforted by the sight of Fletcher's long, broad fingers cradling hers. She finally looked up. "I still don't understand why he would want to kill me?"

"Several reasons, although the most prominent is to blame you for his disappearance—set it up to look as if you'd murdered him. That way, no one—especially Korie—would come looking for him. Then the passport and money in your office would explain your own plans to disappear after you killed him."

"Which just gives me more motive for killing him." Maggie had never felt so lost.

Fletcher paused and looked her over. "Yes."

Maggie turned to stare at the wall. "I really thought he still loved me. Or at least liked me."

"He did."

Maggie squinted, her mind confused. It refused to accept both possibilities—love and murder. "I don't see—"

"You and I both know how different Aaron really was from what most people thought," Fletcher said. "That public persona he had—so liberal, womanizing, easygoing—was a front. He was some of that, but it was only a little bit of his surface. He was a complex man."

Maggie nodded. "He once told me that few people knew him as he really was and even fewer of them really liked him."

"You were one of them."

Her heart twisted again. "Yes."

"He thought you'd want to help him."

Maggie stared at him. "By dying?"

Fletcher licked his lips. "There's a lot of evidence here that

Aaron wasn't exactly rational during his last days." He told her about Bill's comments. "Even people who weren't around him all the time noticed that something was terribly wrong."

Maggie's mind skimmed again over the last weeks of Aaron's life. Fletcher certainly had a point there. Aaron's anger had been out of control. He'd hit Lily, and Maggie had never known him to hit a woman. There was the fight with Jamie—so convenient for her when she needed another suspect, but now…

"Jamie. He'd never thrown anyone out before. Asked them to leave, yes, but not a fight, nothing physical."

"If you think about it, other things will pop up in your mind as well."

She took a deep breath and let it out slowly. "Do you think it was the baby?"

He shrugged. "Maybe. Maybe the long-term effects of the booze finally kicked in. Maybe what happened with Korie was the last straw. I do think he would have loved that child, once he got over the shock of it, no matter who the father was. Her abortion may have just pushed him over an edge he was already tottering on. And I know that the man we were with before he died was not the same person I had been friends with for all these years."

Maggie pushed off the bed and paced a bit, pressing her hand to her injured ribs. "So by being that way, he took someone with him. Pushed someone else over the edge enough to kill him."

"That's what seems likely."

"But who?"

Fletcher paused. "You know the players, Maggie. You tell me."

She smiled. "Want me to do your job for you?"

Fletcher sat straighter on the bed and grinned. "No. I want to hear how you think."

She stopped. "You care about how I think?"

He looked down for a second, and his fingers twitched, missing his pen. "Just talk to me, Maggie."

So she did, starting with the day Aaron died. "Seeing the bottle, I really thought Lily might have done it at first, which is why I hid the bottle when I found it. It was just my impulse."

"To protect her."

Maggie nodded, then watched as another realization came over Fletcher's face.

"You settled her case out of court."

Surprise flashed through her. "You know about that?" At his nod, she grinned. "Maybe you are Judson after all."

Fletcher cleared his throat and she continued, more seriously. "Then I came to my senses. She couldn't. When she's angry, she's like a mad cat, more spit than claws. Even holding a bottle, her impulse would have been to leap on him with her nails or throw it at him, not turn into a home-run slugger."

She started to pace again. Fletcher, almost amused, crossed his arms and waited. "For a while, I thought it was Korie, but she's just money. She would have gone for a lawyer." She stopped, looking at him. "I told you this, didn't I?"

"Keep talking."

She paced again. "Then all the motives kept pointing at me, so I started thinking of other people who might have a logical motive. He'd certainly made people angry, but enough to kill him? He'd fired Edward. No biggie there. I'm sure he's lost clients before. If Lily wasn't sleeping with him, that rules out any feelings on her part, and Scott wouldn't fight for her, not while he was spending time with Korie. It would need to be someone who would either benefit only from his death, or suffer greatly if he continued to live. That really just leaves me—" She stopped. "And Scott."

He nodded. "Yes."

"You think Scott killed him over the manuscripts?"

"With what we know now, yes. From what Susan told me, Aaron may have just stolen them to punish Scott, with no real intention of publishing them. Although Scott wouldn't have known that. But nothing is certain yet."

She frowned. "What does that mean?"

He stood up and reached for her hand. "It means we can prove nothing."

Her mouth dropped, and she waved one hand in the direction of Aaron's office. "But we have all this stuff!"

He shook his head. "It's all circumstantial. It gives motive, but not proof. And it's less motive than you have. If an arrest had to be made today…" His voice trailed off.

Her shoulders dropped. "It would be me."

He nodded.

"So what do we do?"

"I need Scott's DNA."

Her eyes widened. "That's not a problem. He eats at my table every night. What else?"

He shrugged. "We wait. See if Edward finds anything in the financials. See what the DNA shows. If Scott's DNA is on the bottle, Tyler could get a warrant for his cabin. We can do more work with Aaron's computer, but I don't know if we'll find anything that constitutes proof."

"I could search his cabin."

Fletcher shook his head. "No. We're pushing the envelope being here, but Aaron is the victim. With Scott, it'd never make it to court."

She stared at him a moment, her mind still flying. Then she grinned. "I have an idea."

TWENTY-TWO

Judson looked over Lee's notes. His young partner fidgeted and paced, trying not to hover over Judson's shoulder. "So, do you think it'll work? It's not entrapment. Not even close."

Judson looked up at him, somber. "Do you realize what a risk this is to you?"

Lee froze. "Well, yes!" He leaned over the desk and tapped the paper. "But isn't it worth it? Isn't getting this woman's family justice worth any risk?"

Judson stood up. "No, it's not. If this doesn't work, you could get hurt. So could her sister. That alone makes this foolhardy. I don't want you to go through with it."

Lee crossed his arms. "Her sister wants this."

"She's a civilian. She has blinders on. You should have a more objective point of view."

"This will work."

Judson stepped away from the desk. "Whether it will work isn't the point."

Fletcher stretched out on his bed, staring at the ceiling of the cabin and trying to get his head straight. He didn't like Maggie's plan, but there wasn't a lot of choice between it and waiting for something else to happen.

Like another attack on her.

He closed his eyes. The injuries to her face were still prominent, and she could barely breathe with that broken rib. All because he couldn't figure out who'd slammed Aaron with a champagne bottle. Despite how close they were, he still felt inadequate, as if his skills had been absorbed by his grief over his best friend.

Inadequate. Except, he realized, when Maggie looked up at him. Her eyes were a rich blue, and they seemed to hold all the innocence in the world. She had dated the most worldly man he had ever known, yet the word "worldly" would be the last one he would assign to her. Her fire, her belief in her sister, her adoration for Aaron were all tempered by an unawareness of how devious and evil people could be. Fletcher didn't know if he'd ever be able to forget the shock on her face when he told her Aaron had planned to kill her.

He shouldn't have, but the realization had caught him almost as off guard as it had her. Aaron wasn't that kind of man. Or he hadn't been. Fletcher searched through his memories of the last few months, looking for any clue during their visits that Aaron had stepped over the edge. He didn't want to believe it, but the evidence they'd found betrayed that belief. Aaron had been stressed beyond the breaking point, and he had become almost a Jekyll and Hyde character—normal around most people, crazed with a few and certainly while alone.

Fletcher sat up, running his hand through his hair. This was going nowhere.

Pray.

The thought came out of nowhere, and Fletcher hesitated a moment before his obstinance kicked in. "No," he said aloud. "I do *not* need to pray. It's been too long and I certainly don't need to start now." Instead, he reached for his cell phone and flipped it open. Dialing Tyler's number, he walked to the desk, searching the drawers for a pen, until the young police chief answered. "Did Maggie call you?" Fletcher asked.

"Yep. Are you two sure this will pull Scott into the open?"

Fletcher sighed. "Nope. It's a gamble, but it's better than sitting on our hands. Did you get those papers off to Edward?"

"Sure did. I grabbed Judge Baker after church yesterday, put through the request, and Edward pulled what he had, then I had the banks courier over everything else this morning."

"You had them sent by courier?"

"You said you were in a hurry."

Fletcher grinned. "Thanks. When did Edward say he'd be through?"

"Maybe as early as this evening. You might want to give him a call."

"I will. Anything else?"

"Not really."

"Thanks. See you in an hour or so."

"You got it."

Fletcher folded over the phone and set it aside. He resisted pacing, but the inaction was driving him nuts, and he didn't feel like attacking another tree.

"You work out too much."

Fletcher rolled his shoulders and rubbed a sore spot at the base of his neck. "And you don't do enough."

"Too old. Hurts too much. Why do I want to work that hard in the short time I have left?"

"Why do you keep talking about dying?" Fletcher tossed Aaron a towel and grabbed one of his own. They settled into the sauna and eased back against the hot wood. Fletcher cherished the feeling.

"This is probably not good for my blood pressure," Aaron grumbled.

"Considering your liver probably looks like a block of iron,

I'm not exactly surprised you have high blood pressure. The workouts could help that, you know, along with whatever other problems you're hiding. But none of them are going to kill you anytime soon. Now hush and enjoy the baking."

"How do you know I'm hiding problems?"

"Because you talk more when you're drunk than you do sober."

Aaron paused, then burst out laughing. "Okay, me boyo. Point well made. Obviously, I need to stop drinking. The doctors love me. Want my picture in their textbooks." He wiped the sweat off his face with one hand. "But don't be surprised if I don't live much longer."

Fletcher opened one eye. "Why do you say that?"

The older man shrugged. "I'm Irish. We just know these things." He paused and looked over at his friend. "I'm serious, Fletcher. Don't be surprised."

Fletcher opened both eyes. "You almost sound as if you're planning something."

Aaron shook his head. "No. Just a feeling."

Fletcher walked onto the cabin porch and looked out through the dusky light of sunset. "What were you trying to tell me, Aaron? And why didn't I follow up with you?" He turned and went back in. Time to follow up now. He picked up his cell and dialed Edward's number.

Maggie paid the rest of the bills she had forgotten on Thursday night. She checked her e-mail, to see if she had responses from the three she'd sent. There were two, and she read them with a smile. Good news. It would help set the stage for tonight. She printed them out and carried them to the main room where she left them at her place on the table. She also dusted her office. She dressed, then re-dressed, trying to find something businesslike, that didn't constrict her breathing any more than it already was. She finally decided on one of her favorite long skirts with an elastic waist, and a shell with a matching sweater.

I can't believe how nervous I am. When she tried to sit, she merely bounced both feet and twirled strands of her hair around one finger. Getting up, she went to the kitchen to prepare for the evening meal, which would be delivered in a few minutes.

"You are so obsessive sometimes. Relax."

Maggie froze. The voice was so clear, she could have sworn she actually heard it. But, no. Not really. He was still very much dead. Her spirit deflated, and she leaned against the refrigerator.

Flashbacks. That's what her mom had called them when her stepfather had died. She'd gathered her and Lily together to talk to them about death and grief and what to expect. Even though they were both grown, she cuddled them as if they were still children. Flashbacks, she had explained, are tiny memories of someone who's gone. They hit when you least expect them, and they can hurt like crazy. All over again. And her mom had been right. Maggie had had plenty of them about Bobby Dunne. Even more when her mom had died.

Now Aaron.

"You gonna haunt me forever, old man?" she said to the ceiling.

"Just so you never forget me, doll. Just never forget me."

"Little chance of that."

Maggie walked out on the deck and looked up at the first stars of the evening. "Look at me! I'm having a chat with a dead man." She'd rather have one with a man who was alive. Very alive. Maggie bit her lip, remembering how strong Fletcher had felt as he'd picked her up after she'd collapsed in Aaron's office.

She blushed at the thought, but it also excited her. What was this...*chemistry*...that they seemed to have? As much as she had loved Aaron and wanted to be with him, she'd never felt this kind of irrational draw to him. And it was irrational. They should be enemies. Fletcher could easily change his mind and have her arrested. She should resent him, want him to leave this alone and let Aaron rest in peace. But there were the attacks, and…she just didn't want him to go away.

Maggie rubbed her arms, shivering a bit in the cold. It smelled like snow, although there were no clouds in the sky. Soon. Thanksgiving was not far away. Maybe when it's all white and pristine again—

"You're wandering again, babe. Stay focused."

Maggie stamped her foot, causing a mild wave of pain to shoot through her torso. "Aaron, shut up! I'm doing the best I can!"

"You, too, huh?"

Maggie yelped, then turned her wrath on the man standing at the foot of the deck stairs. "This is impossible! How do you walk through dry leaves and not make a sound?"

Fletcher grinned. "Practice. And they aren't that dry."

"That's not the point."

He laughed. "I know. I thought you could use some help with the food."

She looked down her nose at him. "The *food?*"

"And your nerves."

"*My* nerves?"

"Woman, do you want help or not?"

Maggie turned to look over her shoulder. "Your timing is pretty good. I think I hear the truck."

Fletcher climbed the steps and held the door open for her. "My dear, my timing is always excellent."

She grinned and took his arm briefly as they walked through the room. She opened the front door for the caterer, and Fletcher helped her bring in the food, since she was forbidden to lift anything heavy. After the caterers left, she started a pot of coffee, then poured some for both of them.

Fletcher walked to the fireplace and stared at the flames. Maggie joined him, wishing once again she could read his mind. "Penny for your thoughts."

He sipped the coffee. "I want to say some things about Aaron tonight at dinner. They're not good."

"Worse than him wanting to kill me?"

Fletcher looked intently at her, his eyes dark. "No." He leaned against the mantel. "Medical things. I don't want you to be surprised." He told her what he'd learned from Edward.

Maggie took them in stoically. They explained a lot, but nothing would ever truly salve the last wounds that Aaron had laid on her. He'd wanted her dead.

"I have something I need to tell them," she said. "Then you can have the floor."

He nodded, and they fell silent. They were still standing in front of the fire, cups in hand, when the first of the writers arrived for dinner.

Fletcher looked down at her. "Let the games begin."

TWENTY-THREE

It was a quiet entry. Frank and Laura arrived first, holding hands. They declined coffee, but Laura asked if she could help, and Maggie gave her bottles of water to put at everyone's place. Dan and Patrick arrived together, chattering a bit about a game they had watched the night before. The men were already into the food when Scott and Lily arrived, exchanging tender looks and soft touches as they went down the buffet line. Carter and Mick followed them in, not speaking at all as they loaded plates with food and joined the others at the table. Fletcher and Tim went through the line together. Tonya finally emerged from her room, just as everyone else was getting seated. Maggie sat down last after kissing her sister, not wasting any time. "I have a lot to say. To all of you."

Scott cleared his throat. "Where's your guard dog?" Lily put a hand on his wrist and he looked away.

Maggie took a deep breath, trying to gather a bit more courage. "Ray has gone home to eat with his family. We don't think there's any more danger to me at this time."

Laura leaned forward. "How can you say that? I'm terrified to walk up here by myself."

"I know," Maggie said, "especially after Sunday. And I apologize for not filling all of you in on what's been happening. It's just all happened so fast—" For a second, her courage failed.

"I miss him," Tonya said.

Maggie looked up at her, grateful. "Me, too. Sometimes I get the feeling he's just in the next room, waiting to come out and scream at me."

Most of the writers smiled. Scott stared out over her left shoulder.

"Anyway," she continued, "I wanted to talk about the Retreat for a few minutes, then get on with some other details, which I hope will help." She twisted the cap off her bottle of water and took a sip.

"Most of you were at the funeral. You heard what Edward said about me inheriting." There was a light murmur around the table. "Well, nothing's settled yet. Korie will most likely contest the will. And I promise all of you I had no idea that he was going to leave it this way." Dan started to speak and Maggie held up her hand. "*However,* one provision of the will that Edward didn't mention had to do with the review process. When Aaron made out the will, he'd asked three of the best authors he knew if they would take over if something happened to him. They had all agreed, in principle, to act as an advisory board for the retreat. I'm sure none of them thought it would be this soon."

Even Fletcher was surprised. Scott glared at her. "Who?"

"Katie Matthews, Martin Scudder and Thomas Banks."

Dan yelped. "Are you *serious?* Banks just won the Pulitzer!"

Maggie nodded. "Today I e-mailed them for confirmation. Katie and Martin have already replied, saying they would assume the review duties."

The burst of enthusiasm spread up and down the table, just as she had expected. Even Scott leaned back in his chair, stunned. Maggie held up her hand for quiet. "But they are busy people, so the process will change some. Admission requirements to the retreat will become more stringent, although everyone here will be grandfathered in, if you wish. Residency will be limited to five—the other cabins will be opened for rental to other writers, although their work will not be part of the process and whatever work they do here will not carry the retreat's imprimatur. The critiques will be done monthly, instead of weekly, with evaluations for continued residency done on a quarterly basis. Once you're in, you have at least three months guaranteed."

They loved it. Scott leaned over to speak above the chatter. "Why did he do this? After all he'd done."

Silence fell. Maggie bit her lip and started to reply, but she couldn't. It would give too much away. Instead, she looked at Fletcher, who nodded.

"Because he knew he was going to die," he said.

"What?" Patrick asked.

Fletcher leaned back in his chair and toyed with his coffee cup, not looking at anyone for a moment. "A few weeks ago, some things happened in Aaron's life that he wasn't prepared for emotionally. He wasn't able to handle it, and it pushed him over the edge. He collapsed in Edward's office one afternoon, ranting like a madman. Edward wasn't sure what happened, so he called his doctor and they checked Aaron in to St. Vincent's, under an assumed name. No one knew."

The writers looked at one another, then waited as Fletcher continued. "They thought at first it was just exhaustion, or perhaps depression. Depression does seem to have been part of it it, but not all. St. Vincent's only confirmed what Aaron's own doctor had already told him." He paused and took a deep breath. "Aaron had been diagnosed with alcoholic cardiomyopathy. His heart wasn't pumping enough blood to his organs and his brain. His doc had told him to reduce his stress, get more exercise and stop drinking. He started seeing a therapist, who put him on some antidepressants. Aaron, however, was still Aaron, and wouldn't listen. He wouldn't stick to a schedule with the meds, so he wound up having some vicious mood swings, especially when he would pick up the bottle again."

Scott set his water down hard. "You are not going to tell me this explains all the trash he pulled."

Fletcher shook his head. "No. It really only explains one thing—his plans to disappear."

Patrick spread his hands on each side of his plate. "He was going to vanish?"

Fletcher nodded. "And take at least two people down with him." He nodded at Scott and Maggie. "He may have lost perspective, but Aaron still knew right from wrong. Everything else was just because of his anger at life. And fear."

Dan frowned. "I knew he had a temper. Didn't realize it was that bad."

"I suspect that's why he believed he wouldn't live much longer. His anger. His flaring out at other people. His depression."

Tonya said, "So he took steps to protect the Retreat."

Maggie spoke up. "Yes. No matter what, he still wanted this to be his legacy."

Laura shook her head. "Maggie, I'm sorry. But I'm still scared. I was already planning to tell you tonight that we—Frank and I—are leaving tomorrow."

Lily sighed. "I don't blame you, Laura. I'm leaving, too. Going back to L.A."

Tim dropped his fork. "What? You're leaving?"

Lily smiled. "Yes. But it's not out of fear. I'm going back to work." She reached over and took Scott's hand, and he nodded, a mild look of resignation on his face. "Scott, too."

Dan grinned. "So you two have put it back together?" Lily blushed, and Dan laughed. "It's about time."

Scott's mouth gaped, then he grinned. "You oaf. Stop spying!"

Dan's next smile bore a great resemblance to a certain Lewis Carroll cat.

Maggie turned to Laura. "I hate to see you leave, Laura, but I understand. You and Frank are not under any suspicion, so I see no reason for you to stay, unless you want to. And you'll be welcome back anytime, if you want to return."

"Thank you," Laura said.

Patrick tapped his fork on his plate. "Honestly, I have no idea why we didn't all run for the hills the minute someone took a potshot at Maggie."

Dan poked him. "'Cause we're writers, which means we're dumb and curious. We wanted to see how it turned out." He nodded at Maggie. "Any news on that front?"

"Actually, yes," she replied. "Tyler will be here in a few more minutes to talk to a couple of us. There's enough information at this point that I think he's close to an arrest."

Dan sat a bit straighter. "I should be taking notes for my next book. Who's on the grill tonight?"

Maggie looked at her sister. "Lily and Scott, to start with."

Lily's green eyes narrowed in confusion. "What?"

Maggie reached for her hand. "You don't mind staying for a while after dinner, do you?"

Her sister looked at Scott, who scooted his chair away from the table and got up, plate in hand. "Do what you want," he muttered as he walked toward the bar.

Maggie looked from her sister to Scott. "It'll only take a few moments."

"I don't care. I'm not staying."

Everyone at the table looked at one another, unsure of what to say.

Dan cleared his throat. "Scott, I have never seen anyone as able to drop tension into a room with a ladle before. It seems to be your specialty."

Scott dropped his plate on the bar with a rattle. He turned to speak to Dan, but his reply was drowned out by the knock on the door. Maggie went to let Tyler in, as Scott motioned for his wife to join him outside. With a glance toward Maggie and Tyler, she did, and they stepped out on the deck.

"Man," said Dan. "I hope they have a great makeup—"

"Dan!" Tonya slapped his arm.

He grimaced, rubbing his injury. "What did I say this time?"

Tyler took one look around the room. "Did I interrupt something?" he asked Maggie.

"No. We were just finishing up. Do you want some coffee?"

"Yes, thanks." Tyler kept watching Lily and Scott through the glass, as did everyone in the room.

Maggie winced. The door was closed, but their words could be heard loud and clear.

"Why do you agree with everything she says?" Scott demanded.

"What is going on with you?" Lily responded. "She just asked us to stay and talk to Tyler. It's not like we don't know the man."

"Oh, just us? I suppose we have special information about Aaron's murder now. What do you think *you* could tell him? You were dead drunk!"

"What has gotten into you? Why don't you want me talking to him?"

"Because I don't like the idea of you talking about us to strangers."

"Is this about the manuscripts?"

Scott stopped, staring at her. "What do you think it's about?"

"I don't know."

He shook his head. "Don't be dumb, Lily."

"And don't you talk to me that way."

"Fine," he said. "Do what you want. You do anyway." He turned and ran down the steps and away from the lodge.

Lily watched him go, then turned to come back into the room, only to find everyone staring at her. She spread her arms wide. "Well, now you know what life in the Jonas household is like."

Dan walked over and took her hand. "And you married him because…"

She sighed loudly. "Because he has such a sparkling personality?"

Everyone laughed, and the mood in the room lightened. Maggie watched as Fletcher eased out the door to follow Scott. She felt relieved. For their plan to work, Scott really needed to be in the room.

The others took their plates to the kitchen, and—assured that Tyler didn't need to speak with them today—headed out. She could still sense the fear that some of them felt…and she didn't blame them. She certainly wouldn't be walking alone until this was over.

Tyler and Lily were getting coffee when the phone rang. They looked at her, but she waved toward her office. "The machine will get it." And it did. She heard the clicks and double beeps from down the hall.

Tyler and Lily headed back to the center of the room, with Lily cozying up to the fireplace. Maggie covered up the food, refrigerating what was necessary.

The phone rang again.

She stared at it, annoyed, and let the machine pick it up.

Maggie poured her own coffee. She felt good. The evening was going as planned, and if Fletcher could persuade Scott to come back with him, maybe they would get to the bottom of this tonight. She wanted it over, no matter what. She picked up her cup, ready to join her sister by the fire and get this thing started.

The phone rang.

TWENTY-FOUR

Judson looked the disheveled Lee over, head to toe. "You're going to need a new suit, kid. And a wrist brace."

Lee grinned. "We got him. It worked."

Judson nodded. "That it did. Not like you planned, but work it did." Judson held out his hand and the younger man shook it gratefully.

Lee squared his shoulders. "So?"

Judson's eyebrows lifted. "So?"

"Does this mean I'm your new partner permanently?"

"Don't get cocky, kid."

"Is that a yes?"

Judson paused. "You may regret it," he said, then turned and walked away.

Lee punched the air with his fist. "Yes!" he whispered, as he followed his partner out of the squad room.

Scott left at a furious pace, and he was almost to his cabin before Fletcher caught up with him. "I thought this thing between you and Lily was settled," he said, moving around in front of Scott. "She talked to me about Aaron and said she was going to work it out with you."

Scott held up his hand at Fletcher. "Look, I'm grateful to

you for talking to Lily, for getting her to open up to me. I mean that." Scott crossed his arms. "I love that woman more than I ever thought I could love anyone. That she conspired with Aaron to destroy my work hurts. A lot. I won't deny that. And I was wrong to hit her."

Fletcher matched Scott's angry pace back and forth in front of the cabin. "Then why the fight just now? Why do you want to keep her from talking to Tyler?"

Scott's temper flared completely. He came at Fletcher, stopping only inches from him, thrusting his finger in Fletcher's face. "Because I know what you want with her! Don't try to con me. I know you're not here because you want to keep my marriage together." Scott turned and stomped several feet away, looking more like an enraged teenager than a man about to lose his wife. "Man, I can't believe I'm talking about this to you! Because I know you want to convince her I killed Aaron! But I didn't, Mac-Allister. I never touched the man!" He resumed pacing.

Fletcher stood still. "Why would we think that?"

Scott stopped and faced Fletcher. "Don't insult me, okay? Just don't. I know Lily talked to you about the manuscripts. You know I wasn't in the cabin when he got killed. You know I had a fight with him just outside the lodge that night."

"What was it about?"

"What do you think? He was stealing my work!"

"Which gives you motive for revenge, if not murder. Not to mention what you'd already done to him by sleeping with his wife."

Scott froze. "What did you say?"

Fletcher met Scott's gaze solidly. "I know about Korie. And the baby."

Scott ran both hands through his hair, then cursed under his breath and walked away.

Fletcher followed him. "Does Lily know?"

Scott stopped, rubbing his hand over his mouth. "No. Not unless you've told her."

Fletcher shook his head.

Scott exhaled in frustration. "Man, what a mistake that was! Korie is…" His hand waved wildly as he tried to find a word.

"I know," Fletcher said.

Scott bent and picked up a handful of rocks, slinging one after the other into the woods, a physical outlet for his irritation at himself as well as Korie. "I can't believe I was so stupid." Light from the windows of his cabin shed an amber glow over the frost-covered ground. The leaves were thicker here, blown into mounds that were now soggy from the fall rains. Their footsteps were muffled.

"I didn't know what to do," Scott said, his voice sounding clogged. He cleared his throat. "I was so angry. I guess I took some of it out on Lily. I'm sure Aaron did. My wife was just caught in the middle."

"What did Aaron say that night?"

"That I deserved anything that I got." Scott took a deep breath. "He stole my work for revenge—he wanted to make me hurt the way he had. He was never going to publish it—just make it unpublishable." He shook his head. "I guess the bad part was that I thought he was right about getting revenge." He sighed again, some of the last fight leaving him. He tossed the last rock straight in front of him, just to be rid of it. It landed about four feet from the side of the house with a thud that reverberated through the trees.

Fletcher froze. "What was that?"

Scott looked at him. "What was what?"

"That sound. What *was* that?"

Scott shrugged. "Oh, that's an old well. The reason this cabin is larger than the others is that it's really old. Was here when Aaron bought the place. He was supposed to fill the well in when we got city water, but he just covered it over with tin. Sounds like that anytime someone drops something on it, or steps on it."

Fletcher stared at him. "Like thunder."

Scott looked confused. "Yeah, I guess. Why?"

Fletcher looked up at the cabin. "Is that the bedroom window?"

Scott nodded, and Fletcher paced off the distance to the well, Scott tagging along. Stopping a couple of feet away, Fletcher bent and found the edge of the well, trying not to step too close to it. He frantically dug leaves away from the edges. The leaves were cold and damp, sticking together in muddy clumps. He pulled handfuls away from one side of the concrete edge of the well, then around the corner.

Scott watched, his eyes wide. "Fletcher, what are you looking for?"

"The missing information."

"What?"

He pulled back more leaves, then was still. There, in the ground, was a boot print, with a grid-patterned sole. He frowned, trying to remember where he'd seen this pattern before, just recently …

In front of the fireplace.

A cold spot of fear clutched Fletcher's chest, and he heard the words in his head, which he thought had referred to Aaron.

"I'm a fan, y'know? It's why I took the job."

"Oh, no," he whispered, as he turned and bolted in the direction of the lodge. As he ran, Fletcher MacAllister found himself doing something he'd refused to do for almost ten years.

He prayed.

Maggie intended to just turn off the ringer, but she saw that the number was Tyler's office. She glanced up at Lily and Tyler again, then snatched up the portable phone. "Hello?"

"Maggie?"

"Hi, Peg, what's up?"

There was a pause. "Is Tyler there yet?"

The edge in Peg's voice made the hair on Maggie's neck twitch. "Yes, he is. Peg, what's wrong?"

"He's turned off his radio again. I need to speak with him. Now."

"I'm going. Peg, talk to me." Maggie started down the hallway.

"Hurry, Maggie. We got a call from the LAPD. They found a fingerprint inside the last envelope from Lily's stalker. They've been trying to track her down all day."

Maggie almost leaped. "So they know who it is? Tell me, you have to tell me!"

"He was in the system, a trespassing charge from breaking into a movie set down in Tennessee."

Trespassing. Tennessee. Realization hit Maggie square between the shoulder blades as she broke into a run, screaming, "Lily! Get down! Get down! Now!"

Lily and Tyler turned toward her, startled, just as the back door burst open and Fletcher and Scott headed for Lily. Scared, the young actress backed up a few steps, putting her in a clear line of fire from outside.

The bullet shattered the window, blasting glass throughout the room. There was no time to react. The bullet struck Lily in the shoulder, and she dropped to the ground. Maggie screamed, throwing herself at her sister. Fletcher and Scott reversed direction and headed for the door, followed by Tyler, who grabbed his radio off his belt, snapped it on then barked sharp orders for help, for officers and an ambulance.

Maggie slid down on her knees next to Lily, who was curled on the floor, clutching at her shoulder. Maggie stripped off her sweater and pressed it to the wound. Lily moaned and tried to open her eyes.

"I'm sorry," Maggie said through her sobs. "I'm so sorry." She pressed the wound with one hand and slipped the other under Lily's head, holding her close.

"So am I," whispered Lily. "This hurts!"

"I know," Maggie answered. "Don't try to move. Tyler called for an ambulance."

"At least you were knocked out."

"Don't you try to make me laugh. I'll never forgive you."

Lily managed a weak smile. "At least it won't be so hard to act if I get shot in the movies." She moaned, her legs drawing up a bit tighter.

"Shut up."

"You think they have good drugs in that ambulance?"

"I know they do. Good ones. No booze, but some really good drugs."

Lily smiled briefly, then closed her eyes, clutching at one of Maggie's hands. "Don't leave me."

"Never."

"I'm gonna tell the world about you."

"Don't you dare."

Lily squeezed her hand tighter, and Maggie watched another wave of pain cross her sister's face. She kissed her cheek. "I love you, little sister."

"I love you, too, Mitten."

Fletcher hit the bottom of the steps first and sprinted to the right, while Tyler bounded straight ahead and Scott veered to the left. A few yards out, however, Fletcher stopped for a moment, his detective's mind taking over. He looked around, his eyes checking every shadow for movement, his ears trying to pick up on anything that wasn't Tyler's frantic crashing or Scott's angry shouts.

He looked back up at the lodge, fighting the urge to check

on the women. He knew Maggie would take care of Lily the best anyone could until the ambulance arrived. Emotions aside, he wasn't needed. The lights of the room seemed to blaze out over the backyard, casting much harsher shadows than the gentle silver of the full moon overhead. On a hunch, he moved quickly back into those shadows, slipping in under the deck, a few feet from the downstairs entrance. He thought he heard the door to the deck open, but he waited silently, clenching and unclenching his fists to keep himself still.

His instincts didn't fail him. A few moments later, with the noises Tyler and Scott were making beginning to fade and the sound of sirens still in the distance, a man walked easily around the corner of the house and under the deck. He paused at the door and pulled a set of keys from his pocket.

"Hello, Tim," Fletcher said.

Tim Miller jumped, flattening himself against the wall. One hand clutched at his chest as he recovered. He peered into the shadows as the openings between slats of the deck cast diagonal lines of golden light across his face. "Mr. Mac-Allister," he said, breathlessly. "Man, what are you doing down here?"

"Waiting on you."

Tim didn't respond. He stood quietly, catching his breath. He squared his shoulders. "Do you have a gun?"

"I do," Fletcher said, keeping his voice even.

"I don't," Tim said. "Would you shoot me anyway?"

"If you run, yes."

Tim nodded. "So it's over."

"Yes. Where's the rifle, Tim?"

Tim pointed out toward the woods. "It's up in a tree about seventy yards out. Strapped to the trunk. It'd be hard to find, but I'll show you if the dogs don't."

"That makes you a pretty good shot."

He nodded, a bit of pride in his voice. "The army. I was real good for a while. I've been slacking off, though. Not enough practice."

"I have to admit that I'm grateful for that."

Tim shrugged. "I hadn't planned on killing Miss Maggie. Just keeping her quiet for a bit."

"Why?"

"She was in my room. She saw the letters. She had to know. She just hadn't figured it out yet."

Fletcher was struck by the image of Maggie on the deck, turning suddenly to tell him something. Something she forgot forever. "She didn't know."

Tim was silent. Instead, he stuck both hands in his pockets. Fletcher stiffened and jerked his gun from its holster. Tim saw the move and raised his hands quickly. "No, sir! Don't. I really don't have anything." Tim jerked his head toward the sounds of the sirens, which were grinding to a halt in front of the house. "I couldn't run now, anyway. It would be dumb, right?"

"Just keep your hands where I can see them."

"Yes, sir."

"So why shoot Lily?"

Silence reigned between the two men. Then Tim cleared his throat. "It was okay, y'know? As long as she was here with Mr. Jonas and all. It didn't matter. I liked watching them, y'know? Together? It was like I could still be with her. It was okay in my head."

Fletcher lowered his gun slightly. "But now she was leaving."

Tim held his hands out, and his voice became even more Southern, almost a parody of the accent. "Yeah! I couldn't stand that, y'know? I have to be with her! It drives me crazy. I've followed her everywhere until now. But I just can't keep going on like this."

"That's why the letters come from all over."

Tim grinned. "I like movie sets. But now…I just thought, if she were gone, then…I would get okay. She wouldn't be in my head anymore."

"And Aaron?"

Tim looked down a moment, then back up at the detective. "He hit her! Then I overheard the fight with Miss Maggie about his drinking, then what he'd done to Mr. Jonas, and I just lost my temper. It made me nuts the way he treated Miss Lily, like she was some kind of a—"

"You plan to use the insanity defense, don't you?"

Tim grinned and stood a bit straighter, the good-ol'-boy routine suddenly gone. "Sounds good to me."

"But this wasn't about you being crazy. This was because Aaron was going to fire you."

Tim hesitated. "Yeah. He did fire me. That night, because he'd found out about me and Lily. He was coming back to tell her and Miss Maggie."

"So this didn't have anything to do with Aaron hitting Lily. You got mad because he was sending you away from her."

"Mama always did say I had a bad temper."

Fletcher stepped out of the shadows. He didn't want to hear any more. "Time for the handcuffs, Tim."

The younger man smiled and turned around, putting his hands behind him. "You know this is just between me and you. Not on the record. And even if you testify, you'll have to say how crazy I am."

Fletcher holstered his gun and pulled his handcuffs from his back pocket and snapped them on Tim's wrists.

"And I will get off. I did before."

Fletcher pulled Tim backward suddenly and whispered into his ear, "That was trespassing. This is murder. And you just confessed to a licensed private investigator. I'm not even acting for Tyler tonight. Just me and Maggie."

Tim twisted sideways, his mouth open. "What?"

"You must have a nice bruise from your fight with Maggie. Maybe even a scrape, if she got you as hard as she thinks she did. Has that healed yet?" Fletcher pushed Tim out from under the deck. Tim stumbled and went to his knees, but Fletcher grabbed his arm and pulled him to his feet.

As his hand closed down hard on the bicep, Tim jerked, trying to pull away. "You're hurting me, man!"

Fletcher slung Tim facedown on the steps of the deck. His prisoner writhed, trying to turn over, and Fletcher drew his gun. "You were running away, weren't you, Tim? Trying to get away. Just you and me, right? No proof. Just an accident. Just like Aaron!"

Tim cried out, "Oh, man, don't do this!"

"Why not? Like you said, no one's around. Who would know?"

"Fletcher!"

Maggie's voice silenced both men. They froze, and Maggie walked to the top of the steps. Fletcher slowly raised his eyes, remembering the sound of the door opening. She'd heard everything. Backlit by the house lights, she looked like a figure of the darkest vengeance hovering over them.

"It's over," she said quietly.

Or a messenger of God's mercy, he thought. Fletcher felt all his tension drain away, and he whispered a quick prayer of thanks, not quite believing what he had almost done. He lowered the gun and stepped away from Tim.

Tim squirmed and started to speak.

"Don't, Tim!" Maggie commanded. "Don't say a word."

He didn't, remaining still until two of Tyler's newly arrived officers came out of the house and gathered him up off the steps. As they herded him toward their car, Fletcher holstered his gun slowly, watching the three men walk away. "How's Lily?"

Maggie came down the steps. Ignoring the red stain, she stopped on the last one so that she was eye level with him. "On her way to the hospital. She'll be all right. It didn't seem to hit anything vital. She's just in a lot of pain." She touched his shoulder. "You knew where he'd go. That he'd come back to the house," she said softly. "That's enough."

He shook his head, still looking at Tim's back. "No. I should have known. I should have seen it sooner."

"But you didn't fire when he reached into his pocket."

Fletcher's gaze snapped back to her. "What did you say?"

"Aaron told me. A long time ago. I've been praying for you. Now you know."

"Do I?" Fletcher's eyes stung and he looked out through the woods.

"Yes. I was watching. You're good, but you're human," she whispered. "You're not Judson."

He turned his head to stare at her, not quite believing what he'd heard. Her eyes gleamed, with both humor and tears, and he relented. "You, too, could be the victim of a horrible accident," he said, his voice low.

She laughed. A genuine, sweet sound of relief, and he reached for her. She moved into his arms easily, as if she'd always belonged there. She kissed his neck, then whispered into his ear, "We have to let him go. Let Aaron go."

He nodded, burying his nose in that sandalwood-scented hair and holding her tightly against him.

TWENTY-FIVE

Winter makes everything look new. Clean, washed by even the first touches of snow. *Like God's forgiveness,* Maggie thought, as she stood at the back wall of the lodge, sipping a steaming cup of coffee and looking out at the woods through the fat, white flakes that were cascading down around the retreat. *At this rate, we'll have a foot before nightfall,* she thought. Her deck was already covered, including, she knew, the red stain at the bottom of the steps. If she salted the steps, by spring the stain would be bleached out. A final goodbye.

She wrapped both hands around the mug, cherishing the warmth. The morning had been pleasant. Most of the writers had left for the holiday while Lily was still in the hospital, leaving only Scott, Lily, Fletcher and her behind to hold down the fort. All four of them had stayed in the lodge house since Lily had returned, with Scott and Lily in the guest room and Fletcher in Aaron's room. Tim was long gone, transferred up to Portsmouth for safekeeping, but it still felt safer to have everyone under one roof.

And more fun. They had stayed up late last night playing board games and talking. This morning, Maggie had gotten up early to drive Scott and Lily to the train, then fixed a quiet breakfast for her and Fletcher. Fletcher had now gone back to his cabin to pack the last of his clothes. He'd not even suggested that they stay in the house alone together, and that respect for her made Maggie admire him even more. She'd also loved cooking for him, and she still clung to the unexpected feeling of desire and comfort that the mere act of scrambling eggs and making biscuits had given her. She grinned. Lily would be stunned. Cookie would be proud.

"Maggie?"

She took a deep breath. That voice. But now it was one she cherished hearing, its low rumble stirring something in her she never thought she would feel.

She turned, setting her coffee on the mantel. Fletcher put his arms around her, and she leaned her head against his chest as he curled his fingers into her hair. "Are you ready?" she asked.

"Mmm?" he asked, his mouth against her head.

She laughed and pushed away from him. "Are you packed?"

He let go of her and took her hand, tugging her closer to the fireplace. "Regretfully, yes."

"I wish you didn't have to go. Everyone's leaving me," she said, her mouth in a playful pout.

He bent and gave her a quick kiss, dissolving the pout. "Did Scott and Lily get off without a fight?"

She nodded. "Her agent called. She got the part, and the film starts shooting after the holidays. Scott's going on location with her, just this time. She also whispered something about getting back into church before she left as well."

He grinned. "Think Scott will go along with that?"

Maggie nodded, her mouth twisted thoughtfully. "Yeah, I do. I think once they get out of this—" she waved her arm around in the direction of the cabins "—drama and get into the more normal and perverse drama of L.A., he'll be fine. You know, he never was violent toward her until Aaron and Korie started messing in their lives."

"Yeah, they had that effect on a lot of people."

"Said the man who once attacked a tree."

"I'm going to regret telling you about that, aren't I?" She giggled.

His eyebrows went up. "Did you just giggle?"

Maggie stepped away from him. "Nope. Not me."

Fletcher took her hands. "There's something else," he said softly.

A twinge of fear shot through Maggie. "What?"

Fletcher squared his shoulders and reached into his coat pocket. He pulled out a piece of paper. "While you were at the train station, I went back over to Aaron's house. At first it was just to make sure I hadn't left anything in the bedroom. But on a whim, I checked his office again. I wasn't sure why. I thought maybe there'd be something else about Scott or Tim—" His voice broke for a second. He swallowed, then continued. "Instead I found this. It was tucked into his calendar. It's addressed to you."

Maggie took the paper slowly, almost afraid of it. She gasped when she saw Aaron's angular handwriting. Her eyes flew to Fletcher's.

"It's dated December twenty-first. Apparently, that was the day he'd planned to make his move."

She swallowed. "Just before Christmas."

Fletcher stroked her cheek. "Just read it."

She did, part of her heart breaking all over again.

Sweet Maggie,

Mea culpa. You may hate me by now, and I cannot deny that I deserve your anger. What I can say is, "I'm sorry." And a little more. Remember that speech Elvis had hanging in his office, "The Man Who Counts"?

You were the one who counted, babe. The one who held my feet to the fire and my backside over the flame. You were my muse, far more times than I can remember or recount. The one who changed my life…and my perspective.

The one I regret leaving.

When this all comes down, things may get rough for you. If you want to escape, look in the bottom drawer of my filing cabinet. It doesn't make up for what I've done, but I dearly hope it's a bandage for the wound.

Love,
Aaron

Maggie's vision blurred, and Fletcher pulled her into his arms one more time. "Not to murder you," he said. "In the fuzz that his brain had become, he took your card to give you a new identity. He still wanted to protect you."

She pushed back from Fletcher. "Thank you."

He stroked her cheek. "It helped me, too." He cleared the tears from one corner of her eye, his fingers touching her so gently that Maggie fought the urge to sigh and moon like a school girl. *Romantic fool,* she scolded herself.

Fletcher rubbed her arms. "You aren't really going to spend the holiday by yourself."

She shook her head. "No. The church is doing a big dinner for some of the families in the area who can't afford it. Lots of kids. I'm going to keep the nursery, then Cookie and I are going to bed down at her cottage and drink hot chocolate and tell each other lots of stories. I'm actually looking forward to it. What about you?"

"My uncle and I are going to get together. I may even cook a turkey. I called a couple of my cousins and persuaded them to get their—get themselves home for a change. And he…um…wants to go to church."

Maggie's eyebrows arched. "Don't tell me God's been poking you in the back, too?

Fletcher snorted. "Why don't you ask Cookie about that?"

"Believe me, I will."

"Have you heard from Korie?"

Maggie slid her arms around his waist again. "She's still not taking my calls. I called her lawyer while you were packing. He said she's definitely going to contest the will. In the meantime, I'm going to pay off her mortgage and sell that house. Edward is helping me with that. I already have a buyer, who— Y'know, I really don't want to talk about all that right now." She tightened her grip on him, loving his smell, the feel of him against her.

Fletcher pressed her against him and kissed the top of her head. "What do you want to talk about?"

"When *will* I see you again?"

"I'm not sure. Soon. I'm going to sit down with my business plan and Edward when I get back and see what's possible. I've got a lot to think about. You. New York. God. I'll let you know."

"I'll miss you."

"Want to hear something funny?"

Maggie closed her eyes. She didn't want to let go of him. "What?"

"Tyler made me an offer."

Maggie pushed back, her eyes gleaming. "Get out! He didn't!"

Fletcher grinned. "Yep. Benefits and everything."

"Hey, at least you know you'll have a place if New York gets too crowded."

He ran one finger down her cheek. "I already knew that." Leaning forward, he kissed her, gently at first, then deeper as one hand cupped the back of her head.

Maggie's chest tightened and she responded fully. Her hands clutched his back, and she trembled at the touch of his hand on her side. As the kiss ended, he searched her face. "Are you okay?"

She nodded, slowly opening her eyes. "When did you say you'd be back?"

Fletcher laughed and released her, holding only to one hand as he picked up his suitcase and walked to the door. He kissed her again, lightly, before heading out to the rental car, which was warming in the driveway, its exhaust sending a light fog up into the trees where it froze on the branches. Fletcher turned once, looking back at her as he tossed his bag into the back seat.

Maggie waved, then watched as the car disappeared up the long driveway. She closed the door and looked around. She took a deep breath, making a mental list of chores and preparations she needed to take care of over the next few days. It was going to be lonely for a while, that was certain. Still, she had a lot of work to do.

But first...

She grabbed her coat off the sofa and headed for the back door. Snow angels were waiting to be made.

Judson looked out the window of his apartment, sipping a specially brewed coffee and watching the snowflakes drift lightly down over New York City. It had been a good week. They had arrested the right man, and justice would be served to all who needed it. Lee had proved himself to be a diligent partner, yet strong enough that Judson would not overwhelm him. Everything was in its rightful place.

He was, in the end, content.

THE MAN WHO COUNTS

It is not the critic who counts, not the man who points out how the strong man tumbles or where the doer of deeds could have done them better. The credit belongs to the man who is actually in the arena, whose face is marred by dust and sweat and blood; who strives valiantly, who errs, who comes short again and again; who knows the great enthusiasms, the great devotions; and spends himself in worthy causes; who at the best knows in the end of the triumph of high achievement, and who at the worst, if he fails, at least fails while daring greatly, so that his place shall never be with those cold and timid souls who know neither victory or defeat.

—Theodore Roosevelt

Dear Reader,

There are times I believe that following Jesus' command to "love one another the way I loved you" is the hardest instruction He ever gave us. Our friends and family aren't always that easy to love! They're human; they make mistakes, just as we all do. And sometimes those mistakes go so completely against our faith and beliefs that we don't know what to do. Do we, in fact, continue to hate the sin but love the sinner?

This is the trial set in front of Maggie Weston as she deals with the mistakes made by her friends, her family—even herself—in *A Murder Among Friends*.

Friends can be both a help and a hindrance in your life. That's the joy of journeying through life hand in hand with them, and good friends don't give up just because one of them stumbles. I hope you'll take Maggie and Fletcher's struggles and triumphs to heart as you read, remembering a few of your own friendship journeys.

Blessings,

Ramona Richards

QUESTIONS FOR DISCUSSION

1. Maggie's quick prayers to God and reliance on Scripture help her to deal with Aaron's death. How has your faith sustained you through the loss of someone you loved?

2. Do you say little prayers to God throughout the day? Why or why not? Do you think this is what Paul means when he advises us to "pray without ceasing" (1 Thessalonians 5:17)?

3. When Maggie finds the champagne bottle, she knows people will think Lily is the killer, even though Maggie does not. She's torn between protecting the sister she loves and what she knows is right—turning in the bottle. How do you feel about the path she chooses? How would you have handled the situation?

4. Has anyone you loved ever put you in a position of choosing between your faith and your loyalty to them? How?

5. Throughout the story, Maggie's faith influences Fletcher, even though she never talks to him about her beliefs. Instead he finds that he admires the way she lives it. Have you ever been strongly affected by how someone lives out his or her beliefs?

6. Do you think your faith shows in how you live as well as by what you say? Why or why not?

7. Maggie's romantic relationship with Aaron dissolves, in part, because she won't sleep with him. Has a stand you've taken because of your faith ever damaged a relationship? How did you respond?

8. Do you freely discuss with your friends how your ideas and beliefs may differ from theirs? Do you think being friends with someone whose values are different from yours can strengthen or weaken your own? Why or why not?

Love Inspired®

SUSPENSE
RIVETING INSPIRATIONAL ROMANCE

Don't miss the intrigue and the romance
in this six-book family saga.

THE SECRETS OF STONELEY

**Six sisters face murder, mayhem
and mystery while unraveling the past.**

FATAL IMAGE
Lenora Worth
January 2007

**THE SOUND
OF SECRETS**
Irene Brand
April 2007

LITTLE GIRL LOST
Shirlee McCoy
February 2007

DEADLY PAYOFF
Valerie Hansen
May 2007

BELOVED ENEMY
Terri Reed
March 2007

**WHERE THE
TRUTH LIES**
Lynn Bulock
June 2007

Steeple
Hill®

Available wherever you buy books.

REQUEST YOUR FREE BOOKS!

2 FREE INSPIRATIONAL NOVELS
PLUS 2
FREE
MYSTERY GIFTS

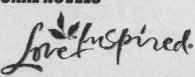

YES! Please send me 2 FREE Love Inspired® novels and my 2 FREE mystery gifts. After receiving them, if I don't wish to receive any more books, I can return the shipping statement marked "cancel." If I don't cancel, I will receive 4 brand-new novels every month and be billed just $3.99 per book in the U.S., or $4.74 per book in Canada, plus 25¢ shipping and handling per book and applicable taxes, if any*. That's a savings of 20% off the cover price! I understand that accepting the 2 free books and gifts places me under no obligation to buy anything. I can always return a shipment and cancel at any time. Even if I never buy another book from Steeple Hill, the two free books and gifts are mine to keep forever.

113 IDN EF26   313 IDN EF27

Name	(PLEASE PRINT)

Address		Apt. #

City	State/Prov.	Zip/Postal Code

Signature (if under 18, a parent or guardian must sign)

Order online at www.LoveInspiredBooks.com

Or mail to Steeple Hill Reader Service™:

IN U.S.A.: P.O. Box 1867, Buffalo, NY 14240-1867
IN CANADA: P.O. Box 609, Fort Erie, Ontario L2A 5X3

Not valid to current Love Inspired subscribers.

Want to try two free books from another series?
Call 1-800-873-8635 or visit www.morefreebooks.com

* Terms and prices subject to change without notice. NY residents add applicable sales tax. Canadian residents will be charged applicable provincial taxes and GST. This offer is limited to one order per household. All orders subject to approval. Credit or debit balances in a customer's account(s) may be offset by any other outstanding balance owed by or to the customer. Please allow 4 to 6 weeks for delivery.

Your Privacy: Steeple Hill is committed to protecting your privacy. Our Privacy Policy is available online at www.eHarlequin.com or upon request from the Reader Service. From time to time we make our lists of customers available to reputable firms who may have a product or service of interest to you. If you would prefer we not share your name and address, please check here. ☐

LIREG07

Love Inspired SUSPENSE

TITLES AVAILABLE NEXT MONTH

Don't miss these four stories in March